TIDE OF *Resolve*

TIDE OF *Resolve*

Restored

Part 4

Mary E. Hanks

www.maryehanks.com

Suzanne D. Williams Cover Design:

www.feelgoodromance.com

Cover photos: micromonkey @ iStock; Andrei Monkovskii @ iStock

Author photo: Ron Quinn

Visit Mary's website:

www.maryehanks.com

You can write Mary at

maryhanks@maryehanks.com.

For Lance

You were, and are, a sweet "little" brother.

Thanks for sharing your gifts. Your worship times have been such a blessing.

For Jason

Book ten! Thanks for cheering me on and helping me believe I could.

When you pass through the waters,
I will be with you;

Isaiah 43:2

Basalt Bay Residents

Paisley Grant – Daughter of Paul and Penny Cedars

Judah Grant – Son of Edward and Bess Grant

Paige Cedars – Paisley's younger sister/mom to Piper

Peter Cedars – Paisley' older brother/fishing in Alaska

Paul Cedars – Paisley's dad/widower

Edward Grant – Mayor of Basalt Bay/Judah's dad

Bess Grant – Judah's mom/Edward's wife

Aunt Callie – Paisley's aunt/Paul's sister

Maggie Thomas – owner of Beachside Inn

Bert Jensen – owner of Bert's Fish Shack

Mia Till – receptionist at C-MER

Craig Masters – Judah's supervisor at C-MER

Mike Linfield – Judah's boss at C-MER

Lucy Carmichael – Paisley's high school friend

Brian Corbin – Sheriff's deputy

Kathleen Baker – newcomer to Basalt Bay

Bill Sagle – pastor

Geoffrey Carnegie – postmaster/local historian

Casey Clemons – floral shop owner

Patty Lawton – hardware store owner

Brad Keifer – fisherman/school chum of Peter's

James Weston – Paul's neighbor

Sal Donovan – souvenir shop owner

Penny Cedars – Paisley's mom/deceased

One

Paisley Grant took a deep breath and sucked in her belly, pressing her lips together to stop any air from escaping her mouth. If she pulled in her waist another half an inch, she'd be able to fit into the wedding gown her mother-in-law, Bess, chose from the bridal shop rack. But if the dress was this uncomfortable, how could she even wear it to her vow renewal ceremony?

Molly, the mid-twenties consultant, had cinched up the bodice's structured fit with ribs until Paisley couldn't take any more tightening.

"Undo it, quick!" she said through gritted teeth. The form-fitting ivory-colored dress was pinching off her air supply. She feared she might pass out. Or tear the dress. "Hurry."

"Of course. Stand still." Molly fingered the fasteners.

When the last clasp released, Paisley burst out the breath she'd been holding. "Oh, my. That was close."

"Not this one, huh?" Bess smoothed her hand over the lacy material on the sleeve.

"I'm sorry, but, no. Not if I want to breathe while your son and I promise to stay married to each other." Sliding the fabric off her shoulders, glad to be free of the tight gown, Paisley accepted Molly's help.

"Be careful. Step out of the dress cautiously."

"I'm trying." Paisley had already tried on five dresses, so she knew the strict routine.

When her legs cleared the fabric, Molly whisked the dress away, muttering about people needing to be more sensitive about the expense of such delicate fabric.

Paisley bit back a groan.

She and Bess had made a day trip to Eugene, Oregon, about sixty miles east from Basalt Bay, to find the perfect dress for her to wear for Judah's and her vow renewal ceremony coming up in six days. *Six days! Yikes.* Maybe she'd been a tad hasty in setting the date so soon. But the look on Judah's face when she asked him if seven days would work had been priceless. And the kiss he gave her afterward—*deep blue sea in the morning!*—she'd never forget that. It made her more determined to get everything accomplished so they could restart their life together, beginning with choosing a knockout dress neither of them would forget.

Bess had seemed overjoyed to accompany her on this spur-of-the-moment wedding dress hunt. And when Paisley told her she could choose a couple of gowns for her to try on, Bess acted downright giddy. Although, it soon became apparent their tastes in styles varied greatly. But, still, Paisley enjoyed trying on some of her mother-in-law's more elaborate choices.

"Oh, no. I forgot to take a picture of that one." Bess handed Paisley her shirt.

"No worries. I couldn't eat or dance in it, let alone breathe, so it's not a contender."

"Okay, if you're sure. You looked lovely in it."

"Thank you." She slipped her shirt back on while she waited for Molly to bring out the next dress. Hopefully, a more comfortable one.

Her thoughts wandered back to the first time she and Judah got married. The adrenaline rush of sneaking off and not telling their parents. Not having to purchase expensive clothing for the ceremony. Only her and Judah standing before the judge, making their secret, forever promises.

All good memories, yet she had different expectations now. She wanted her family to be there. And she dreamed of strolling down a church aisle wearing a lovely gown. She imagined Judah's delighted expression, seeing her walking toward him dressed in something stunning. That was worth whatever headache she might have to go through today in trying on dresses.

Bess strolled around the racks set up along the perimeter of the dressing area, browsing through plastic-wrapped dresses. Every now and then, she held up a frilly gown and asked for Paisley's opinion. "How about this one?" She lifted an off-white knee-length dress from the rack.

"It's nice, but I have my heart set on a long one."

"Oh, right. How about this one?"

"Too puffy."

"Okay. I'll find something else." Her mother-in-law didn't seem to mind Paisley's refusals.

"Thanks for doing this with me. It was kind of you to drop everything you were doing and join me on this shopping trip." Paisley sipped from the water bottle Molly gave her earlier.

"I'm honored you asked me." Bess glanced over her shoulder as if checking on the consultant's progress. "Will your sister be one of your attendants?"

"No, I don't think bridesmaids are needed in a vow renewal."

"You sure?" Bess pulled a peach-colored dress from the rack.

"Not really, but—" Paisley stepped down from the small circular platform in the center of the room. "Things are unsettled between Paige and me. Just family stuff."

"I'm sorry. I didn't mean to pry." Bess cleared her throat. "Forgive me?"

"No need. Family dramas aren't pretty."

"Boy, don't I know that?"

Of course, she did. The Grants had plenty of family drama. Even now, Bess was staying in the guest room at Judah's cottage after having left her abusive husband. Then, when she found employment at the local grocery store—her first job since becoming Mrs. Grant—her mayoral-louse-of-a-husband became enraged about it. Everyone in Basalt had heard about that fiasco.

Molly shuffled back into the dressing area with her arms full of white shiny fabric. "Here's just the one. I'm sure you're going to love it." She helped Paisley step into the center of a full petticoat and shimmied the satiny dress up to her waist.

Bess helped with removing Paisley's shirt, then grabbed her cell phone.

Once Molly buttoned up the back of the gown—which seemed to take forever—Paisley smoothed her hands over the pearl-laden dress. Earlier when she saw this one, the tiny gems reminded her of sitting on the beach and running her hands over pebbly sand. But now that it was on, and with the scratchy fabric brushing against her legs, it felt stiff and bulky. Still, she stepped up onto the platform and swished the material back and forth.

Bess took several photos with her cell camera. "Oh, that's lovely. It's like a ball gown. Judah would be amazed at how royal you look."

"Royal? No one ever said that about me before." She was more the adventurous, mischievous, take risks sort of girl growing up.

"No?" Bess's smile widened. "Well, you, my dear, are princess material. Just ask my son."

Paisley laughed. Bess was so supportive and kind about her and Judah getting back together. She loved her for that.

If things were better between her and Paige, she would have asked her sister to join her today. But ever since they had that disagreement about Craig Masters, they hadn't cleared the air. And then there was the matter of her sister's harsh comments about Paisley leaving Judah for three years. Somehow, she had to bridge the gap between them, but she hadn't figured out how. And she wasn't going to let it spoil today's outing, either.

"What do you think?" Bess's question brought her back to the present.

Paisley ran her palm over the bumpy surface of the dress, still thinking of the feel of the sand—the roughness of it.

"It really is perfect. You'll be a beautiful bride." Molly probably made such statements to encourage a purchase.

Paisley stared at her reflection in the mirror and gulped. *I'm remarrying the man I love, the man I want to spend my life with, but do I need a super expensive dress to do that in?* She'd missed doing this before when she and Judah eloped. Seven years ago, she wore casual clothes before a judge. Now, she agreed with Bess.

She did look like a princess. However, the dress was too frilly and stiff for her.

Maybe this plan of hers about picking out a fairytale wedding dress and sashaying down the aisle was all wrong. Maybe she didn't need the white dress and trimmings. Perhaps a simple, yet nice, dress would work just as well.

"What are your thoughts about this one?" Bess took a couple more snapshots, her gaze dancing with anticipation or approval.

"Uh, well"—she hated to disappoint Bess or Molly—"it just isn't me. Sorry."

"You sure?" Molly tugged gently on something at the back of the dress.

"What's the price on this one?"

Molly quoted a number that went far above Paisley's mental budget for a wedding dress. Even though Judah had given her his credit card and told her not to worry about the cost, she didn't want to spend that much. Sure, it would be a day to remember for the rest of their lives, but she could enjoy that with a dress under two thousand dollars.

Molly unfastened the long row of buttons at the back and helped Paisley step away from the fabric, then sighed as if personally disgruntled with her wedding gown choices.

Bess, on the other hand, strolled toward the racks with a bounce to her step and a smile on her face as if unfazed by Paisley not liking any of the dresses so far. "Here's a cute one." She held out an A-line gown. It looked like something from *Pride and Prejudice*. "Or this one."

"They're pretty." Paisley's enthusiasm was waning. How many more gowns would she have to try on before she found a dress she loved?

"I'll be right back." Molly gathered up the dress as if handling a baby, then strode into the next room.

Bess walked back and passed Paisley her shirt and the bottle of water, kindly second-guessing her needs. "Which one do you want to try on next?"

"Maybe something simpler."

"Not the puffy ones, huh?" Bess grinned.

"Probably not." She didn't want to offend her mother-in-law who'd chosen the fancier gowns.

When Molly returned, Bess met her at the archway between rooms. "You've been so helpful, but could we skip over the gowns we picked earlier? Do you have something simple, yet lovely, that Paisley could try on instead?"

"Simple, yet lovely? Tall order." The consultant squinted at Bess like she was feeling put out by the request.

"I know. But you can do something along those lines, right?" Bess smiled encouragingly. "The ones I picked out aren't the bride's style."

"I'll see what I can find." Molly cut a glance at Paisley, then scurried back out of the room.

"Thank you." Bess was a gem for stepping in like that.

Paisley still had to find an office supply store where she could get invitations printed while they waited. Also, she wanted to get a few personal items for her new married life.

"How many people are you planning to invite to your event?" Bess went back to browsing through the wedding gowns.

"Twenty, or so."

"Maybe I could help you make a list." She whirled around. "I hope that's not too imposing."

"Not at all. Now, Aunt Callie? She'd demand that I invite all her friends. Definitely imposing."

Bess chuckled. "Okay. You tell me if I'm butting in."

"Thanks for being sensitive about it. This getting-married-again gig is uncharted territory for Judah and me."

"But you're doing great! I'm thrilled for you both."

"Thank you." It was nice to know she had such a positive mother-in-law.

Molly shuffled back into the dressing area, her arms clasped around two gowns. One bright white. The other ivory. "I thought you might not have noticed these as they were on the farthest rack. Clearance items, actually." She lifted one gown, gently shaking down its fabric, then she did the same with the other one. Holding them side by side, she extended them for Paisley's perusal. "Would you like to try either of them? Or both?"

The ivory one with short sleeves and a soft-looking train caught Paisley's attention. There was something warm and inviting about it.

Bess came around and stood by her, making "ooh" and "ah" sounds.

"Since we were married before, ivory might be best." She pointed at the ivory-hued gown. "May I try that one first?"

"Absolutely." Molly set the white one on the rack as if working with fine china.

"It's so beautiful," Bess murmured. "While I like both, if you prefer the white one, it's okay for you to wear white. Who cares about those outdated rules?"

"Aunt Callie would care." Paisley chuckled. She removed her shirt and handed it to her mother-in-law.

"Ah, I see."

Molly undid the hidden zipper in the side of the dress. Then she bent down for Paisley to step into the empty circle.

As soon as the silky fabric slid up her legs, Paisley smiled at the cool feel. The material wasn't thick like some of the previous dresses. It didn't strangle her breathing. She put her hands into the armholes, and the cloth molded comfortably to her body. She gazed at herself in the mirror to check out the fabric's movement. "I like it. Simple, yet elegant."

Bess snapped pictures, making happy sounds of approval. "I love it too. Is this the one?"

"I think so." Paisley shuffled over to the mirror, being careful to hold up the length of fabric, wanting a closer look. Running her hands down the sides of the dress, it felt almost like she was smoothing her hands over water. She twirled and the dress swished softly across her bare feet. "I'll take it." *Judah, just wait until you see me walking down the aisle to you in this!*

Molly clapped.

Bess cheered too.

"Do you want to know how much it is first?" Molly sounded hesitant.

"I suppose I should." Even if it were a higher price, Paisley might not be able to refuse, now that she'd found the one she liked. But then, the attendant told her the price, and it was half the cost of the last dress—perfect!

After Molly helped her out of the gown, Bess asked, "How about if I take you out for lunch after we get this all squared away? My treat."

"Sounds wonderful. I'm famished." That would give her a few minutes to put together a guest list. "And I need some shoes. Something to match." She pointed at the dress Molly was putting into a plastic sheath.

"I know just the place." Bess grinned.

If everything between now and their vow renewal ceremony went as smoothly as today, Paisley couldn't ask for more.

Two

Later that day, Paisley sat beside Judah in the pastor's office twisting her engagement ring around and around her finger, seeking a little anxiety relief. A few minutes ago, before Pastor Sagle left the room to take a call, he asked her a question that made her cheeks burn and her heart pound to a furious cadence.

"Why did you leave Judah three years ago?"

She didn't answer, just sat there staring back at the minister. Why did he have to start their marriage counseling session with that kind of question? Wasn't he supposed to offer them advice about their future marriage—how to deal with finances, how to disagree fairly, how to put the other spouse first? Maybe even be encouraging about their attempts to restore their relationship. Why dig up old problems?

Thankfully, the pastor's phone rang. A reprieve from embarrassment.

Now, to keep herself from sprinting from the building—or saying 'phooey' to this whole bridal-stroll-down-the-aisle thing—she perused the pastor's messy desk in front of her, searching for a distraction. Cluttered papers, a dirty plate, fork, and crumpled paper towels. Nothing interesting. She focused on a calendar spread across two-thirds of the desk surface, partially covered by the other stuff. Judah's and her names leaped out at her from a square marking today's date. "Reconciling" was printed in bold letters, too. Looked ominous. As if reconciling might even be a bad thing.

She shuddered and twirled her ring again.

"You okay?"

"Will be. Once this is over."

"I agree with that." After hearing the pastor's blunt question to her, did Judah wonder what queries might be thrown in his direction?

"Want to get out of here?" She leaped to her feet. "I'm game to leave if you are."

"Pais, why? We're already here." He tugged on her hand. "Let's do this. Get it over with, okay?"

She groaned. Too bad he wasn't feeling spontaneous. "Fine." She dropped back into her chair. "But whose business is it why I left? Other than yours and mine."

"No ones."

"Exactly." She huffed. "I don't feel like discussing that stuff with the pastor. Or with anyone, other than you."

"I get it." He stroked her hand between his. His touch was obviously meant to comfort her. "It'll be okay."

Would it be? Coming here for premarital—or re-marital—counseling might have been a mistake. But Pastor Sagle told her on the phone he wouldn't perform any marriage ceremony unless the couple came in for counseling, even if they had been married before.

That left City Hall, or else hunting for an alternative venue in another city. Even Judah had mentioned the possibility of getting married at the local government building. She was the one who hated the idea. Mayor Grant officiating? No, thanks. A mental image of him sneering down at her, or him saying something derogatory during their vows, made her temples throb and her neckband squeeze her throat. She slid her index finger beneath the band, trying to loosen it. Was the heater turned up too high in this office?

"You okay? You seem tense. Try to relax."

"I'm trying." Yet, an emotional weight pressed down on her chest. What else might the pastor ask her? What other private matters might he try to pry out of them? Her breathing became erratic. "I think … I need to get out of here." *Inhale, exhale.* "Away from his questions. I don't mean … run from you."

"I'm glad to hear that. But I can see—" His eyes widened. "Oh, sweetheart." He wrapped his arms around her, smoothing his hands down her shoulders and back. "I'm right here. We're in this together."

"I know. Thank you." She pressed her cheek against his jacket and closed her eyes, controlling her reaction by imagining herself out on the peninsula, breathing in the sea air. The world looked and felt different from here, too, sheltered in the arms of the man she loved. Oh, good, she was breathing easier, more freely, now.

"Remember what I told you the other day?" He stroked his fingers over her hair. Ticklish sensations.

What did he tell her? Oh, right. If she ever felt tempted to run, she should run into his arms. If only for a moment, this was her running to him, staying with him, promising him forever. "I remember." But then, she pictured Pastor Sagle opening the door and finding them cuddling. She settled back in her chair and took a couple of deep cleansing breaths.

Judah jumped up and strode toward a three-gallon water dispenser in the corner. He grabbed a miniature paper cup, filled it with water, then brought it back to her.

"Thanks." She swallowed the water.

He filled another cup and drank it himself, then refilled her cup, before he sat back down. He took her hand in his again, but the way his knees bounced up and down, he might even be as nervous as she was.

She glanced at the pastor's calendar again. On yesterday's date, "Edward Grant" was scrawled in the memo. Did that mean the mayor had a session with the pastor?

Even if Judah's dad got counseling, and even if he honestly changed for the better, Paisley hoped Bess never accepted him back into her life. She loved her mother-in-law and wanted the best for her. And she was certain Edward Grant was *not* the best for her. How the woman stayed married to the cad for over thirty years was beyond her imagination.

Pastor Sagle opened the door and Paisley dropped Judah's hand as if she'd been caught doing something wrong. Silly reaction.

"Sorry for the delay. Now, where were we?" Pastor Sagle crossed the room and sat down behind his desk.

Did that mean he forgot his previous question? If so, good.

"If memory serves me correctly, you two skipped this part of the process the first time, didn't you?" He glanced at Judah, then met Paisley's gaze. He picked up a pen and tapped the calendar. "Normally, these meetings are one session of two hours, once a week, for six weeks."

"What?" Judah's voice pitched high.

"Six weeks?" The words stuck in her throat.

"We were hoping to have our ceremony in six days." Judah leaned forward and crossed his arms over the edge of the desk. "What would we need to do to make that happen? Any chance we can fast-track this since we've already been married for seven years?"

"Fast-track it, huh?" Pastor Sagle ran his hand over his hair, smoothing down gray strands. His narrowed glance homed in on Paisley. "You were apart from each other for three years, right?"

"Uh-huh."

"Maybe you could use some counseling beyond fast-tracking, hmm?"

She gulped.

Judah clasped her hand again. "You're right, we didn't do well in some areas before. But we're committed to working on those things. Paisley and I have discussed our past. God has answered my prayers in bringing her home. That's what matters."

It was nice of him to stand up for them like that.

"All well and good, but for me to perform your vow renewal, I need to be certain you're both ready for this step."

"Oh, we are. No worries there." Judah winked at her, and she nodded.

The pastor scrawled something on the calendar.

"We want to be together, married." Paisley hoped to add clarity. "It's better for us to do that than to continue acting like we're single, right?"

Pastor Sagle leaned back in his chair. "What about family matters?"

"What family matters?" Judah's hand tightened around hers.

Was the pastor angling for more information about their families? About the mayor, perhaps?

"Bess, for starters. She's staying at your house, isn't she?" He sent Judah another stare as if that might even be his fault.

He released her hand. "What does my mom have to do with anything?"

"A mother in the house on the wedding night?" Pastor Sagle shrugged.

"Oh, that." Judah's cheeks hued red.

Paisley should have guessed there'd be more embarrassing topics.

"My mom's staying with us for now. Maybe Paisley and I will go away on a little honeymoon." He met her gaze as if to ask what she thought.

A honeymoon escape sounded perfect. A drive to the dunes or Coos Bay. Anywhere along the coast would be awesome if they were together, alone.

"Did you hear me?" The pastor gave her a stern look.

What did she miss?

"Have you thought this through?"

Why did he seem so troubled about them getting back together? Did he think their remarriage wouldn't last? Or had his possible conversation with the mayor negatively influenced his thoughts about Judah remarrying her? The mayor had despised her for her whole life, it seemed. She could only imagine what he might say about her.

"Do you mean the honeymoon, or renewing our vows?"

"You left before." Pastor Sagle spread out his hands toward her.

So they were back to that.

Shouldn't he be saying something positive about them getting married again? As Judah said, God had brought them back together. It was kind of like the story of the prodigal son. She came home. Judah welcomed her with open arms. Now they were ready for a celebration.

The silence in the room grew heavy.

"You're right." She swallowed, determined to speak honestly. "I did leave before. And I'm sorry about that. But now, I'm back to stay. I love Judah. I want to be married to him." She met her husband's gaze and smiled at him.

He slid his arm over her shoulders.

"That's good, but about the question I asked before?" The pastor picked up his pen again and rolled it between his fingers. "I'd still like to hear the answer."

"Respectfully, Pastor Sagle, why Paisley left is a private matter between her and me." Judah eyed the minister. "What we want to do is go on in God's grace, married, sharing our lives. We'd like your blessing. And the blessing of our family and friends. Can you help us make that happen?"

Pastor Sagle returned his stare for a good twenty seconds. "Three sessions work for you?"

Judah let out a soft groan.

"Three sessions in six days?" Paisley didn't try to subdue the surprise in her tone.

"Better than six in six weeks, hmm?"

Maybe they should get married at City Hall. If only they could find a way around Mayor Grant being involved.

Three

Judah returned from their marriage counseling session feeling a bit discouraged. Why was Pastor Sagle so abrupt? Why wasn't he more compassionate about their desire to reconcile?

Needing a task, he decided to clean out his drawers in the bedroom, making room for Paisley's things for when she moved back in. He started with the drawer in his bedside dresser that had accumulated papers and mailers over the last few years. As he shuffled through the pile, he flinched when he saw a familiar, wrinkled scrap of paper. With trembling fingers, he touched the frayed edges. He knew better than to read the words. Still, as if they had a mind of their own, his fingers smoothed out the crumpled paper over his jeans.

I don't love you.

The muscles in his chest clamped at the remembrance of an old wound. He closed his eyes long enough to recall the first time he read those words from Paisley. How they seared his spirit with gut-wrenching pain that lasted about a year.

There's someone else. Always has been. You should get on with your life without me.

Thank God he didn't follow her advice. Otherwise, he might already be married to someone else. However, in the years she was away, he never allowed himself to get interested in anyone else—even when women like Mia Till pestered him to date them, or to find comfort with them. Instead, he kept the faith. Kept his thoughts true to his wife. Kept his vows. And he prayed daily for God to give back to him and Paisley the love they'd lost.

And He did that. Wasn't their getting back together a testimony of God's grace? Judah should be focusing on that and rejoicing. And he was. But even as he read the words Paisley wrote to him three years ago, he couldn't ignore the burning sensation in the middle of his chest.

In those days after she left him, he read this note many times. Wept over it. Threw it at the wall. Retrieved it. He even slept with it clutched in his hand a few times. But, man, he shouldn't be contemplating that today. Shouldn't be reliving it—especially when they just talked with the pastor. And with only six days until their vow renewal, his mind shouldn't be focused on what happened three years ago.

Yet, like a tragedy that a person never wants to remember again, but whose mind keeps going over the details, Judah's thoughts replayed past emotions. Even now, when he knew he and Paisley loved each other and were eager to recommit to their vows, the words tore at him. "*I don't love you.*" Were there ever more powerful and anguished-filled words for a husband to hear from his wife? He drew in a long breath.

Wait. Enough! How many times had he told Paisley that the past was the past? It was done. Finished. That's right. So, starting right now, what should he do with this scrap of paper and the hurtful memories attached to it? No need to hang onto it like a keepsake. He never wanted it to be lying around to use as ammo in a future argument between them. And, honestly, he'd rather not see it again.

However, tossing a piece of their past in the trash, as if it didn't happen, felt weird, too. But wasn't forgiveness like that? Letting go. Acting as if the wrong never happened. Not giving it the power to sting. He wanted them to have a fresh start. A new beginning. He didn't want her to ever find this and feel guilty about it, either.

Making his decision, Judah squashed the paper in his hand, gripping it until it became a tight one-inch ball. Then he marched into the only bathroom in the house and lifting the toilet lid—closed because his mom was staying in the guest room—hurled the wadded note into the water. He hit the flush knob and watched the crumpled paper swirl into the whirlpool and get sucked down the pipe. Good riddance. He flushed again. What a relief. He should have done that years ago.

He drew in a deep breath, a healing breath, then exhaled, hoping any negative thoughts or memories could be expunged as easily. He trudged back into his bedroom, determined to put that old business behind him. It had probably only bothered him because of Pastor Sagle's question about why Paisley left him. Why, didn't matter. What mattered was they were recommitting themselves to their marriage.

He resumed the task of sorting out his drawers.

In between working at C-MER, Coastal Management and Emergency Responders, and sleeping, he'd spent most of his spare time over the last two weeks remodeling the beach cottage. He'd taken extra steps to make this room into a warm, inviting space. Paisley said she wanted to decorate using beach tones. So they painted the walls cream-colored and made one feature wall deep sea blue. Only trim work remained. He already put the mattresses back in the frame and headboard. Even washed the bedding. The flooring wasn't finished, but he couldn't do anything about that before their ceremony.

He hoped Paisley would be comfortable here, despite the flood damage and any tentative emotions she might be experiencing, considering it had been a long time since they shared a space. Was she looking forward to the romantic side of their marriage as much as he was? He should probably take her some flowers or plan a beach walk with her, or maybe have a picnic dinner before their vow renewal. He mentally slotted time for them to be alone, or go on a date, before their next marriage counseling session.

Finished with the drawers, he scooped up a roll of painter's tape from the floor where he'd previously left paint supplies. He climbed up the stepladder and unrolled a line of tape and pressed it along the doorframe. He still hadn't decided about the floor covering. Either carpeting or vinyl planks. For now, it wasn't a priority. The plywood was new, although rough to his bare feet.

Mom strode into his room from the guest room. "Want some help with painting before my late shift starts at the store?"

"Sure, I'm going to do the door trim." He pointed to the supplies. "You could paint a window frame if you want."

"Absolutely." She shuffled across the room.

"Seen anything of Dad this week?" Judah still had concerns that his father might show up and cause her problems on the job. "He hasn't been by the grocery store while you're working, has he?"

"Nope."

"Is he—"

"Can we not talk about your father?" She pried open a small can of paint, seemingly avoiding eye contact with him.

"Oh, sure." He didn't mean to make her feel uncomfortable. After their appointment with the pastor, Paisley told him she saw his father's name penciled in yesterday's date on the calendar. Dare he ask Mom about that? "Did you hear anything about Edward having counseling with Pastor Sagle?"

"I said—" She sighed. "No, I don't know anything about that." She stirred the paint with one of the wooden stirring sticks, then poured navy paint into a small container. "I thought I might make some cookies later. Is that okay with you?"

"That's always okay with me." He grinned, imaging her homemade chocolate chip cookies. But then he remembered how she used to bake cookies whenever she had bad news or disciplinary measures to dole out. As if that might ease the unwelcome information. "Why do you want to bake?" He wished she'd face him and look him in the eye when she explained.

"Can't I make cookies without you being suspicious?" Her chuckle sounded forced. She seemed intent on cleaning smudges of paint off the container with a rag.

His mind wandered to other times when she baked to soften bad news. The time his father grounded him for a month. When Mom's brother, Abe, died. The first time Edward demanded that Judah not date Paisley. "Is there something you're not telling me?" Now, he sounded like a parent. He turned on the ladder and leaned his back against the doorframe, since he hadn't put any paint on it yet. "What is it?"

"You've been a gem to let me stay here." She smoothed her wet brush up and down the side of the window frame. "I appreciate how you opened your home to me and made me feel so welcome."

Uh-oh. Where was this conversation going? "Mom, you're welcome to stay here as long as you want. Even Paisley is fine with your staying after she moves back in. There's no rush for you to leave." And certainly, no reason to return to her previous house with the mayor.

"She's a dream for being willing to let her mother-in-law remain in the house during her second honeymoon." Mom lifted her paintbrush and tapped the air as if punctuating her point. "But this is a small home. Three's a crowd, as they say."

"I don't want you to feel that way."

Finally, she faced him, looking embarrassed. "I know. But I've already made other housing arrangements." She smiled, then cringed.

"You have? Where might that be?" His protective instincts arose in him.

"It's somewhere more convenient for getting to work. Walking distance, actually."

Not back to Dad's, then. "Where are you thinking of moving to?"

"Kathleen Baker—you remember her?—invited me to stay with her at Miss Patty's rental." Mom grinned. "It's small. Temporary. But we're going to hunt for something bigger after I get more financially secure." She continued painting. "Kathleen and I have become friends. She's an artist, you know."

"No, I didn't know that." He wanted to argue and tell her she shouldn't make such a drastic move so soon after leaving his dad. What if Edward got the counseling that she told him to do? Not that Judah wanted her to reconcile with his father, unless he experienced a real, transforming change in his heart.

The man had already used up his second and third chances. "Is that wise?" He couldn't help being concerned about her well-being.

Eyebrows furrowed, Mom turned toward him. "What do you mean?" Her voice sounded stern as if warning him not to cross her. "I'm a grown woman. I'm finally making my own decisions."

"I know. And, yes, you are. But being with family at a time like this is important."

"Of course, it is." Her voice softened. "I won't be going far. We'll still see each other." She gave him a tender smile. "After all you've been through with Paisley, you of all people know how hard it is to work through rocky marital waters."

"Are these just rocky waters? Or do you want a more permanent separation?" He was prepared for the latter. He hated to push, but with her talking of moving out, he was curious about what she may have decided.

She gave him another stern look as if he'd crossed an invisible line into her privacy.

"I'm sorry, Mom." He sighed. "But if Dad were willing to undergo personal rehabilitation, would you be open to, I don't know, counseling sessions together?" Far be it for Judah to try to meddle between his parents.

Mom painted some more before answering. "A lot would have to change. I don't expect any miracles in my marriage. Or in your dad's behavior. I'd rather he left me alone. Let me live my own life." A pause. "I still believe in second chances and God's grace. But your father was abusive. I'm under no obligation to stay married to him. You'll have to accept my decision about that."

"Of course, whatever you decide, I'm here for you." He

cleared his throat. "I wouldn't want you to be in an unsafe environment, either."

"Good." She sighed. "Thank you."

Judah had gone through his own dark time when he had to accept he and Paisley might get divorced, might never reconcile. But then, a tenacious trust and belief that God would work things out came over him. He prayed and held onto hope like a drowning victim to a flotation device. However, he couldn't blame his mom for not having that same expectation after the way his father treated her.

"Just so you know, you can stay here for as long as you want."

"Thank you. But you and your sweet bride need time to figure out your lives together." She sighed. "Time to be alone, don't you think?"

"I suppose." But he didn't want his mother feeling like she had to leave, or that he and Paisley didn't want her here. "I wish things were different for you. That your life was more peaceful and stable."

"Me too. But it will be. I'll make sure of it."

If only Judah felt as confident as she seemed.

Four

Paisley had spent the last two days splitting her time between finishing up tasks at her father's house and working on the remodel at the cottage in anticipation of moving out there. In just a few days, she'd be living at the beach house, becoming Judah's wife, again. Every time she thought about taking that step, her heart rate sped up. She was eager to be with him. To share their waking up and going to sleep times. And even though he told her she could come home whenever she wanted to, she'd waited for them to renew their vows. Hopefully, she made the right decision.

Now, she was at her dad's house, folding the load of jeans she removed from the new-to-them dryer he'd picked out in Eugene a week ago. Yesterday, a delivery truck arrived with the gently used appliances—washer, dryer, fridge, and oven—that were mismatched greens and golds and looked made in the 70s. At least, they worked, and her dad didn't seem to mind the eclectic styles.

Ever since the laundry machines were installed, Paisley kept them running, washing and drying clothes, towels, and bedding. She sniffed the jeans she was folding, hoping they didn't smell musty anymore. It would take days to process the dirty, smelly things that had accumulated in the last month since the hurricane. Some items were in too bad a condition to salvage. But they were moving forward in the aftermath of the disaster. If only that were true of her attempts at mending the emotional scars of the past. She still needed to talk with her sister again.

Someone clomped up the steps and thudded across the porch. That better not be Craig Masters. His habit of showing up unexpectedly drove her nuts.

When no one knocked, she hustled over to the plastic-covered window. Aunt Callie, not Craig, rocked in the ancient chair. That she didn't call out with her usual tea request seemed odd. Something must be wrong.

Paisley hurried to the door and opened it. "Aunt Callie, hello. Do you want to come inside?"

"No. I'm exhausted. Just going to rest." She waved a colorful pamphlet like a fan in front of her face. "Got any sweet tea, Paisley Rose?" There, that sounded more like her.

"Not yet. I'll make you some in a jiffy."

"Good. Make plenty. Might take a while for me to get rested." She shut her eyes, still rocking.

Paisley scurried back into the kitchen and put a kettle of water on. She'd heat a cup of water in the microwave to speed up the process, but she tried that before and Aunt Callie scolded her, saying she could taste the difference.

"Almost done?" Aunt Callie called from the porch. "I'm parched."

"Coming!" Paisley hunted through her recent purchases to locate a package of oatmeal cookies. Her aunt would expect snacks with her tea.

With the refreshments ready, she carried the tall glass of iced tea and a plate with two cookies outside. "Here you go, Auntie."

"About time." Aunt Callie grabbed the glass and took a long swig. "Oatmeal, my favorite." She downed one of the cookies. "Have a seat, Paisley Rose." She didn't ask, just commanded.

"Okay, sure." Paisley dropped into the other rocker.

"Have you seen this pamphlet?" Aunt Callie flapped the small booklet in front of her and glared.

"No. What is it?"

"The mayor"—she said "mayor" like she plugged her nose—"wants folks to think kindlier of him than he deserves. Just when we're getting our impeachment campaign—*Grant Can't Last*—rolling, this happens. Mark my words, we won't rest until Edward is cast out of Basalt Bay politics." She thrust the brochure toward Paisley and cleared her throat like she was having a phlegm attack. "He doesn't deserve such praise, I can tell you that."

"So, you and Mrs. Thomas still plan to impeach Mayor Grant?"

"Course, we do. Soon as Maggie returns from her buying trip for the inn. She says she can't do anything until her business is running again. Then, just wait. We'll be knocking on doors and passing out our own pamphlets." Her aunt leaned forward, her double chin creasing to the sides of her cheeks. "You haven't seen anything until you watch Maggie Thomas, Patty Lawton, and Callie Cedars go after something they want." Smugly, she tipped her face one way, then the other, her gaze dancing with mischief or evil plots.

Maybe this was where Paisley got her mischievous side.

Aunt Callie pointed at the pamphlet. "Go on. Read it."

"Okay. 'Mayor Grant Serves Basalt Bay with a Heart of Gold,'" Paisley read the headline and nearly choked. "Heart of gold?"

"Hogwash." Aunt Callie harrumphed. "He serves himself, that's what."

Paisley continued reading, "He works for our community because he's a man of integrity." Her jaw dropped. "Who wrote this stuff? Mia Till?"

"Or that braggart who Maggie thinks is hot."

"Craig Masters?" Paisley snickered, recalling the conversation when Mrs. Thomas commented on his good looks.

"Who else would say such affirmations about Edward Grant?" Aunt Callie pursed her lips. "Someone from his payroll, no doubt. Someone paid to invent flattering news."

"It says he's a man of the people, too." Paisley didn't try to hide her eye roll.

"Of the sea snakes, more likely." Aunt Callie slurped her tea glass dry.

"No sea snakes around here, Auntie."

"Other than whoever wrote this garbage."

Paisley let the pamphlet drop in her lap. "It's not even an election year. Why all the fuss?"

"He must've caught wind of our plans to impeach him. Bigmouthed tale whisperers. Wait till I discover the tattler. I'll give her a piece of my mind." Aunt Callie held out her glass, her eyebrows raised.

Paisley grabbed it and strode inside for a refill. When she got back, her aunt had torn the pamphlet into a pile of pieces.

"That's what I think of Mayor Grant's 'heart of gold.'" She rocked in the chair extra-hard as if taking out her frustrations on the outdoor furniture. "He must be shaking in his boots to put out a pompous pack of lies like that."

Paisley handed her the tea and ice-filled glass. "What are you going to do now?"

"As soon as Maggie returns, we'll have a secret meeting where the mayor's spies can't hear." She rocked forcefully, her gaze aimed toward James Weston's house across the street. She gripped Paisley's hand. "Would you join us? You don't like the mayor any more than I do. We could use some youngsters to help us figure out how to oust the crook and who should replace him."

"Auntie, I'm marrying the man's son in five days. How can I take part in a group to remove Judah's father from City Hall?"

"Pshaw." Aunt Callie released her hand. "You've been wronged by that two-faced mayor. We've got to stand up to tyranny, even if you share his last name. Pity, that."

Paisley's stomach clenched just imagining some of the things the mayor had said to her in the past. And ever since Craig insinuated that Edward was involved in that near-assault on her three years ago, Paisley felt more suspicious of the mayor than ever.

"So, what do you say?" Aunt Callie made a pleading face as she vigorously rocked the chair.

Before Paisley could respond, a crackling sound came as a warning a mere second before the chair imploded. Aunt Callie's hands flailed in the air, groping at nothingness, as the chair toppled over with her in it. She landed with a thud and a whimper on the wooden floor.

"Aunt Callie! Auntie, are you okay? Are you hurt?" Paisley dropped to her knees and crawled to her aunt, assessing the damage. Broken wood from the rocker was scattered across the porch. Aunt Callie lay slumped over as if dazed or knocked out. But the heavyset woman was breathing. Paisley touched her arm. "Are you okay, Auntie?"

The older woman wiggled her legs and groaned. "What happened? Where am I?" She glanced around and seemed disoriented.

"Are you hurt? Should I call for medical assistance? Do you need to go to the hospital?" Paisley fired questions. "I'm so sorry you hurt yourself."

"That terrible, rotten chair." Aunt Callie smoothed her hand down her hip and groaned. "I'll live, I suspect, but I don't know how I'll ever get up."

Neither did Paisley. If only Judah were here to help. What about her father? If he heard that loud crash, surely, he'd come running. "Does anything feel broken?"

"Not that I know of. Why didn't you toss that chair in the trash years ago?" Aunt Callie's voice got louder. "My brother should have thrown it away."

"I know." Paisley didn't want to make things worse by saying Aunt Callie shouldn't have been rocking in it so hard when she knew it was in bad shape. She turned toward the house and yelled, "Dad! We need your help."

Across the street, James Weston, her father's longtime neighbor, stepped out of the door of his house, then bent over as if retrieving a paper, his gaze aimed toward them. Had he heard Aunt Callie's moans?

"James!" Paisley stood and waved. "Can you come over and help us, please?" She pointed toward her aunt lying on the porch.

Aunt Callie smacked her leg.

"What?"

"Stop that caterwauling. I don't want *him* seeing me spread out like a smashed eagle." Her cheeks flamed brilliant red. She tugged on the bottom of her shirt. Smoothed her hand over her hair—as if her appearance mattered when she couldn't even stand up. "Did he hear you?" Aunt Callie leaned up on her elbow. "Is he coming over here? How embarrassing."

"What's the trouble?" James shuffled across the street.

Did the thinly built man have the stamina to help lift Aunt Callie? Maybe Paisley made a mistake in asking for his help.

"My aunt fell, and she's hurt."

"Oh, leave me be." Aunt Callie huffed.

James stopped below the steps, a worried expression crossing his face. "You okay, Callie?" His voice got super soft. "Where's Paul? He should be helping too."

"I called, but—Dad!"

"My niece is making a fuss over nothing. Go on with whatever you were doing, James. Don't worry about me. We'll figure this out ourselves." Aunt Callie glared at Paisley, then pushed first her elbow, then her hands, against the porch, gritting her teeth. Paisley got under her left arm and helped her to a sitting position. That took all of Paisley's strength. She brushed some dirt off her aunt's arm. Aunt Callie slapped her hand away. Still feeling feisty, apparently, despite the tears on her cheeks.

"Here, let me help." James climbed the stairs and dropped on one knee beside Aunt Callie. "Can you hold onto the column?" He nodded toward the chipped board extending from roof to floor.

"I think so." She wrapped one arm around the solid column, then heaved herself forward, moaning.

Paisley squeezed in close to her side, assisting her the best she could.

James clutched her other arm. "Remember when we were kids and Paul shimmied up this board to get to the roof? Said he could see the ocean better from up there." James chuckled, lifting and supporting Aunt Callie.

"I remember." She clutched the column, huffing. Between the three of them helping, Aunt Callie finally stood, albeit wobbling as if she might topple over again.

"You okay?" James breathed deeply like he might have overexerted himself.

"As well as can be expected after such a tumble. Wretched deathtrap chair." Her normally loud voice got quiet, whether due to embarrassment or her proximity to James, Paisley didn't know. "Thank you, James." She smiled timidly at him.

Paisley glanced back and forth between the two, curious about her aunt's soft tones and smiling face.

"You're welcome, Callie." He tipped his dapper hat and winked at her.

For a second, it seemed as if they both got lost in each other's gazes. Or caught up in something of the past. Did they have shared romantic memories? Paisley pictured her aunt attending a high school prom, and James asking her for a slow dance. Or maybe the two of them strolling on the beach, or wading in the sea, holding hands. Maybe she'd ask her aunt about it later.

James cleared his throat. "Looks like you're right as rain now, Callie Cedars."

"Told you so. Just a fall. That chair's fault." She gulped but continued chattering. "Pauly should have tossed it away before the hurricane. I told him so a hundred times. Does he ever listen? Does anyone?"

James chuckled. "It was an oldie but goodie, no doubt about it."

Paisley and Judah used to sit in those chairs when they were dating. She and Mom sat there and discussed Paisley's pregnancy, years ago, too. The chairs really were old.

"Here"—James grabbed a few pieces of what remained of the rocking chair—"I'll throw these in the trash."

"Thank you." Paisley scooped up the arm rails and a few chunks of wood.

"What's this?" James picked up several scraps of paper Aunt Callie tore up. He put two together as if trying to make sense of the words.

"Never mind about that." Aunt Callie tugged them from his hand, letting the pieces fall again. "Disturbing news is all." Her face flushed as she sat down in the remaining rocker. She stepped on the stray pieces of the pamphlet as if hiding them.

"Something about the mayor?" His eyebrows rose.

"You for or against?" Aunt Callie's voice turned gruff. In five seconds, her face went from looking like a rosy-cheeked schoolgirl to a hostile woman.

"Aunt Callie—" Paisley tried to warn her.

"For or against whom, or what?" James paused, his arms loaded down with wooden chunks.

"Like you don't know."

"Honestly, I have no idea. How could I know what you and those yakity-yaks talk about?"

Aunt Callie put her hand to her chest. "Why, I never."

James shuffled the pile of wood in his arms, a tense silence building between them. "I'd better take care of these." He strode down the steps, then rounded the corner of the house toward the garbage cans, mumbling.

"Aunt Callie, why did you treat him that way? He's our neighbor. He was being nice, even helped you stand up."

"He drives me nuts. Always has." She rubbed her hip and scowled.

"You okay? I'm worried about you." Paisley couldn't stay perturbed at her aunt for long, especially when she was injured.

"I need to go home and lie down." She stared toward James' house again as if lost in thought. "I'm tired of men thinking a woman can't do anything but talk. I got news for James and Pauly. Just watch me do something!"

"I don't know, Auntie." Paisley took a risk of antagonizing her. "You seemed to like our neighbor just fine when he helped you stand up. When you two were looking at each other with lovey-dovey eyes. He's kind of cute for an old guy."

"Paisley Rose!" Aunt Callie jabbed her chubby index finger toward her. "Don't you think for a second that I find that pig-headed man attractive." Her glare intensified. "Don't you dare say one word about this to Pauly, either. Or Maggie. You hear me?"

"Okay, okay." She sure got worked up about someone she didn't find attractive. "Are you hurting badly? Should I call for emergency help to get you to the hospital in Florence?"

"No. I just want to go home and lay down. I ache all over." Her eyes got teary. "Haven't fallen in years."

James shuffled back around to the front of the house. "Where's your dad?" He addressed Paisley, his gaze avoiding Aunt Callie's. No wonder with the way she nearly bit his head off.

"He's inside somewhere. I'm surprised he didn't hear me shouting for his help."

"He's hiding from me." Aunt Callie squinted.

James broke into a grin. "He's reverted back to that strategy, has he?"

Aunt Callie's grimace transformed into the schoolgirl grin from earlier. "I guess he has."

By the way they exchanged glances, Paisley was convinced James and Callie must have a past together. Maybe not sweethearts. But friends. James had, after all, lived across the street from the Cedars' house his whole life. Paisley's thoughts flitted between the possibility of them being jilted lovers to the girl-next-door who admired the friend of her brother.

"You can go in and talk with him if you want." She rocked her thumb toward the front door.

"Don't mind if I do." He trudged up the steps.

"Thank you for your help, James." Aunt Callie said his name softly.

He nodded, his gaze on her for a moment, then he entered the house. "Paul, you in here?"

A muffled response sounded like Dad might be upstairs. Perhaps, hiding from Callie as she said.

"You're going to need help getting home." Paisley smoothed her hand over her aunt's shoulder.

"Might just sit here and get my bearings."

"Okay." Paisley traipsed down the steps and retrieved from the lawn the unbroken glass that had held Aunt Callie's tea.

"May I have another glass of sweet tea? Nothing like tea to settle a person's nerves."

"Sure thing." Paisley walked through the house to the kitchen, glad to have a task. She paused to listen to the men talking in the hallway upstairs.

"You hear about the recall campaign?" Dad asked.

"Is that what Callie's yammering about?" James replied as if trying to keep his voice quiet but failing. "Can you imagine what this town would be like without a Grant at the helm?"

"My son-in-law's a Grant." Dad sounded proud of the fact.

It was nice he valued and loved Judah.

"Yeah, but for how long?"

"How long what?" Dad's voice deepened.

"The Cedars record for marital bliss is short-lived, wouldn't you say?" James chuckled as if he told a joke.

A steely silence followed.

Paisley gulped.

"Just 'cause you and Callie never …" Dad's voice faded.

James and Callie never what? So her guess might be correct about her aunt and the neighbor. Hmm. They were both single after all this time. Was it possible they still cared for each other?

Five

Judah stared at the scaled drawing of the peninsula on his desk at C-MER. What might the public's reaction be to the replacement of the old protective barrier? By later this afternoon, he'd have access to a 3-D model his engineering team was creating. Then he'd have a better idea of what solutions to recommend to the crew who would be putting together a proposal for a man-made dike.

Ever since duo hurricanes wreaked havoc on the coastline, he knew something would have to be done to reconstruct a safer solution for Basalt Bay. The peninsula hadn't held up under the intense pressure of two rounds of vicious winds and the ensuing tidal surges. Now, they were in a time crunch to prepare their town for any possible future strikes. Although, he hoped that would never happen.

Sighing, he perused the drawing. Once the proposal was finished, there would be lengthy discussions with Mike Linfield, his manager, who would then make recommendations to upper management. Eventually, someone would have to address the city council and Mayor Grant, maybe even speak at a town meeting. Hopefully, that person wouldn't be him.

At least he still had his supervisory position. So far, no news to the contrary had crossed his desk, even though there were previous hints of changes in the ranks. Even yesterday, Mike told him Craig Masters was scheduled to go before a board of inquiry about the complaints he filed. After that, who knew what might happen to Judah's position? In the meantime, he was keeping busy, hoping for the best, and trying to prove his worth as a valuable C-MER employee.

As far as the needed improvements to the peninsula, one person would hate it—his wife. Paisley loved the peninsula. Didn't she recently say she'd like to build a house at the end of the peninsula so she could wake up to the nautical view every morning? She'd hate to see her favorite place for experiencing the sea torn up and replaced with a rock wall. But it couldn't be helped. Safety had to come first.

Mia flounced into his office, wearing a low-cut white blouse and turquoise skirt with several necklaces jangling at her neck. "Hey, boss." She winked at him, bringing his attention to her heavily made-up eyelids.

He looked away, groaning inwardly at her outrageous flirtation. "Good morning." He set down his pen. "What can I do for you?"

"Now, that's a loaded question if I ever heard one." She giggled.

"I didn't mean anything by it." He felt a need to explain due to his past problems with her flirtations.

"Right." She plopped down on the chair opposite him and crossed her arms over his desk. Over his blueprints.

Her perfume scent was strong. He wished she'd move back. Preferably, to get out of his office and stay out of it. Didn't she have work-related tasks to be doing in her own space as the company receptionist?

"The mayor and I would like you and the little wife to come to dinner tomorrow night." Her obviously-whitened teeth gleamed brightly next to her red lipstick.

"What do you mean, you and my dad?" He didn't want to hear of any talk about those two being together. Especially not when he still hoped his dad would get counseling and try to make peace with his mom. Even if his parents didn't get back together, his dad ought to at least admit his wrongs and apologize before he moved on with his life with another woman.

"The mayor and I are still working on the city's reconstruction plan." Mia tapped the blueprint with a plum-colored fingernail. "We're both stoked about all the accomplishments the renewal groups are doing. Your dad is such a great leader."

Right. Why was she here gushing about the mayor?

"About dinner?" She leaned forward, edging her elbows across the blueprints. "Eddie wanted me to ask. He's eager for you guys to talk over what needs to be done for the good of the town."

Eddie? Her familiar, almost intimate, reference to his father twisted the proverbial knife in his gut. He clenched his jaw to keep himself from telling her off. As far as he knew, his father didn't even approve of anyone calling him that nickname. How did Mia get away with it?

"It'll be fun to get together. No reason to let past disagreements get in the way of business, right?" She crossed her legs and swung her high heel like she had all day to sit around doing nothing. "Bury the hatchet and all of that, hmm?" She squinted at him. How aware of his parents' problems was she? Did she know his father had a dark side that she should beware of and avoid at all costs? "Can I tell Eddie you're in?" Mia stood and smoothed her hands down her skirt.

"I'll talk with Paisley. See if she has time. Although, we're pretty busy right now." He could imagine her response—*no way!*

"Oh, right. I heard you two are planning to renew your nuptials. How quaint."

He ignored her impolite assessment. Hopefully, his father wouldn't bring her along to their vow renewal as a plus-one. How awkward would that be? Might be heated words exchanged between his mom and dad. That's all he needed on one of the most important days of his life.

He pressed his fingers against his forehead, willing away tension.

"What if Paisley doesn't want to meet up?" Mia curled her index finger toward his chest, then pulled it back toward herself like she was reeling in a fish. "You'll still have dinner with us, right? It's not like you have a ball and chain around your neck *yet.*"

He gritted his teeth. "I'll attend if I want to"—it wasn't like Paisley would ask him not to—"but like I said, we're busy." He ran his palm over a crumpled edge of the blueprint. Did Mia crinkle it on purpose?

"Come on, your dad wants to talk with you." A hard edge crept into her tone. "What harm is there in chatting with him?"

Plenty of harm, depending on Edward's demands. "You can tell the mayor that he and I, and only he and I, can get together for a talk any time after work this week." He nodded toward the door. "Please shut the door on your way out."

Both of her fists landed on his desk. She leaned forward, her eyes glinting. "Listen, Jude. It's not my fault your dad left your mom. Stop blaming me."

Who did she think she was speaking to him that way? He leaped to his feet, his shoulders tightening. "First, don't call me 'Jude.' Second, my dad did not leave my mom." Not that he had to explain anything to her.

"Whatever." She shrugged and her necklaces clinked together. "I'm not some homewrecker. It's not my fault they didn't get along."

"Didn't get along? Is that what he told you? You ought to sprint away from 'Eddie' while you can." Judah leafed through some papers to calm himself down. "We're done here. In the future, I'll thank you not to mention my father to me during work hours."

She held a steady glare at him for about ten seconds, then she whirled around, stomping across the office. At the doorway, she paused, her back toward him. "Remember, you and I both know how you got this job." Then she strutted around the corner.

What was she implying? That he'd been asked to return to C-MER in some underhanded way? He wadded up a scrap of paper into a ball and hurled it into the trash. He'd had all he could take of the receptionist's insinuations.

Where was Craig? The two of them needed to have a discussion. Then he'd talk with Mike Linfield, if necessary. He planned to get to the bottom of Mia's and his father's intimations that the mayor may have pulled rank and gotten him this position.

Angst burning in his chest, he strode out of the office in search of Craig's cubicle. Judah should have had a conversation with him before now. He should have tried to make peace, even if it cut him to the core. Being a Grant, humility didn't come easily, but he was determined to get beyond that.

As soon as he entered the work area where a half-dozen cubicles were clustered around the center of the space, with a few others lining the outer wall, he heard feminine laughter. Mia's voice? Why wasn't she at the front desk where she belonged? Something needed to be done about her fraternizing and flirtations with employees.

He passed by Jeff's and Todd's cubicles, then rounded his old partition. Craig sat behind the desk where Judah had spent much of his eleven years with C-MER, when he wasn't out in a skiff on the ocean watching the coastline. Mia pranced about in front of the man's desk as if acting out a story or telling a joke. Craig covered his mouth with his hand and guffawed. His laughter sounded odd after the grumpy behavior he'd exhibited over the last month.

Mia wagged her index finger. "Don't you talk to me that way." Was she mimicking Judah? Or his father?

"Breaktime over yet?" He leaned his arm over the partition and met the startled gazes of the other two.

"Oh, Judah." Mia's hands landed on the center of her chest. "You startled me."

At least she got his name right this time.

Craig stared at him without any laughter or welcome. His dark eyes squinted as if Judah were intruding.

"I was delivering a message to Craig, that's all." Mia grinned at her old supervisor and winked.

"Are you finished?" Judah fought to keep his tone civil.

"Sure am, boss." She scooted past him. Giggling, she waved at Craig. "Too-da-loo."

Craig nodded at her, following her with his gaze. "I didn't have anything to do with that."

"Not encouraging her, are you?"

"What's it to you? Oh, right. Her and your father."

"Not that." Judah glared at the other man but refrained from saying something rude. "I wouldn't want harassment charges brought against anyone here."

Craig rolled his eyes. "You and your dad are the most suspicious people on the planet. Must run in the family."

That got Judah's hackles up. He didn't like being compared to his father. But he forced himself to focus on what he walked over here to do. "Meet me at your"—he swallowed—"my office in five minutes. There are things we need to discuss."

Craig tapped his fingers over his keyboard, staring at the computer screen. Obviously, he wasn't concerned about Judah outranking him now.

"Did you hear me?"

"Yep."

"Okay."

Judah said hello to a couple of his previous cubicle buddies on the way back to his office. Mentally, he coached himself to discuss only job-related topics with Craig, and not dig up things they fought about in the past.

Fifteen minutes later, Craig shuffled into the office and dropped into the chair opposite Judah. He slouched over, his eyes appearing glassy. Looked like he'd aged twenty years in the last week. "*Whaddya* want to see me about?" Did he just slur his words? "Let's get it over with."

He wasn't drinking on the job today, was he? Probably nerves. This awkwardness affected both of them—Judah sitting in Craig's old chair; Craig working in Judah's former cubicle. All the problems with Craig and Paisley, then Craig and Paige, still hovered between them. Not to mention all the weird vibes during that community dinner five days ago.

If only Craig knew that Judah saved him from a ton of cleanup work when he stopped Paisley from mud bombing his house. He almost snickered at the remembrance, until he met Craig's icy glare.

Judah cleared his throat. "I wanted us to have a chat about our new seating arrangements."

"You mean me sitting in your cubicle flirting with your old girlfriend?"

Is that what Craig thought? That Judah was jealous of him and Mia? A rebuttal leaped into his thoughts—Mia had never been his girlfriend. Instead, he said, "No, I wanted to ask you how this happened."

"What happened?"

"My dad said—"

"What does big-daddy-o say? That he wants the best for his boys?" What did Craig mean by that? "Why did you ask me to come in here?" He gazed around the room as if noticing the changes.

"I haven't switched much of anything in here other than picking up the garbage." Judah couldn't ignore that offense. "Thanks a lot for the mess you left me."

"No problem."

"I'd like to know the chain of events that led to my getting this job." Judah glanced around the office that used to be Craig's. Was it difficult for the other man to be in here now? "I'd like to know I got this position fairly."

"Fairly?" Craig guffawed. "Think about it. How could you have gotten my job? I had seniority. A clean record."

Not so clean. However, if Judah mentioned that it would only add fuel to the fire. "That's what I'm trying to figure out. I don't want a job because my father forced it to happen."

"Sometimes you're hilarious, Grant. Didn't get that from your dad."

"I'm sure I didn't."

"At least you had a mom who cared for you."

The change in topic and Craig's gentler tone surprised him. "What's that supposed to mean?"

"Nothing. Just be grateful for what you have."

Mia danced into the room with a plate of sliced bread. "Hey, guys. One of the wives brought in a couple of loaves of freshly made banana bread. I split them up. Want some?"

"No, thanks." Why did she keep popping into his office, interfering, disrupting his work?

She leaned down by Craig and whispered something. What was she up to now?

Craig sat up straighter. He reached over to take a slice of bread, but his hand shook.

"Here you go." Mia pulled a napkin out from under the plate and set a piece of bread on it, then handed it to Craig. She did the same for Judah.

"Thanks," he said, even though he told her he didn't want any. He set the homemade food on the desk. "If you'll excuse us? We're in a meeting here."

"Oh, right. Sure. Want some coffee?"

"None for me." Judah's irritation level increased. Something was going on with these two, whether romantic or devious, he couldn't tell.

"I'll be right back with a cup for you, Craig." Did he even say he wanted coffee? Had she seen his hand shaking?

Leaning forward, Craig pressed his fingers against his temples.

"Are you okay? Are you sick?"

"I have a headache."

"Sorry." Judah pondered what they were talking about before Mia intruded. "May I ask what happened for you to get sent back to the cubicles?" By questioning him, Judah dared to incur Craig's wrath, but he was determined to get some answers.

"Man, I don't—" Craig grabbed the trash can and lost his breakfast in it.

Judah jumped up and strode out of the room to give him a minute of privacy.

"Sorry, man." Craig trudged past him, the wastebasket extended from his hands, a grimace on his face. He headed toward the men's restroom.

So much for an honest and open discussion. Judah returned to his office—*phew*—and yanked open the window. Maybe he'd shut the door and work in the lobby until the air cleared out.

Mia waltzed into the room with a cup of coffee. "Did Craig—" She clamped her mouth shut. Her eyes widened, and she backed out of the room.

That was one way to keep her out of his office. Judah scooped up a file and followed her, closing the door. "He's not feeling well."

"The flu's going around." She offered him the cup. "Could you use some coffee now?"

"Why not?" He took the mug and trudged toward the front end of the building to sit on the leather furniture that faced the sand dunes. This side of the building was Mia's domain, but he'd do his best to stay clear of her.

A few minutes later, Craig landed in the seat next to him. "Maybe I should head home."

"Yeah, sure. Too bad about your illness." Judah glanced over his shoulder and observed Mia talking on the phone. She laughed and, as if noticing him watching her, danced her fingers in his direction. Ignoring her gesture, he turned back toward Craig. "Can you drive home safely?"

Craig shrugged. "About the other thing. Your promotion."

"Yes?"

Craig jerked a couple of times. Did he almost fall asleep?

"Maybe you should go rest in the sick bay. Probably shouldn't be driving." They had a small office with a cot that some of the crew used to sleep on when they were on call overnight. Even Judah slept there in the past.

"Yeah, that sounds right." Craig stood, swayed. "I'm beat."

Did he have a hangover? Judah hated to report him. But he wasn't in any condition to go out on a skiff if an emergency call came in.

Craig stumbled on his way to the sick bay. Judah hopped up and escorted him back to the room a few doors from his office. Craig groaned and collapsed on the narrow cot.

"Sleep it off, huh?" Judah tapped the light switch and stepped from the room.

"It was the mayor."

"What?" He paused and stared into the darkened space.

"Edward has something he's holding over Linfield." Craig coughed, maybe gagged.

"Something like—?"

"Money. Secrets. Favors. Same as me. Your dad has a lot of people in Basalt who owe him big-time. He doesn't let them forget it, either. That's where he gets his power. His success." Craig belched. "We got switched, you and me."

He wasn't making sense.

"My office. Your cubicle." He hiccupped. "My cubicle. Your office."

"Right. Get some sleep, man." Judah closed the door. He stood there for a moment, replaying Craig's words. *Your dad has a lot of people in Basalt who owe him.* Was that true?

Six

In Aunt Callie's kitchen later in the afternoon, Paisley threw together her version of homemade soup by opening several cans of premade varieties—chicken noodle, beef barley, vegetable, steak and potatoes—and dumping them together. She filled up a large pan that should last her convalescing aunt for a few days.

Aunt Callie lay in her bed, bemoaning her sore hip but arguing against going to the doctor. "Is Pauly coming over?" Her eyes lit up as she slurped the soup Paisley gave her.

"Not today. You know how he is."

"A stubborn, grouchy old coot, that's what." Aunt Callie harrumphed. "Grudges run deep in that man's soul."

Paisley had learned that the hard way.

Aunt Callie took a few bites of soup. "This is good. What is it?"

"A Campbells, Progresso, and Wolfgang Puck combo."

"Canned soup?" The older woman scowled. "Didn't anyone teach you to cook, Paisley Rose?"

"Mom tried. I've burned too many things to care." She thought of Judah. "Fortunately, I married a man who likes to cook."

"Lucky you." Aunt Callie put another spoonful of soup in her mouth.

"Indeed." Paisley was lucky for more reasons than Judah's ability to grill a fabulous steak. She pictured his baby blues gazing at her like he could see into her heart. Him linking pinkies with her. His tender kisses. She sighed. Then she focused on something she'd been meaning to ask her aunt. "A couple of weeks ago, you mentioned something about my dad being stubborn and not talking to you around the time he married Mom. What happened?"

Aunt Callie's spoon stalled midair. "Doesn't matter."

"Doesn't it?" Paisley smoothed her hand over the patchwork quilt. "Isn't there still a squabble going on between the two of you?"

"Siblings quarrel. You know that as well as I do." Slurping her soup, she gave Paisley one of her squinty-eyed glares.

"You mean Paige and me. I'm talking about you and Dad. Why the bickering after all these years?"

Aunt Callie pushed the bowl into Paisley's hands. She wiggled her back against the mound of pillows and closed her eyes as if to ignore the question altogether.

Paisley took the dishware to the kitchen sink and ran some water over it. It was time for her to leave anyway, although she would have liked to hear her aunt's answer. She traipsed back into the bedroom to say her goodbyes and found Aunt Callie in tears.

"Auntie, what's wrong? Are you in that much pain?" She adjusted her pillows. "Shall we call for an ambulance?" She wouldn't be able to get her aunt into Dad's Volkswagen by herself. Even getting her home after the accident earlier today had taken James and Dad to get her settled. Fortunately, her father came out of hiding long enough to be of assistance.

"No, no. I'll be okay."

"What is it, then?"

"Your question got me thinking is all." She sniffed and patted the side of the bed where Paisley sat before.

Was her aunt going to honestly talk to her? Or was this a ploy to get Paisley to stick around a while longer? She had things to do. Invitations to pass out. But she sat down and faced her aunt. "What's bothering you?"

"She was an odd one, your mom. Didn't approve of social gatherings or frivolity." Aunt Callie heaved a sigh. "Standoffish, she withdrew into her art. Nothing wrong with that mind you, but she withdrew so far into herself it was hard to reach her."

That wasn't news to Paisley. Although, to hear anyone speak of the past in such an open way was surprising. Dad never did. He said he couldn't speak ill of his late wife. "But Dad loved her, right?"

"He said he did, although I never knew why."

"Auntie!"

"Well, it's true." Aunt Callie groaned. "I shouldn't say anything. I told myself I wouldn't. Pauly would rather take his secrets to the grave."

"What secrets? What happened? Please, tell me."

"Maybe it is time you knew." Aunt Callie's lip trembled like she was on the verge of crying again. "You see, Pauly loved another before your mom."

"What?" Paisley sat up straighter on the bed. "He said Mom was his one true love."

"Pshaw. He was gaga over Sue Anne Whitley." She said the woman's name like it was a treasured memory. "Several of the local boys fell for her, even Edward Grant"—her tone changed at the mention of his name—"although he was younger than her."

"What? Dad and Edward went after the same girl?"

"That's right. But she loved my Pauly something fierce. Made Edward crazy with jealousy." Aunt Callie stared out the window as if watching events from long ago. "Sue Anne and Pauly were mad about each other. Can't-live-without-you stuff."

"I can't imagine Dad being 'gaga' over anyone, especially someone other than Mom." She couldn't even remember him being affectionate with her.

"The man was a romantic back in those days. And Sue Anne was my best friend."

"So what happened?" Paisley pulled her legs up, wrapping her arms around her knees. "They obviously didn't get married."

"No, but I thought they would." Aunt Callie made tsk-tsk sounds. "Never saw two people more in love. Dancing. Holding hands. Stealing kisses. Making plans for the future."

"Dad dancing? No way." Why hadn't she ever heard of this before?

"Back then he did. Pauly and Sue Anne were good dancers too." Such a look of longing for yesteryear or some unseen memory captured her features. A tear dripped down her cheek.

Paisley gulped. She didn't want to push her aunt into a painful discussion, but she needed to hear the rest of the story. "Something must have broken them up. Did Mom come between them?"

"They argued. Couples do that." Aunt Callie tossed her hands in the air. "Didn't mean they'd break up for good. They took a few days to cool down, think things over. Sue Anne told me she felt bad about whatever she said. Pauly said mean stuff too. Not that I heard, but he was my brother for goodness' sake. He could mouth off. Look how he holds a grudge!"

Ignoring that, Paisley tried imagining her father as a young, handsome dancer. He and Mom never seemed that happy. Did Dad ever regret choosing her over Sue Anne? "So they never got back together?"

"Nope. Penny's family moved to town that weekend. Their family had suffered a loss. A younger sibling drowned in the sea."

"Drowned? Maybe that's why Mom hated the ocean." Why didn't she ever say anything about it? Even when Paisley lost the baby, her mom hadn't seemed empathetic. "How did Dad end up with Mom if Sue Anne was so charming?"

"Who knows? When Pauly met Penny, he heard her story and felt bad for her. Who wouldn't? Didn't mean he had to marry her." Aunt Callie snorted. "He told me he liked how different she was from the local girls. Never danced. Rarely went out. So sad."

Some of Paisley's childhood daydreams of her parents being romantic at some point in their lives crumbled.

"Of course, the whole *we-both-have-P-names* drove me nuts. Like that was a sign from heaven." She made more tsk-tsk sounds. "Pauly was on the rebound. They married quickly. Said they'd name their kids 'P' names, too, which they did."

Paisley contemplated her sibling's and her names—Peter, Paisley, Paige. And Paige even named her daughter Piper, carrying on the tradition.

Her aunt put her fist to her mouth like she was holding back a sob. "Nearly broke Sue Anne's heart. Once Pauly made the decision, he wouldn't back down. So stubborn and prideful."

"What happened to Sue Anne?"

"Married a Coast Guard fellow and moved east." Aunt Callie sighed. "She and I lost contact. I always regretted what happened between them. I couldn't let it go for the longest time."

"And the squabble? Why the bitterness between you and Dad after all these years?"

"Before the wedding, I told him what I thought of him jumping into marriage with a girl he barely knew when he loved Sue Anne." Aunt Callie shuddered. "He could have been happy all these years, instead of tiptoeing around Penny."

She let out another long sigh. "Now, I don't mean to say I wanted you and your siblings to be anyone other than who you are. But if only you could have seen your daddy." She smiled and Paisley figured she was imagining her youthful brother.

Maybe Dad understood her unhappiness in her marriage, and her trouble with Edward Grant, more than he ever let on. Perhaps, he would have been an ally had she talked to him.

"I hope this revelation doesn't shock you."

"Not really." It made her feel more compassionate toward her father.

"You asked if Pauly loved Penny."

"That's right." Did her dad find happiness, even if her parents didn't act romantic toward each other? They had three children. Although, even she knew that didn't guarantee happiness.

"Maybe he did, given the years they stayed together." Aunt Callie folded and unfolded her hands. "But after seeing him with Sue Anne, I never once saw him act that way with Penny."

"It's a tragic story." Although, Paisley couldn't picture her father being as jovial as Aunt Callie made him out to be, either. "What else happened between you two?"

"What makes you think anything else happened?" She reached for a glass on the nightstand. Paisley jumped up and handed it to her. Aunt Callie took a long swallow of water. Stalling?

After setting the glass back down, Paisley resettled on the edge of the bed again. "Come on, tell me. I suspect there's more to the story."

"I may have said some other things to Pauly that I shouldn't have." Aunt Callie's lower lip protruded. "I didn't mean to alienate my only sibling, again."

"What did you say to him?"

"After Penny passed on, I told him that now he should find a warmhearted woman like Sue Anne."

"What?"

"I know. That was harsh. I didn't mean for him to run out and marry someone right then. Terrible timing." She made a strangled-sounding cry. "I apologized, but he hasn't forgiven me."

Paisley patted her hand. She knew firsthand about making mistakes and people holding grudges. "He doesn't like talking about the past, but don't stop trying to get him to talk things through. Your relationship is worth it, right?"

Her aunt shuffled against the pillows, scooting down into the covers. "All that talk about the past is exhausting."

"You should get some rest. Thank you for telling me about Dad and Sue Anne. Mom too. It helps me understand our family better."

"Can't say as I ever understood your mama." Aunt Callie

shook her head, blinking slowly like she was sleepy. "Like that pantry business."

"Wait." Paisley's chest tightened. "What do you know about that?"

"I know I didn't approve. And it created a bigger rift between Pauly and me."

"So you knew about the pantry?" Paisley's heart thudded in her ears. She took several deep breaths. "Tell me, please." The things she heard today mattered and were a part of her family history. But this, *this* was something she desperately needed to hear.

"When I found out she put you kids in the pantry and left you in the dark as punishment, I came unglued." Aunt Callie drew in a nasal breath. "I confronted Pauly. Would have raked Penny over the coals too, but he forbade me. Said he wouldn't speak to me again if I stirred up trouble."

"Oh, Auntie." Hope clawed to the surface of Paisley's wounded spirit. Someone had tried to rescue her. "What else did Dad say?"

"He said I didn't have kids. It wasn't my business." Aunt Callie coughed like she'd been talking too long. "I threatened to call the police or Social Services."

If only she had. If only she'd taken the time to find out how badly Paisley's situation became. But, realizing her aunt had tried to help, even threatened to do something, made her feel closer to her. She leaned her head against her shoulder. "Thank you, Auntie."

The older woman patted Paisley's head. "He kicked me out of the house, but it was our family home. I could go there any time I wanted." Aunt Callie pulled a yellow-flowered hanky from beneath her pillow that looked small in her hands, a vintage pattern from the '70s. She twisted it between her fingers. "That's when I got the idea to stop by and ask for sweet tea. It would be unneighborly of them to refuse." She chuckled lightly. "It gave me a chance to peek in the window and check on you children. I couldn't let my nieces or nephew be in trouble and not help. But your mama didn't like me hanging around, spying on her."

Too bad Paisley wasn't aware of her aunt's efforts back then. Here she'd considered her little more than a blabbing gossip.

"You said, nieces." Paisley touched Aunt Callie's wrist. "Did you think Paige was locked in the pantry too?"

"She was."

"Really?" Tears flooded Paisley's eyes. She'd always considered her sister the favored child, while she was the worst kid in Basalt. "Paige could do no wrong. Why lock her up?"

"Who knows? You and Peter challenged Penny's need for solitude. Maybe Paige did too."

Paisley remembered how she and Peter usually played outside where the sound of their voices couldn't affect their mother's fragile peace of mind.

She sat quietly for a few minutes. So did her aunt. Maybe they were both pouring over the details of the past. She had one more question to ask before this conversation ended. "Did you and James have a thing back in the day?"

"'A thing?'" Aunt Callie coughed as if she were choking. "What are you talking about?"

"You never had a crush on the neighbor boy? Not even in school?" Paisley kept pushing despite her aunt's spider-killing glare. "I noticed the way you spoke softly to each other, your gazes sparkling. It seems like a romantic history to me."

"Romantic?" Aunt Callie's face hued as red as a tomato. "I'm warning you, none of that nonsense. And don't you dare whisper a word of it to Maggie. Now, I'm tired. You should go." She huffed and turned sharply away from Paisley.

"Was he sweet on you?" Paisley grinned impishly.

"Too long ago to matter. Now, goodbye." She shuffled deeper beneath the comforter.

"Fine." Paisley kissed her aunt's cheek and left her to get some sleep.

All the way back to her dad's house, her thoughts churned with the things Aunt Callie had told her. Hopefully, one of these days she'd get the chance to talk with Paige about it, too.

Seven

Judah stood by his desk staring at a cryptic text from Mike Linfield. *Meeting in my office. Five minutes*. No subject reference. No information. Was Judah supposed to bring any blueprints or files?

Mia slinked into the doorway, grinning. Why couldn't she stay on her side of the building? But her job included delivering messages and mail, so Judah had to put up with her random intrusions. Maybe that's why she was here. No reason to expect her flirtatious nature was the cause of this visit.

"You're on your way out, huh?" She nudged the door closed and leaned against it, crossing her arms.

Irritation crawled up his neck. "What's going on?" By the twinkle in her eye, his first impression was correct. She did have ulterior motives.

"I must tell you something."

"Okay. But I'd rather keep the door open."

She didn't move. "You know that meeting you're about to go to?"

"Yes. What about it?"

"Any way you could skip it?"

"Now, why would I do that? Mike asked me to meet him." And what business was it of hers?

"Just hear me out, okay?"

"Fine." Judah checked his watch. His five minutes were over. "Talk fast. I have to go."

"Here's the deal." She swayed forward as if exaggerating the swing of her hips and smiled in a predatorial I-have-power-over-men expression.

Not over him. He picked up a file off his desk and thumbed through it, avoiding her gaze.

"Your father wants to see you before you talk with Mike about the peninsula." She smoothed her hand over the edge of his desk. "Then he needs a face-to-face meeting with Mike."

So, his father, the great manipulator, couldn't help but control something else in Judah's life?

"What, you're working for my dad now?" Maybe he should suggest that she give up this job and go work at City Hall. And good riddance. But he didn't want her hanging around his father full time, either.

"I'm volunteering with the town reconstruction committee, that's all." She shrugged. "Although, I may have mentioned something to the mayor about what I saw on the blueprints."

"You may have?" He bit back a growl of frustration. C-MER's plans weren't top secret. But why was she yapping about work-related projects to the mayor? "And you saw these blueprints how?" By cozying up to some engineer, no doubt. He didn't need information getting leaked to the locals when they were only at the preliminary planning stage of the peninsula's reconstruction.

"I saw the drawings on the boys' desks. No biggie." She lifted one shoulder then lowered it. "It's not a secret, right?"

The boys being whom? Todd? Craig? Jeff?

"It's not a secret, but there's an unwritten code of confidentiality here. What are you doing talking with the mayor about company business?" She'd already crossed the line too many times with excessive flirting. Now she was passing company information? Maybe he should report her. End her affiliation with C-MER once and for all. But ratting on a coworker wasn't his way of doing things, despite how he felt about her right now.

His work phone buzzed, and before he could reach out and grab the receiver, Mia beat him to it.

"Hey, that's my—"

"Yes, sir," she spoke into the receiver in a breathy voice. "Uh-huh. I'll tell him."

Sir? Most likely Mike Linfield. What would his boss think of Mia answering Judah's phone in a sultry voice like that? Or of them being behind closed doors? Not that Mike or any other employee knew about that, but gossip traveled fast in the small group. He covered the distance from his desk to the door in a few steps. He grabbed the knob, pulling the door open just as Todd strode past. His coworker gazed at something beyond him. Mia? *Ugh.*

"Sorry that I detained him, sir." Her lilting voice caught his attention again. "He'll be right there."

Judah rushed back to his desk, scooped up the file he'd been working on for the last few days, then strode for the open doorway.

Mia dropped the phone and charged ahead of him. She thrust out her hands as if that move had the power to stop him from exiting his office. "We haven't finished our discussion."

"Oh, yes, we have. In the future, don't close my door, don't answer my phone, and do not discuss C-MER business with the mayor. Got it?" He glared at her. "Otherwise, you may find yourself looking for another job. Now, get out of my way."

Her jaw dropped, but then she seemed to shake off his rebuff. "Please, listen to me first."

He groaned then shuffled back to where he was standing before as if to acquiesce to her wishes. But when he heard her following him, he pivoted like a basketball player and dodged around the opposite side of the desk and exited the doorway.

"Judah!" Her heels clicked after him. "Wait! You have to hear me out."

No, he didn't. He stomped toward Mike Linfield's office. After knocking on the manager's door, he entered and shut the door, stopping the receptionist from joining them. Swallowing down his frustration, he tried to appear calmer than he felt. Mia was pushing the lines of flirtation, and insubordination, too much.

Mike talked on his cell phone and held up his finger in a wait-a-minute signal. Judah remained by the door in the office that wasn't much bigger than his own.

"Yes, I understand." Mike's voice turned abrasive. His face reddened. "You assume I'm responsible for that?" A pause, then, "Good day, Mayor!" He slammed the phone onto his desk. "You and your father are like night and day, aren't you?"

"Pretty much."

Mike pointed at the black chair across from him. "Have you been talking with Mayor Grant about our plans for the peninsula?"

"Me? No, I have not." He dropped into the seat. Hadn't Mia just admitted to telling the mayor about the blueprints? Should he mention that to Mike?

His boss squinted at him. "I'd hoped you would keep our project plans to yourself until they're finalized."

"Of course, I would." His face heated up at the implication that he'd blabbed to someone who could cause them difficulty.

"I'm not a fan of Mayor Grant. Never have been."

"I've hardly even spoken to my father since Hurricane Blaine hit." There were reasons, personal reasons, for that other than the hurricane.

Mike thumped his fist against the desk. "Then it appears we have a mole in our ranks."

"I have a hunch who that might be, although I'd rather not say until I have more information." He didn't have any reason to protect Mia's position in the company, no reason to keep the peace at all costs, yet he still didn't like the idea of ratting out a coworker.

Mike squinted at Judah again. Did he still suspect him of compromising their project? "We have a problem with your plans for the peninsula."

"We do?" Judah's shoulders tensed and he leaned forward. "What is it?" Would he be expected to put in extra hours to correct the problem? On the week of his vow renewal ceremony when he planned to spend more time with Paisley?

"The mayor"—Mike grimaced like he'd bitten into a lemon—"wants the town council to discuss our plans, and vote on it, before we move forward with anything. And he means *anything*."

So, Edward had found his own way to discuss this with Mike. What was Mia's powerplay back in Judah's office? A stall tactic? Control?

"We're only at the initial phase of the project. Why should anyone vote on it? Why does he care?" As soon as he said the words, he pictured his father's obsessive need to run everything.

"That's what I asked." Mike tossed up his hands.

"What we're doing is for the safety of the town and for the tourist industry." Judah dropped the file he brought onto the desk and nudged it toward Mike. "We've been working on a solution that will provide safety for the coastline for years to come. He should be grateful for our efforts."

"One would think." Mike riffled through the papers in the file. He tapped his finger against an image of the proposed dike. "He claims the peninsula is considered a historical landmark."

"If so, it's an unsafe one. Something must be done. Otherwise, we'll have to post security and not allow anyone access to it." Paisley would hate that. So would other longtime residents. "All the signage on the beach will be an eyesore for tourists, too."

"You don't have to tell me that." Mike eyed him intensely. "So, you and your dad don't get along, huh?"

"You could say that."

"Any way you could patch things up so the mayor will work with us?" Mike glanced out the window as if avoiding Judah's gaze now. "That's one of the reasons we rehired you. To be a liaison between C-MER and the town council—namely, the mayor."

What? He was hired because of his family ties with Mayor Grant? That news felt like a slug to his gut. He wasn't hired because of his experience or his years on the job? Any pride he felt in his accomplishments over the last week disintegrated.

"How shall we move forward with this project?" Mike ran his fingers over the edge of the photo.

After what he just heard, Judah didn't care much about the proposed project, but he schooled his features. He had to focus on the job. Then he'd ponder what Mike said later. "The team has spent hundreds of manhours pounding out the details. We don't want that time wasted."

"No, we don't." Mike peered at the miniature printouts of the original blueprints, his jaw clenching and unclenching. "The recent storms have squeezed our financial reserves to the max. We need the town's goodwill. And their financial backing."

No wonder he was catering to the mayor's wishes—money.

Judah sank back into his chair.

"I need you to be our peacemaker with the city."

Peacemaker? Judah felt anything but diplomatic when it came to Edward Grant.

"In fact, I'd like you to have a chat with the mayor today." Mike tapped his fingers on his desk surface. "See what you can do to smooth things out. Take Mia with you."

"Mia? Why?"

"She and the mayor have been seen around town together." Mike's chuckle sounded forced. "She may be our foot in the door at City Hall."

"I'd rather not be involved with—"

"Oh, right. She's not what you had in mind for a stepmom, huh?" Mike guffawed.

"She's not my—"

"Just kidding." Mike palmed the air. "Take it easy."

Why would his boss even say such a thing?

"I realize," Mike spoke quieter, "she could be the leak."

He knew? Yet he didn't care?

"Or it might be Craig." The manager opened a mint tin and popped one into his mouth. "But we have to knock this project out and soften the mayor's attitude about it. And, while it pains me to say it, groveling for approval and financing might be required."

"Begging the mayor for help? No, thanks. The man's my father. Isn't that a conflict of interest?" Judah stood in a huff. Too late, he realized he probably sounded rude. "No disrespect intended. I appreciate the job here, but wouldn't it be better if Jeff, or even Craig, went to City Hall instead of me?"

Mike squinted at him. "We all have a price to pay to keep our positions. Today is your turn."

A veiled threat? Like if he didn't do this task he'd be released from C-MER? "I'd rather not work with the mayor, if at all possible."

"Even if it means losing your job?" A gleam hued Mike's eyes to almost silver.

He needed a job, but at what cost? Could he even talk to the mayor on a professional level without their personal problems muddying the waters? And bring Mia along? What about her being the one who was yacking about company business?

"Judah?"

"Yes, sir. I'll give it my best shot." What else could he say? He hadn't spoken with his father in ten days, ever since he showed up at the cottage ordering Mom around, and she threw a glass of water at him.

"That's what I want to hear. When you meet, focus on the safety aspects of the project." Mike rocked his thumb toward the door. "Let me know how it turns out."

Judah would have preferred a couple of days to come up with a plan that might have a measure of success. How would he face Mia and his dad working together without saying something that might jeopardize the project?

Hating the task ahead, he strode to the receptionist's desk. Mia stared at her computer screen, her shiny fingernails tapping the keyboard. She didn't even glance his way. Ignoring him now?

He cleared his throat. "Mike wants you to accompany me to a meeting with the mayor today. Set it up, will you?"

"Of course, I will." She broke into a wide grin as if all were forgotten. She lifted her cell phone. "You know, Todd asked me why you and I were meeting behind closed doors." She made a couple of exaggerated winks. "I had to tell him the truth."

"That being?"

"I can't resist a man like you. Never could." Wink, wink.

He groaned.

"Shall we ride over to City Hall together? Maybe get a drink on the way back?"

"No, I don't think so." Not in a million years. "I'll drive my truck. Let me know the time of the meeting." He marched to his office and shut the door. Without sitting down, he picked up his cell phone and tapped Paisley's name.

"Hi, you," she answered softly. "What's up?"

"Stuff's happening. Mia—" He ground out her name.

"What did she do now?"

He briefly related what transpired over the last hour.

"Anything I can do to help?"

He appreciated that her first response was to assist him. Not expressing anger over Mia's involvement, although it probably frustrated her as much as it did him. With the way the receptionist kept insinuating herself into his personal life, and now with the way she was doing that with Edward, it troubled him.

"Maybe nothing terrible will come of the meeting or the other stuff about Mia." Her voice went quiet.

"She suggested we ride together. I declined."

"Good for you. But, Judah, look, I trust you. Really, I do."

"Okay. Thanks."

"Just don't forget who you're dealing with—a mastermind of flirtation. Perhaps, a genius of manipulation. Be careful, okay?"

"I will."

"Oh, and Judah?"

"Yeah?"

"Thank you for wanting to keep things honest between us." She took a breath. "I'm lucky to have you in my life again."

The tenderness of her words made him eager to finish the workday so he could see her again.

"Want me to grab something for dinner?" He could stop by Lewis's and get some deli food. "We could have a picnic before our session with Pastor Sagle."

"That sounds great."

He loved her voice. Loved hearing her soft tones.

"Only four days left until I get to hold you the way I want to hold you." He grinned even though she wouldn't be able to see his expression.

"Ditto." She chuckled and the sound washed over him. "Will you have time to squeeze in a meal with me?"

"I always have time for you."

"I like the sound of that."

So did he.

Knowing they would meet up later would help him get through the uncomfortable meeting he still had to face.

Eight

For fifteen minutes, Judah sat at the ten-foot oval conference table at City Hall, waiting for Mayor Grant and Mia. Was this part of Edward's strategy to keep him feeling apprehensive? More manipulation?

Mia finally sashayed into the room, her high heels tap dancing across the floor. A strong scent of floral perfume surrounded her. Judah's shoulders and neck tightened—a normal reaction around her these days. "Where's Eddie?" She glanced out the door's glass window. "I thought he'd be here by now."

"He must have been detained." A bitter taste filled his mouth. That the C-MER receptionist would dare to call his father such a casual name irked him. But he was here under orders to smooth ruffled feathers. Not to make a scene. Although, part of him wanted to do that very thing. Stomp out of the room, leave the city building, maybe dust off his shoes.

"I'll be right back." She left the room, but her scent lingered.

Was there any way he could talk to the mayor alone? Have a man-to-man talk with him about Mia Till? Once and for all, he'd like to find out if their friendship was more than business. Not that he cared to hear details about an affair.

The door opened and Mayor Grant strode into the room with Mia clinging to his arm. They both laughed, leaning in toward each other, whispering. Could the day get any worse? They deserved each other. Manipulator and manipulator. Only, what if Edward treated her like he'd treated Judah's mom? Mia didn't deserve that. No one did.

Edward sauntered toward the executive chair at the end of the table. "Judah."

"Mayor." Judah addressed him in his official capacity, although he was tempted to call him "Eddie" as Mia did.

"One other person will be attending this meeting." Mia dropped into the seat next to the mayor, across from Judah, and patted Edward's arm.

"Oh? Who's that?"

"You'll see."

The door opened again, and Craig shuffled lazily into the room. He gave Judah a cursory nod and sat next to Mia. Why was he attending? Shouldn't he be back at work?

"What's the deal with the committee needing to pass approval on a preliminary plan?" Judah jumped right into the topic.

The other three chuckled like he said something humorous.

He sat up straighter, trying not to look as insignificant as it seemed they were trying to make him feel.

"You want to take this one, Eddie?" Mia batted her fake eyelashes at the mayor.

"Sure." He smiled at her as if bedazzled, but in the next instant, he scowled at Judah. "The town council must approve and vote on any changes to the coastline within the city limits, prior to any actions by C-MER, per the city charter." He tipped his head and squinted as if Judah were a foolish child. "If you were doing your job, instead of just talking about doing your job, you'd know the public record too."

His words chafed, but Judah forced himself not to respond in a similar tone. "I wasn't aware the town charter demanded a vote when a hurricane had hit the coastline. When people's lives were at stake. Emergency repair work to the peninsula is essential for public safety." He tapped the file he brought. "Someone could step off the end of the peninsula and struggle in the crashing waves. The water's deep. We're all aware of the whirlpools. But an unsuspecting tourist might not read the signs. Might fall in and get swept away. Then who will be to blame? We don't want anyone to get hurt or die due to negligence. Something needs to be done ASAP."

"Aren't you biased since your wife is the one who took a careless tumble into the sea?" Craig gave his usual smirk.

"What I'm saying, *Craig*, is the town we all live in is trying to recover from a hurricane. Two, actually. In an emergency, we must make decisions for the good of all, without going through cross-the-T-and-dot-the-I protocols. Even you must recognize that, Mayor."

Edward returned a pelting gaze, squinting like he was thinking.

Judah pressed ahead. "If a lifesaving surgery were needed, a doctor wouldn't quibble over a signature. The same goes here. Emergency work needs to be done on the peninsula now."

"Good thing we came here so you could explain all of that to us." Craig snorted.

"What's your problem?" Judah shoved against the table and stood, towering above his coworker. He'd had enough of the other man's snide attitude.

Craig leaped to his feet also. He leaned forward and reached out as if to grab Judah by the coat sleeve.

"Settle down, you two." The mayor pounded the table. "I'll have none of that in my building!"

Mia's chuckle irritated Judah. So did her grins and unprofessional hand touches with the mayor. Good grief. His parents weren't even divorced yet—and he was tempted, with the riled way he was feeling, to say so. Instead, he sat down slowly.

Craig dropped onto his seat too.

"It's reasonable to assume the council might not vote on an emergency lifesaving situation." Edward gave Judah a hard stare. "But we need the town pulling together if financial aid is expected from the city. Is it?"

"I guess it is." He figured the mayor knew it was.

"Then procedures must be followed." Edward crossed his arms. "C-MER must put on the brakes until we get things sorted out. You can expect things to be different now."

"Different how?" Judah's voice deepened with his emotions.

"The citizens of Basalt Bay don't want C-MER controlling our coastline. Never did. Now we're prepared to do something about it." Edward stroked his chin. "We've had enough interference from outside sources."

Mia clapped for the mayor like he'd played a game-winning point.

Edward swiveled toward her in his chair and bowed his head slightly, then turned toward Judah and scowled again. "You'll have to address the whole committee before you move forward with any further plans, understood?"

"I thought this was the committee."

Mia laughed. "No, silly. This is just a few of us who I could pull together for a quick meeting. The mayor's a busy man. Our council people have jobs."

"You, Craig, and I could have met at work." These stall tactics were a waste of his time.

"But Eddie couldn't accommodate that." Mia wrote something in her notebook.

Eddie. The bitterness he felt at the familiarity of her nickname for his father hit him again.

The mayor stood. "I have another appointment. Leave a copy of your proposal with Mia. She'll distribute duplicates to the members. We'll meet again in say … two weeks?"

"No way. That's too long." Judah shoved away from the table and stood also. "I want a meeting tonight."

"Tonight?" The mayor blanched.

"What?" Mia screeched.

"This proposal, these plans, must move forward without delay. Didn't we just agree that emergency measures need to be taken?" Judah kept talking so no one else would speak. "If I must address a full committee, plan on a voting session tonight. Signs are up on the peninsula. But that won't stop some kid from wandering out there and slipping into the sea." He glared at Craig, visually challenging him to argue. What did the mayor hold over the guy's head to make him act like a puppy on a leash, so willing to comply?

"That might not be possible." Mia gesticulated frantically. "People have lives. Plans. Can't expect me to get the whole council here on a whim."

"Why not? The city has given same-day notice about other community meetings." He gave her a brief smile. Maybe not such a nice one, but this charade of them working together for the good of the town was over.

Mia and the mayor exchanged eye rolls and glances.

"Fine. I'll try," she said in a perturbed tone.

"Let's say at seven o'clock?" Edward strode from the room.

Judah slid the file to Mia, then tromped out of the building. Nearly to his truck, he heard heavy footsteps.

"Judah, wait." A male voice.

He whirled around, tense. "What do you want?"

"Look"—Craig stopped next to him—"I wanted to say thanks for not mentioning about yesterday to Mike. I'm sure you figured out why I was sick." He sounded sincere, maybe embarrassed that Judah knew he'd been hungover. "I shouldn't have come to work like that."

"No, you shouldn't have." Judah relaxed a little, although he was still irritated with how Craig acted in the meeting. "Why are you caught up in this?" He nodded toward City Hall. "The peninsula is dangerous. A hazard before the hurricanes hit—you know that. It's much worse since Addy and Blaine."

"Not because Paisley stupidly fell in?"

"Not just because of her accident. Although, I know what it's like for one of those whirlpools to nearly drag you to your death."

"You're right." Craig kicked at a rock. "Political stuff shouldn't come into play when people's lives are at stake."

"Exactly. Too bad you didn't say that inside."

"I wish I could explain." Craig toed the cement.

"Why can't you?"

"Not here."

"Yoo-hoo! Craig, need a lift back to work?" Mia shouted.

"Yep. Coming." Craig stared kitty-corner across the street as if lost in thought, or else staring at the art gallery. Thinking of Paige? "I never meant—" He cleared his throat. "Just watch yourself. And Paisley. There are things underfoot that could get—"

"Craig, come on," Mia demanded. "I'm leaving."

He took a couple of steps toward her.

"Wait." Judah pointed at his truck. "You want a lift back to work? We can still talk."

"And look more suspicious to the mayor? No, thanks." Craig glanced at City Hall. "I bet big Daddy Grant's in there watching us."

Judah gazed at the fortification that had weathered two mega-storms almost unscathed. When he turned back, Craig strutted toward Mia's sports car, laughing, and saying something about his mission being accomplished. She giggled and waved at Judah.

Did Craig just try to dupe him into believing he cared? Or was Craig playing Mia, tricking her into believing he told Judah something that he didn't?

Nine

Mid-afternoon, Paisley hauled a couple of garbage bags out to the trash can behind her dad's house. When she rounded the front corner again, Judah stood on the porch.

"Hi. What are you doing here?" Her heart skipped a beat at this unexpected, but most welcome, surprise.

"Hey, Pais." He scrambled down the steps, grinning, arms spread wide.

She met him halfway across the yard and hugged him. Laughing, Judah lifted her and twirled her, gazing up at her like he was delighted to see her. Talk about making a girl feel like a princess. He adjusted her in his arms, bringing her face, or her mouth, in alignment with his.

"What are you—"

His soft lips caressed hers, silencing her. His kiss grew in intensity, and she matched his ardor, kissing him back, running her fingers through his silky hair. They lingered in each other's arms until she recalled where they were—in Dad's front yard—and who might be watching—James Weston, or one of the other neighbors. She broke their kiss. Judah lowered her slowly to the ground, their gazes locked, both smiling.

"Hey." He stroked a long strand of hair away from her cheek.

"Hey, yourself." She smoothed her hands over his navy dress shirt, still encircled in his arms. "This is a nice surprise."

Leaning his forehead against hers, he sighed. "I was driving by and couldn't resist seeing you, if only for a couple of minutes."

His hold on her loosened, but she didn't back up.

"How did the meeting go?" She linked their pinkies, wanting him to stay close to her for as long as possible, wishing he didn't have to go back to work.

"Not great. That's one of the reasons I stopped here. I wanted to explain in person that I have to cancel our plans for tonight."

"Ah, really?" Not that she'd mind skipping the counseling session. But the picnic? That she'd miss.

"I'm speaking at a city council meeting this evening, in front of the mayor and the others. Not looking forward to it. But it will take from now until then to prep." He groaned. "I'm sorry I won't have time for our picnic, or for that meeting with Pastor Sagle."

She swallowed down her disappointment. Things like this happened in the real world. He wasn't trying to distance himself from her. If he were, would he have stopped by to see her like this? Kissed her like *that*? "Um, think the pastor will be upset about us postponing?"

"Hard to say. You want me to call him? Or could you?" He gazed at her with a perplexed look. "I wouldn't ask, only—"

"Sure, I can tell him." Although, she dreaded being the bearer of bad news to the minister who already seemed to doubt their remarriage would work. "I'm going to take an invitation over to Paige's, so I'll be walking right by the church."

"Great. Thanks for understanding. I love you."

"Of course. Love you too."

He kissed her again, slowly, then trailed ticklish kisses from her lips to her ear. "Just four days. Can't wait."

"Me, neither."

One more heated kiss on her lips, then he pulled away.

"Call me later?" she asked, a little breathless.

"I will." He winked, then walked backward to his truck as if he didn't want to lose eye contact with her. At the pickup, he waved, then left.

So, no romantic picnic tonight, after all. Sigh. But it was sweet of him to stop by for those few delicious moments.

She climbed the steps to her dad's, then entered the house, wondering what Pastor Sagle would say about rescheduling tonight's session. *No session, no ceremony?* Ugh. Maybe she ought to investigate alternatives to walking down a church aisle. A beach wedding would be wonderful, although the fall weather might be too cool.

Should they reconsider City Hall? She and Judah could stand in front of the mayor while they said their vows. But after the horrible things he said to her before she left Basalt, and considering the ugly names he called her since, even inviting him to their ceremony was a stretch. What if he said something rude to Judah's mom, or hurt her in some way?

Paisley groaned. Then she rounded up the last of the invitations and stuffed them into her coat pocket.

At the church, she knocked on the door with a metal plate that read "Pastor." Footsteps sounded, then the door opened. The silvery-haired minister, standing in stocking feet, extended his hand and shook hers. "Paisley, aren't you early for our appointment?"

"About that … Judah has an emergency meeting with the mayor and the city council. I'm sorry, but would it be possible to reschedule?"

"Oh, dear." His smile turned downward. "These sessions are important before we can move forward with a ceremony. We're running out of days."

"I know." Boy, did she. "But his meeting couldn't be helped."

Pastor Sagle scratched his scalp and shuffled back to his desk. He leaned over the calendar, then scribbled something with a pen. "In three days, I have an opening, following our meetings for the next two evenings, but it'll be sandwiched between two other couples' sessions. How does three-thirty to five-thirty on Sunday afternoon work for you?"

"We'll make it work. Thank you. I'm sorry to cause you this inconvenience."

He stared back at her and nodded.

She remembered the invitation. "Oh, here." Pulling the envelope out of her pocket, she scurried over to the desk. "I didn't know if we're supposed to invite you to the ceremony since you're the one officiating, but here's an invitation." She set the ivory envelope on his calendar.

"Thank you."

"You're welcome." She backed up toward the doorway, wanting to make a quick exit, hoping he wouldn't ask her anything embarrassing as he did two days ago. "I'll make sure we're here next time. Promise."

"That's good. Uh, Paisley—"

Uh-oh. She didn't leave fast enough. "Yes?"

"I've been meaning to ask how things are going between you and Edward."

"Oh, Edward?" The switch in topic stumped her for a

moment. What could she say about her father-in-law that wouldn't sound awful? "Um, well, he and I don't see eye to eye on a lot of things."

Pastor Sagle's sudden boisterous laughter reminded her of Santa Claus. "I'm sorry. I didn't mean to pry or laugh. Your honesty is refreshing."

"Thanks, I think." No one had ever complimented her for being honest before. Although, Judah recently commended her on being stubborn, which didn't sound like a compliment at all.

If he wanted honesty— "Edward has crossed some lines and done some mean things I can't condone."

"Neither should you."

That was a relief. Although, she still felt nervous, uncertain, about what was acceptable to say to a pastor. "I guess you, being a minister, have to respect the mayor. Or be neutral, anyway."

"Sure, sure." Pastor Sagle chuckled again. "Grace covers a lot of our blunders, doesn't it?" He removed his glasses and tapped the air with them.

"I believe it does."

"You and Judah must have experienced some of that grace to come to the lovely agreement of renewing your vows as you have." He seemed a lot more caring and friendly than he had the other day.

"That's true."

"And the mayor?" He took a few steps away from his desk. "Is he not deserving of such grace?"

Oh, so that's where he was going with this conversation. Angst twisted together like a braid in the middle of her chest, making her feel suffocated.

"Your delay in answering probably means you need more time to ponder that question."

"I do. Yes, thank you."

By the way he stared at her with that kind look in his eyes, she didn't know if he was letting her off the hook or postponing the inevitable. Would he expect her to answer him when she and Judah came for their next counseling session?

"Just four days until the vow renewal, huh?"

A lighthearted topic, finally. "Yes. I still have a few invites to pass out."

"You'd better take care of that."

"I will. See you at our appointment tomorrow." She was eager to leave. Would it seem improper if she ran out of the building?

"We'll work out the arrangements for the ceremony then." Pastor Sagle followed her into the hallway, still in his socks. "Did you say you were preparing your own vows?" He seemed to be thinking. "Or was that another couple?"

"I'm not sure." She and Judah hadn't discussed it. Were they going to make up their own vows? If so, she'd better get started. "It's probably more personal that way, don't you think?"

"I do, but it's up to both of you. Talk about it. Let me know tomorrow."

"Okay. Thanks." She didn't run down the hall, but she hurried.

Coming up with their own vows. Six hours of counseling sessions. All the preparation for the ceremony. This vow renewal was getting more complicated than she first imagined. But getting to be with Judah again, becoming his wife and living with him again, was worth every ounce of effort. No doubt about it.

Ten

From the church to Paige's house in the subdivision, Paisley pondered whether she should ask her sister to be her maid of honor. When she and Judah eloped, she hadn't needed attendants. Asking Paige to stand by her during the upcoming ceremony sounded like a nice thing to do. A sisters' thing. But considering how their last conversation turned out, would there still be awkwardness between them? If so, even Paisley's attempt to reach out to her sibling might not improve the situation.

She knocked on the back door of the blue house where she, Dad, Judah, and even Craig, for a short time, had waited after the hurricane. A warm feeling came over her as she glanced around the backyard, thinking of the firepit they built. Someone had filled it in and set the swing set back up. Craig's doing?

The door opened. "Paisley? What a surprise." Paige smiled tentatively. "Come in."

"Thanks. I, uh, want to give you this." Paisley handed her the invitation then entered the house that already felt homey and familiar to her. "It's an invitation to our vow renewal ceremony on Monday night. A small gathering. Just close friends and family."

"I'm so happy for you. Judah is just—" Tears flooded Paige's eyes, and she shrugged, acting like she couldn't speak. Why was she being so emotional? "He's a great guy." She sniffed a few times. "You're so lucky to get to be with him again. For you to have each other … for the rest of your lives." Her shoulders sagged, heaved.

"What's wrong, Paige?"

"It's just, it's just, Judah is—"

"Yes?" Was she upset that Paisley and Judah were getting back together? That didn't make sense since she just said he was a great guy. Oh, a *great* guy? As in—? No, surely not. She didn't mean— What if *she* had feelings for Judah? Paisley swallowed down her shock at the thought. A ridiculous thought. Yet, why else would Paige react like this? When she found herself in trouble with Mayor Grant, who did she seek for advice? Judah. In Paisley's absence those three years, did her sister, perhaps, depend on him? Become fond of him? Ugh. Paige probably meant something else entirely.

Judah had assured her that in the years she was away he never dated, hardly looked at a woman. Yet, what if he had a secret admirer and didn't even realize it?

"He's the best man I've ever known."

Something about her sister's woebegone look made Paisley want to yank back the invitation and leave.

Did Judah ever have dinner here? Stop by for chats? He told her that he attended Piper's birthday. Did he stay afterward and talk with Paige? Comfort her? Paisley inwardly groaned at where her imaginings had taken her. She didn't want these thoughts—especially not the week of their vow renewal.

An awkward silence filled the space between them. She glanced around the kitchen, forcing herself to think of Judah and her fixing food—his infamous glop—after the hurricane. Not of him doing stuff here with her sister.

Paige tore the envelope open. She held up the card and read, "You are invited to a simple vow exchanging ceremony at the Basalt Bay Community Church, Monday at six p.m., for Judah and Paisley Grant. No gifts, please."

"That's why I came by. I want you to know what's going on." Paisley wouldn't say anything about the maid of honor business. Not now. Not with the riotous, envious, emotions nearly choking her.

"Thank you for inviting me. I wouldn't miss it." Paige set the card and envelope on the table. "Can I bring Piper?"

"Of course. It's just a small gathering."

Paige rolled her upper lip between her teeth. Then sighed. "What I said about Judah … I don't want you to get the wrong impression."

"Okay." Although, it was a little late for that.

Paige stared at the floor. Slowly she lifted her chin and met Paisley's gaze. "Judah was kind and helpful to me and Piper while you were gone."

"You don't have to explain."

"I think I do." She stared out the window. "He wasn't judgmental about me being pregnant or being a single mom, like some others in town who shall remain nameless. He was considerate and extended grace."

Like Paisley imagined. That's who Judah was. What he was like.

"You weren't here." Paige exhaled loudly. "I don't know, maybe he took your place in my heart. He came to Piper's birthdays. Checked in on us, made sure we had supplies, that sort of thing."

"Sounds like Judah."

"Exactly. And you didn't seem to value him." Paige covered her mouth with her hand like she was surprised at her own harsh words.

Paisley felt sickened by them. "You don't know anything about the overwhelming loss I went through. How alone I felt." She took a step toward the door. Time to get out of here. Yet, she hesitated. Wasn't she done running?

"You're right." Paige gulped. "I'm sorry. I shouldn't have said that. And I'm sorry for not being more understanding of you during your time of grief." Her voice softened. "I should have reached out to you, and I didn't."

Her admitting that soothed some of the ache in Paisley's heart. But, still, she needed to find out about Paige's possible feelings toward Judah. And if he'd ever reciprocated. "Did you, or do you, care for … my husband?" Done beating around the bush, she went for the truth. "Did you love him?"

Paige stared at her, jaw dropped, as if shocked by such a forthright question.

Judah would be shocked, too, if he overheard. What if her little sister had carried, perhaps still carried, a torch for him?

"Did you?"

"Sure, I loved him … like a brother." Her soft sigh let Paisley know it cost her. "Although, in honesty—that's what you want, right?—I could have cared for him in other ways. Not because he tried anything, because he never did. Never would." She swayed out her hands. "I'm a single mom. Lonely. He was lonely without you. I could have reached out to him, but I didn't. And he wouldn't have gone along with anything happening between us—even if I'd tried, which I didn't." She glared at Paisley as if her look alone should convince her.

"Judah has always loved you with some you're-the-only-one-for-him kind of love. So there's nothing for you to worry about when it comes to him and me."

Maybe just one thing. "Did you wish for more?" Not that Paisley would ever want to hear that she did. But she had to know, or the question would always haunt her and stand between them.

"Does it matter?"

"It does." Heaven help her.

"Then, yes. Of course, yes." Paige seemed to be fighting her emotions.

That wasn't the answer Paisley wanted to hear. She swallowed hard and opened the door, needing fresh air. Maybe she'd sprint back to her dad's house and try to forget this conversation ever happened.

Paige clasped her arm. "I'm sorry if that hurts you. But who wouldn't wish for more? The man is a saint for waiting for you all that time."

That's what it came back to. Her leaving. Him waiting for her. Her unworthiness of him. Paige's assessment that he was a great guy replayed in her thoughts. Why did it take Paisley so long to recognize what she had before she lost it? She wouldn't easily let go of that again.

"I've had two loves in my life." Paige wiped her fist beneath her eyes. "Both went sour. I needed to talk with someone sympathetic. Judah was that for me. He talked to me about God. His forgiveness and love. But nothing romantic happened between us, whether I wished it did or not."

Did Judah ever suspect Paige's attraction? He never mentioned it. But, of course, he wouldn't. He acted like he cared about Paige and Piper as family, nothing more.

She should go. She needed time to think over all of this. But she wasn't about to let Paige's revelation cause trouble between Judah and her, either.

Paige cleared her throat. "I wasn't the only one if rumors were true."

"Meaning?"

"Some single women in town dubbed him the 'hottest bachelor in Basalt Bay.'"

Oh, right. Paisley had heard that too.

"They were waiting for him to get over you."

She felt a lurch in her chest. "Mia Till? Lucy Carmichael?"

Paige nodded. "And a few others."

So, single women were lined up hoping her marriage to Judah would fail? But what did she expect? That women wouldn't notice a nice, good-looking bachelor-type in a small town like Basalt? What if he hadn't been as honorable? He might already have moved on. And no one, including her, would have blamed him. That made her feel humbled and pleased he waited for her. That he loved her still.

And with all he'd forgiven her for, how could she think of holding something against her sister? She had to learn to let things go too.

"I'm sorry for entertaining such thoughts." Paige toyed with her bare fingernails. "I'm embarrassed to admit it."

"Thank you for being honest with me."

"Are you going to tell him?" A shadow crossed Paige's dark eyes.

Would she? "What good would it do? Except we're promising not to keep secrets from each other."

"Right." Tears filled her sister's eyes.

But Paisley wanted to mend the past with her too. "I need

your word that to the best of your ability you won't have such thoughts again. And never act on them."

"I never would. He's Piper's 'Unca Dzudah.' My brother-in-law. That's all."

"And my husband."

"Yes, of course. I wouldn't do anything to jeopardize that." Paige chuckled nervously. "I couldn't, anyway. Look at his track record, Paisley. He loves you like you're the sun to his moon. You're the tide to his beach. He keeps wanting you. Will always want you." Her voice went soft. "If a man loved me like that, I'd sing and dance in the streets."

While her description of Judah's love for Paisley painted a lovely picture, the idea of her reserved sister singing and dancing outside publicly was humorous. Something else came to mind. "You said you had two loves. Craig and who else?"

"Piper's father."

"So Craig isn't her dad?"

"No, he isn't." Paige squinted at her. "I don't want to talk about him, either. He's not involved in Piper's life. I'm raising her on my own."

"Why?"

"Because he—" She clamped down her teeth. "Just the way it is. My decision."

"Okay, fine." Paisley would wait until Paige was willing to discuss it, and the two of them were feeling closer and more honest with each other, if that time ever came.

What about her being Paisley's maid of honor? Could she even ask her now after Paige confessed to having a crush on Judah? Paige was her only sister. But the room felt electrified with tension and suspicion and past hurts.

Still, something within her prodded her to reach out. To

try to bridge the gap. "Would you, possibly, be willing to stand by me during the ceremony?" She forced the words past her reluctance to ask.

"You mean like a bridesmaid?" Paige shrugged and swept her hair off her shoulders.

"Or a maid of honor?"

A few moments of silence passed.

"I'm honored that you'd ask. Thank you." Paige hugged her. "Of course, I'll stand with you."

"Okay." Paisley took a full breath. "Good."

Hopefully, by the time four days passed, whatever negative feelings she still felt toward her sister would drift away.

Eleven

Standing before the Basalt Bay Council members, including Mayor Grant, Craig, Mia, and six others whom he mostly knew from around town, Judah gave his presentation. He described C-MER's plans for public safety in a way he hoped might reach those who weren't at the first meeting. But by the scowls on the committee members' faces, no one was impressed with his data. However, the peninsula needed surgery, not just a Band-Aid fix. They had to agree on a strategy to provide public safety for the future of the townspeople and the tourist industry, and he was the one commissioned to persuade them to act.

"It's unlikely that a storm will ever reach our shores with hurricane-force winds as it did twice this year." Judah figured most people who lived along the Pacific assumed that. "But the fact remains, those hurricanes barreled up from Mexico, surprising meteorologists and oceanographers with their intensity and hard-hitting strikes along the coast, even while people were saying it would never happen. For the sake of our citizens, and any visitors to Basalt Bay, we must work together to provide better safety measures along the western seaboard. Any questions?"

He took a long swig from his water bottle, waiting for responses. Three hands shot up. He pointed at an older gentleman he knew as Fred. "Yes, sir?"

"What makes you think your new dike would outlast Hurricane Catarina or Cecily better than the old one?"

"Good question." Judah set down his water bottle. "Doing something is always better than doing nothing. I'm confident that the model our engineers are designing will serve our community better than the one built sixty years ago. There are no guarantees, but we have the latest technology and the stats from hurricanes on the East Coast to ensure a quality outcome."

"No guarantees. As I thought," the man grumbled.

The next question was similar. More negative discussion followed. An hour later, they'd gone around in circles about modern technology and a lack of funding and back again.

"Who's ready for a vote?" Mayor Grant tapped his watch.

"Wait! Does anyone else have any questions?"

By the tired, or bored, looks of the committee, they were ready to go home. How would Judah explain the dismal meeting and lackluster vote to Mike Linfield?

"Could I ask one thing?" The other woman who was present besides Mia raised her hand. What was her name?

"Yes, absolutely."

Mia shook her head and frowned as if telling the woman not to bother with any more questions.

"I'm Sue Taylor. I live just beyond the cannery at the old Milner place."

Sue. "Oh, sure. I know which one." Judah had walked by there plenty of times on beach walks. He remembered her father, a stern man who had the tenacity to stand up to Mayor

Grant in a few community gatherings. Did Sue have any of her father's formidable traits?

"My family has lived in Basalt for over a hundred years, but I recently returned to take care of my mother. Mayor Grant was kind enough to offer me a seat on the council in my father's place since he passed away a few months ago." Sue cleared her throat.

"I'm sorry about your dad." Judah smiled, hoping to put her at ease.

"Thank you. My concerns may sound trite, but since I'm here, I'm going to participate."

"Good. What did you want to say?"

"I heard that a woman fell into the sea out at the point and nearly drowned. Is that true?"

"Yes, that was my wife. I experienced the destructive power of the sea that day, too." Just remembering the encounter gave him cold sweats. He wiped his forehead. "That's one of the reasons I'm passionate about getting the peninsula fixed properly and promptly. I don't want what happened to Paisley to happen to anyone else. If the whirlpool could nearly crush a stronger man like myself, a child wouldn't stand a chance."

"This is old business." Mayor Grant thumped the table with his knuckles. "Mia, move forward with a vote."

"Yes, Ed—"

"Hold on." Judah held up his hand. "Go on, ma'am. You still have the floor." If he had one positive voice here, he wasn't going to let the mayor run roughshod over her.

"Thank you." Sue nodded at Judah, then turned toward the others, seemingly avoiding meeting the mayor's gaze. "We've heard facts and figures tonight that don't sound reassuring. But I've heard enough to be troubled, and I'm sure some of you are too, about someone almost drowning just by stepping off a rock in front of our city. I played on the peninsula as a kid. You all probably did too."

A few nods.

"It's the way it's always been." The mayor harrumphed. "People have to be careful. Judah's wife was clumsy. Her foolish recklessness—"

"Hey. Let's keep this discussion civil." Judah shot his father a tense warning.

"Do we want that kind of danger in our front yard?" Sue's voice went soft like she felt nervous speaking up. "Do we want to be responsible for someone being injured when we could have done something? I'd hate for anything like that to happen to one of my grandkids."

"Me too." "That's right." A few people murmured responses.

Judah nodded, relieved that some were responding positively. "That's the purpose of the proposal we're working on at C-MER. To create a safer place for everyone. I, too, used to climb over the rocks at the peninsula. So did Paisley. But the hurricane caused severe damage. It's up to us to find a safe resolution, whatever the price might be."

"Easy for you to say." The mayor leaned over and whispered something to Mia. She snickered.

"We're not trying to make a financial hardship for the town." Judah stepped closer to where Sue sat since she was the one who seemed the most interested. "We want to ensure public safety. That requires people talking together, working over new ideas—like we're doing here—and coming up with a plan that's effective and reasonable."

The mayor's scowl deepened. Craig closed his eyes and looked ready to fall asleep.

Sue raised her hand. "Judah, would you mind stepping out of the room so we could discuss this without you being present?"

"Yes, certainly." That she wanted to continue the conversation must be a good sign. He scooped up the papers he brought that were spread out in front of him. "Thanks for your time." He headed for the door.

"You too, Mayor."

Judah paused to listen, intrigued that Sue would dare to oust the mayor from the room.

"What?" Edward thundered. "I'm in charge of this meeting. I have a right to—"

"She's correct, Mayor Grant." Mia chuckled. "The committee has the right to discuss any matter without either of the opposing parties present. It's in the city charter."

"That's ridiculous. Nobody tells me—" Edward grouched about delays and that no one had the authority to make him leave. But, moments later, he stomped past Judah. He didn't pause when he reached the hallway but kept marching farther away, muttering to himself about needing a break and a drink, anyway.

Judah strode down the hall and leaned against the wall. He closed his eyes and sighed. Did he say enough to persuade the group to act in favor of the proposal he presented? Should he have said more about the types of dikes they were considering? Had he given enough information about the safety aspects like Mike wanted him to do? He remembered the blank expressions of the council members while he was speaking. When it came to a vote, would they side with the mayor? He applauded Sue Taylor for being brave enough to move for a private debate. Too bad Mia and Craig, the naysayers, were still in there.

His thoughts roamed to Paisley. What was she doing? Was she disappointed by tonight's canceled date like he was? Did she convince Pastor Sagle to reschedule their counseling session?

"Judah." Mia's demanding voice. "We're ready. Where's your dad?"

"I don't know. He went that way." He nodded down the hall before pulling away from the wall.

She stomped by him, tapping her phone with her fingernails as her heels simultaneously clicked the shiny floor. "Don't start without us!"

Judah didn't appreciate her commanding tone, but she was right. The mayor should be present to hear the results of the private session.

When Judah reentered the conference room, most of the members didn't meet his gaze, leaving him less than hopeful things would go his way. He dropped into the chair he vacated earlier and glanced at Sue. She was busy writing something down, so he couldn't read her expression. In the past, he would have shot the breeze with Craig. Not happening today. Would they ever be friends again?

The mayor and Mia strode back into the room, her arm linked around his. The sight of them cozying up together shot annoyance through Judah.

When they sat down, Mia took charge. "Okay, let's get this over with. Sue?"

The woman who led the charge for getting Judah and Edward to step out of the room folded her hands on the table in front of her. "We've decided to go along with the C-MER plan for reconstructing the peninsula, despite some of the members' concerns that it doesn't resolve the whole problem."

"Awesome. Thanks." What a relief. His boss would be ecstatic to hear of the better-than-expected outcome. Surely this would guarantee Judah's promotion.

"However"—Fred shuffled on his chair—"we don't have a financial solution. That'll be up to the mayor's office to figure out a plan."

"Now, hold on!" Mayor Grant slapped the table. "You can't make that call without my vote, without me being present."

"No disrespect, Mayor, but, yes, we can." This time, Sue didn't seem to have any trouble facing the mayor.

"One more thing I'll have to take care of," Edward muttered.

Mia patted his hand sympathetically. "How about if we reconvene in two days after we've had time to establish a cost analysis. That can't be worked out in this meeting."

"Sounds good to me." Judah scooped up his coat and empty water bottle.

"You can't mean that you *all* voted and are siding with this C-MER employee?" The mayor's face turned wine-colored as he glared at each of the attendees.

This C-MER employee? How about his son who was trying to do a positive thing for the town? Shouldn't he be appreciative of that?

"Mayor, we're thankful for your fine leadership." Fred's gaze was fixed on a piece of paper he was twisting in his hands. "But we agree we should move forward on the 'something' Judah mentioned instead of doing nothing like we have been doing."

Mayor Grant groaned and pressed his fingers against his temples.

The group dispersed quickly.

Before heading out to the cottage, Judah stopped his pickup in front of Paul's dark house so he could see Paisley. It was strange that the lights were turned off considering it was only nine o'clock. Was Paul already asleep? Did he dare knock on the door and disturb him?

He got out of the truck and crossed the yard. Maybe he could knock quietly, or else toss a rock at Paisley's bedroom window. Just reaching the porch, he heard the rocking chair's rails tapping the floor in a slow, steady rhythm, almost like a heartbeat. He barely made out a form in the darkness in front of the window. "Pais?"

"I wondered if you'd stop by. Couldn't resist seeing me, huh?"

"No, I could not."

In the next second, she was in his arms, wrapping her arms around his shoulders, kissing him like they'd kissed earlier today. Mmm … she smelled nice. Good thing he stopped by. He was glad for her warm welcome too. Relieved she wasn't upset with him for canceling their picnic.

A tapping at the window frame next to the plastic window interrupted their romantic embrace. Paul's silhouette partially filled the window. Apparently, he'd turned on a light in the living room. "I'm watching you two." His gruff voice came through the plastic.

"Is he serious?" Judah felt like a teenager kissing a girl on her parent's front porch.

Paisley snickered. "He must have forgotten we're still married." She stepped away from him and shuffled toward the window. "I'm okay, Dad. It's just Judah."

"Hello, Paul." He waved.

The older man lifted his hand but still stood there like a guard.

Great. Judah sat down on the edge of the porch and patted the wooden floor next to him, inviting Paisley to join him. That shouldn't bother Paul, right?

She dropped to the warped floorboards beside him. "I don't know what's gotten into him. Maybe he's feeling more protective of me since I nearly drowned."

"I can understand that." He felt protective of her too. Still, he'd prefer some alone, unobserved, time with his wife. "Think I can get away with putting my arm over your shoulder?"

"You can try."

Hoping his father-in-law didn't come out on the porch swinging a bat or a broom, Judah eased his arm over her shoulder and pulled her in closer to him. When no more banging sounds came from the window, he relaxed. "This is nice. The way every night should end. You and me sitting next to each other."

"Mmhmm." She leaned her head against his shoulder. "I wish we had the sea for our view, instead of the neighbors' houses."

"We have a perfect view at our cottage."

"True."

What would she say if he invited her to come home tonight? He respected her wishes to wait until they said formal vows to each other, before they were intimate, but still, he wondered.

"Just four more days." She gazed at him, her eyes twinkling.

He pictured four days spread out like massive sand dunes he had to traverse across before he could reach her. Too bad he was so impatient. Any amount of time was worth the wait to be together again. *She* was worth the wait. *Remember that, Grant.* He sighed. "I just stopped by for a few minutes so I could see you. Sorry about missing our picnic and session earlier."

"Couldn't be helped, right?" Did her voice suddenly sound tight? "How'd the meeting go?"

"Better than I imagined." He filled her in on the details, emphasizing Sue Taylor's role in the outcome. It was idyllic sitting by his wife, chatting as if they were already remarried, and sharing their lives together, except for the fact he was going to be driving home alone. "I should go. Suppose your dad's still watching?" If so, Judah would forgo any goodnight kissing. Maybe just a smooch on her cheek.

"I don't know." She shrugged. "Um, Pastor Sagle wasn't too pleased with us rescheduling."

"I'm sorry to have put you in that predicament."

"It's okay. So tomorrow night, for sure, right?"

Did she doubt? Was she worried he might cancel again?

"Absolutely." Trying to keep things light, he added, "Tomorrow night we'll face the lion, er, the pastor, together."

"Good." She kissed his cheek. "Four more sleeps and we'll be together for the rest of our lives."

Oh, yeah. He'd hike four of the world's tallest, most challenging sand dunes to finally be with her.

Just four more sleeps.

Twelve

The next day dark clouds dominated the sky, but even the intermittent downpours couldn't dampen Paisley's spirits. Only three days remained until her and Judah's vow renewal ceremony. Three days until she'd get to wear that amazing wedding dress and become Mrs. Judah Grant in more than name only. That is if they made it to their three required counseling sessions. Thinking of those meetings took some of the spring out of her step.

But when she contemplated some of the things she'd done in preparation—putting her wedding dress in the closet at the cottage and distributing invitations—her upbeat feelings returned. She'd also added some personal touches to the beach house. She picked up a few scatter rugs from the hardware store to lay over the plywood flooring in the bedroom. She bought sparkling cider and a few special snacks the two of them liked. Brownies. Fancy pretzels. Hummus and crackers. She wanted to be ready for their post-ceremony private celebration. Their romantic celebrations.

They still hadn't talked about a honeymoon, other than Judah mentioning it in Pastor Sagle's office. But, considering they were living in the aftermath of the hurricane, they might have to postpone a trip until spring or summer. That would be okay. Just renewing their vows and enjoying married life with Judah would be wonderful.

Today, she planned to go by Bert's to have that talk with him about possibly returning to work at the Fish Shack. Judah texted her this morning that he heard Bert planned to reopen in a few days. Great news. She needed the work. Having a job would help her feel more settled here in Basalt. Of course, it wouldn't be a glamorous position, but who cared about that?

She stared at herself critically in the mirror in her childhood bedroom. Holding out a strand of her long, messy black hair, she checked for split ends. A trim would be nice. Should she do any special grooming before the ceremony? Get her nails done? Highlights in her hair? For a special day like a vow renewal ceremony, she wouldn't mind adding a little wow factor.

She still carried Judah's credit card in her wallet. He said she could get anything she wanted for the ceremony. How about doing something fun with her hair or getting her nails done? Would Paige come along with her? They could drive to Florence and make it a girls' day—a bachelorette party. Forget applying for a job. She could talk to Bert any day.

Paisley was glad she'd decided to let go of those personal things Paige confided in her, and her hurtful accusations. Not that she could completely forget, *yet*. But she and her sister needed a new beginning too. Having a fun day together would be a great start.

Was Paige at home or at the gallery? Paisley could text her, but she'd check at her building first. If Paige wasn't there, she'd head over to the subdivision and enjoy a walk.

Grabbing her coat, Paisley went outside. She strolled down the route she'd walked thousands of times before. Down Front Street, past James Weston's house, past Miss Patty's rental. She paused in front of Nautical Sal's Souvenirs and waved at Sal who was still cleaning up stuff around his destroyed shop. Poor man. Every time she saw the damaged building, she felt bad for him.

At the art gallery, Paisley noticed the plywood door stood ajar. Paige must be inside. She gave the wood a push. "Paige?" She trudged into the darkened space. A cool breeze hit her from the glassless window facing the ocean and caused the door to slam shut behind her. She jumped, startled.

"What are you doing here?" Edward's snarly voice made the hair stand up on her neck.

"Oh, um, is my sister here?" Her heart thudded in her temples as she peered into the darkish room.

"No. Did you expect her?" He stood by the window guzzling from a can. His eyes appeared bloodshot. His face was more haggard than usual. A case of beer, or whatever remained of it, along with a pile of crushed empty ones, sat on the floor. How many had he drunk today? Was he having his own private party here? Disgust over seeing him like this, of being alone with him, made every instinct to run heighten within her.

"I guess. Have you taken over the building already?" She shuffled back toward the door, hoping he didn't notice her aversion to him. Her fear of him.

"I have the right to be here if that's what you mean. You're the one who's trespassing." He held up his can. "But you have a knack for being in the wrong place at the wrong time, don't you?" The way he squinted and looked her over gave her the creeps.

She took a couple more steps. Paige wasn't here. She should leave. Maybe sprint to get away from Edward.

He staggered toward her. "*Thatzz* what you do, isn't it? What all *Cedarzz* do. Cause trouble." He stared at her, squinting and flexing his eyes like he wasn't seeing straight.

She clenched her fists and glanced around for some protection. A jar. A book. Something to throw at him if he dared to come closer.

"You aren't afraid of me, are you?"

"Of course not." She fibbed. He petrified her.

A box sat on the counter to her right. Anything heavy in it?

"Maybe you should be afraid of me." He reached out as if to touch her cheek with his free hand. She slapped it away, which caused him to slosh the liquid from his can down her front. Ugh.

He swore at her.

She brushed the liquid off her shirt. Now she smelled of the pungent scent of beer. She wanted to yell at him. To tell him to stay away from her, but the words wouldn't come out.

He took a long guzzle from the can, then swiveled around and hurled it out the window, giving her the time she needed to race for the door. Unfortunately, his footsteps pounded right behind her. She glanced back and the whites of his eyes almost glowed in the dimly lit room. His gaze locked on hers like she was his prey.

"How much cash would it take to get you to leave this time? For you to leave for good?"

Is that what he thought? Because he gave her money three years ago and told her to leave, and she did, that she'd do the same thing again?

"No amount of money could make me leave Judah. Never again."

"I don't believe it." He scrubbed the back of his hand over his mouth. "My son should have known better than to get involved with you again. A *Cedars*." He spit.

"He loves me." She lifted her chin, daring to defy him.

"He shouldn't have married a tramp like you." Edward reached out and grabbed her arm.

"Hey!" She jerked away from his grip and fell against the closed door. He stepped in front of her, almost touching her, blocking her from pulling open the door.

An overwhelming tightness clawed at her throat. She would not have a panic attack. Not in front of this man. This fiend. She edged to the side of the doorframe. Edward lowered his hand onto her shoulder and leaned his face in toward hers, inches away, his red bleary eyes peering at her. His breath smelled of garlic and beer. "If you tell Judah"—his hot breath huffed on her—"or anyone else, you saw me like this, you'll be sorry. More than sorry." He belched right into her face.

She clamped her mouth shut to stop herself from gagging. She jerked her shoulder away from him. He shouldn't be touching her.

But then, he lifted a strand of her hair and stared at it as if having a hard time focusing. "My son was full of promise until he met you. I had plans for him, but you ruined them."

What plans? How could she ruin anything? She had to get away from him. Avoid him for the rest of her life, if possible. Maybe if she distracted him with a question, he'd step back.

Then she'd open the door and run. "Did you have anything to do with Craig's attack on me three years ago?"

His eyes scrunched to thin slits. "You're the one who flirted. It's your fault he went after you." He swayed, stumbled. "I helped you because I'm a good *citizzen*—not *becauzz* I cared. *Becauzz* I don't care anything about you."

"You're wrong. It wasn't my fault." She grabbed hold of the doorknob, twisting and pulling. But Edward slammed into her, keeping her away from the door. She pressed her palms against his chest, fighting to free herself of his weight. "Let me go!" In those seconds, the way he'd hurt Bess flashed through her thoughts like a red-light warning. "Get away from me!"

He chuckled as if he were amused by her inability to escape. He pinned her arms beneath his grip like a clamp attaching her elbows to the wall. She yelled and fought against him. How did he have the strength to hold her like that when he'd been swaying as if he were drunk minutes ago? "I want to go. Leave me alone, you moron."

"You're coming with me." He dragged her toward the coffee shop.

"No, I'm not!" She flailed her free elbow, striking him in the jaw, the neck.

He groaned, swore, but held her tight, his claw-like hands gripping her arms until it felt like he might break them. Did he even know what he was doing? Or was he soused out of his mind?

"Please, for Judah's sake, let me go."

"Or what?"

"Or I'll scream until Miss Patty hears me." The hardware store was right next door. Surely someone would hear her.

Whatever he thought to do before, his grip slackened. Maybe he was coming to his senses. He glanced over his shoulder. Searching for his beer? Suddenly, he released her.

This was her chance. She scrambled back to the door. Gripping the handle, she rattled the knob. *Come on. Open up.* The swollen plywood door didn't budge. She yanked harder. *Please.*

Right behind her, Edward guffawed and clutched her shoulders—she hadn't heard him cross the space between them. He hurled her toward the middle of the room. She stumbled but caught herself. His strength surprised and horrified her. How would she get away now? The only escape was through the front door that was stuck. The ocean water beneath the window was too shallow for jumping into.

What might her drunken father-in-law do? Didn't he already display that he could injure her? Didn't Bess's bruised face show that too?

Paisley drew in a stuttered breath, still experiencing tightness in her throat. The pressure in her chest felt like a hundred-pound weight pressing down on her. *Stay alert. Breathe.*

He took a couple of menacing steps toward her, his blood-shot eyes scrutinizing her. Was he high on drugs too? Or just out of his mind? She backed up, stiffening her spine, her hands balled, ready to slug him. He undid his belt buckle.

Help me, God. Who cared if she didn't like desperate prayers? She was desperate.

She needed something to throw at him. The beer cans would do damage. She shuffled closer to the case. Edward pulled the belt clear of his pant loops. Whether he meant to hit her with it or do something else, she wouldn't wait to find out.

"Don't move."

Right. Like she'd stand there and not try to save herself. Her next steps would have to be executed quickly. Drop to the floor. Grab two cans. Hurl them at his head. Run. But would the door open this time?

She kept her gaze locked on his as if he were a rattler. One more step.

He let out a roar and barreled toward her. She dodged for the cans. Not fast enough. He rammed into her as he did before, shoving her against the window frame until her waist crimped over the windowsill, her head and upper torso dangling over the water.

She screamed. Her arms flailed air and nothingness. If she fell into the shallow water, she'd probably fall on her head and die. *God, help me.*

Edward looped his belt around her arms and upper torso until her elbows were secured to her sides.

"Please, leave me alone."

He tugged her cell phone out of her back pocket and dropped it into the seawater below.

"No!"

Laughing, he dragged her back inside. She inhaled and exhaled rapidly, relief and fear dueling inside her. As Edward hauled her toward the coffee shop, she yelled and called him names. She knocked a box of coffee supplies to the floor. Some broke open. She shoved against him, fighting him with her hands, her fingernails clawing his arms, his face, but even in his inebriated state, he was stronger than her.

He kicked the back of her legs, and she buckled. He shoved her to the floor. Pinning his knee against her thigh, he cinched the belt tighter around her chest and arms. He grabbed a white rope that looked like a clothesline off the shelf. Did he plan to tie her up?

She wrestled him, squirming, trying to break free. "Stop. Leave me alone. Why are you doing this?"

"Hold still."

She wouldn't. Her fingernails slashed at his cheek.

He groaned and swore. He clasped his hands together and struck her like a bat, hitting the side of her head and shoulder. She toppled to the plywood and winced, but wouldn't cry out, wouldn't give him the satisfaction of knowing he hurt her, or how much she loathed him. Somehow, he got her hands behind her back and tied them together.

"Help! Someone, help me. He—"

Edward clapped his hand over her mouth. "Be silent."

Unable to breathe through her mouth, her anxiety escalated. She tried to bite him. "*Youwonget* away *withis*." Her words came out intermittent and muffled. She inhaled and exhaled rapidly through her nose.

"You'd be surprised what I can get away with. I own this town and the people in it." Edward huffed like he was breathing with difficulty after battling with her. "I've waited … and planned … for this. My son, the future leader of Basalt Bay, will thank me one day." He let go of her mouth and grabbed a long strip of fabric. "Any final words?"

Final? She gulped. "Too bad Bess stayed married to you all those years."

He slapped her so hard her ears rang. She couldn't help whimpering this time.

"Don't speak to me about Bess. She's a better woman than you'll ever be."

"What will Judah think of you treating his wife this way?"

"His wife." He snarled. "He doesn't belong with you. Never did. I'm doing what I should have done years ago. Getting rid of you. Then he'll marry someone respectable."

He planned to get rid of her? Because she wasn't good enough? So Judah would be with someone else? She would have yelled and told him he was crazy, but he wrapped the strip of cloth tightly across her mouth, tying it in back so her jaw was stuck open. The fabric pinched at the edges of her lips. He grabbed a roll of duct tape and roughly wrapped it all the way around her mouth and the back of her head, making a couple of loops. Panic assailed her as the tape blocked her ability to breathe normally. It tasted horrible against her lips and tongue. She felt suffocated even though she could still breathe through her nose.

"When you're gone, Judah will forget you." That sleazy look returned. "Mia Till failed before, but she won't this time."

Mia Till. Paisley tried to argue. Her voice came out garbled around the cloth and through the tape.

Edward leaned closer, breathing over her ear. "I'm warning you—stay quiet. You hear me?"

She nodded, staring into his eyes. But she'd watch for a chance to escape. However, when he tied her legs and feet together tightly, even wrapping duct tape around her limbs, and with her arms secured behind her back, escape seemed impossible. Still, she wouldn't give up. When she got away, and she'd find a way, she'd see Edward thrown in prison. He wasn't getting away with such cruel treatment. And all for what? To stop her from marrying Judah? Did he mean to interfere with their vow renewal ceremony?

"After dark, I'll be back." He stomped across the room.

Good, he was leaving.

Sounds of the door being wrenched open reached her. She waited a second then hit the sides of her right leg and shoe against the floor over and over. *"Yelph! Yelph!"* Her words came out distorted.

"Shut up!" Edward stomped back toward her. Oh, no. He hadn't left. He kicked her legs. She groaned. He leaned down beside her. She sucked air in and out through her nose, watching his intense eyes squint, fearing what he might do.

"You have a niece," he said in a gravelly voice. "You want her to be safe, don't you?"

Piper. All the fight left Paisley. Was he threatening to hurt Paige's child?

"Keep quiet. I mean it, so help me I mean it, or else whatever happens to the little girl will be on your head." His knee pressed against her thigh, his gaze piercing hers. "If you want the child to be safe, you'll do what I say and be quiet. Understood?"

She nodded to pacify him. What else could she do with him leaning over her staring at her like a demon from her worst nightmares?

But as soon as he left, she fought the tape and the rope. She pressed her tongue against the duct tape, loosening it a little on the sides. But the fabric keeping her jaws open kept her from freeing her mouth. She tried to yell, but she realized the roar of the pounding waves coming in through the open window muffled her sounds. Miss Patty probably couldn't even hear her.

Thirteen

Craig strode into the doorway of Judah's office and leaned against the doorjamb. "I hear there's a meeting in Mike's office that you and I are expected to attend."

"I didn't know anything about a meeting." Judah checked his watch. Almost quitting time. He planned to meet up with Paisley before their marriage counseling session with Pastor Sagle. He'd been looking forward to picking up deli food to replace the picnic dinner they missed out on last night.

"You don't have any other plans, do you?"

He did, but he wasn't about to explain his plans to Craig. They hadn't even spoken since yesterday at City Hall. And, between his concerns that Craig and the mayor may have been involved in a plot to coerce Paisley into leaving him three years ago, and his coworker's recent behavior, Judah had tried to avoid him.

"What's this meeting about?" Earlier in the day, he gave Mike a report of all that transpired at the council meeting. The manager seemed relieved to hear it went well. "Are you sure I'm supposed to be there?"

"Would I be standing here otherwise?"

"I guess not." Judah sighed.

"You and I have things to discuss too." Why was Craig suddenly being communicative?

"No doubt, we do." The phone rang, and he answered. "Hello."

"Mia here. There's a meeting in Mike's office in ten minutes. He expects you to attend."

Judah sighed. "All right. Thanks."

"Hey, Judah?"

From his position leaning next to the door, Craig made a show of tapping his watch.

"What?" Judah spoke into the phone.

"I thought you did a good job yesterday." She sounded upbeat. "In the meeting, you stood up against your dad for the town's sake. You can be quite heroic. I was proud of you."

"Oh, well, thanks." Her praise made him uncomfortable.

"No problem."

The call ended and he faced Craig, even though he'd rather finish the email he was writing to one of the researchers in the main office. "Was there something you wanted to discuss? Is it even a good time since we apparently have a meeting in a few minutes?"

"You doubted?"

After all the underhanded things Craig had done, of course, he doubted. He had a few questions he'd like to ask the other man. But getting into an argument on C-MER's dime probably wasn't wise.

Mia flounced into the office, squeezing in beside Craig. "Mike's ready for you two."

"You said ten minutes."

"I did, but he's ready now." She laid her hand on Craig's arm. "How are you doing?"

"Fine." He shuffled away, casting a tight glance over his shoulder.

"I'll be there in a sec." Judah grabbed his cell and tapped out a text to Paisley. He hated to disappoint her again.

Sorry. I have a meeting that might run late.

Without waiting for a response, he strode out of the office, and Mia kept in step with him. "Are you attending the meeting too?"

"Uh-huh. Mike likes me to take notes. I'll walk with you."

Like he had a choice. That she was showing up everywhere he went these days frustrated him. *Mercy and grace*, he reminded himself of the mantra he tried to live by. But his patience was wearing thin when it came to acting kind or tolerant toward Mia Till.

"Come in." Mike waved for them to squeeze into his small office. "Sorry to call a last-minute discussion. But something came up, and it took some time to accumulate the facts. Take a seat, gentlemen." He swayed his hand toward two chairs in front of his desk.

Judah and Craig dropped into those.

"You set, Mia?"

"Yes, sir." She sat in a corner chair, a notepad propped in her hand, a pen at the ready.

What kind of meeting was this that notes had to be taken?

"I'm sorry for all the conflicts surrounding the position

that Craig held, and now Judah has taken temporarily until we can get things sorted out."

Temporarily? That was news to Judah. A knot twisted in his gut. Would he lose his job, after all? Because of yesterday's council decision? Goodnight. The vote went in C-MER's favor. What else could he have done for the company?

"I want to say I'm pleased with the work Judah did as a liaison between us and the city council, namely with the mayor."

That didn't sound so bad. So, Mike was pleased with his work?

"Yes, he did a great job." Mia sighed.

Mike glanced at her. "However, I'm sorry to say we have a problem."

"What's that?" Judah leaned forward, glancing at Craig, who hadn't said a word since they entered Mike's office. Did he know something that Judah didn't?

Mike clearing his throat drew his attention back to him. "The city council has decided they'll need more information and documentation for a private meeting they're holding tonight—before they make any final decisions."

What? "Things were settled last night. What happened?"

"Apparently, it wasn't as settled as you thought." Mike shot Judah a glare.

What had transpired after last night's meeting to bring about this change?

A palpable irritation or unrest simmered in the room. Mike's forehead bunched up with frown lines. Craig's expression remained unreadable. Judah loosened the collar of his shirt.

"Can I count on you two"—Mike nodded tightly at Judah, then Craig—"to work together to gather all the necessary information? Most likely, our cooperation will go a long way in garnering their financial support."

"Tonight?" Judah glanced at his watch. He should be at Paisley's in a few minutes. What would happen if he couldn't make their session with the pastor for the second night in a row?

"Is that a problem?" Mike squinted at him.

"Well, you see—" Surely, Mike knew he had commitments outside of work. But with the tension in the room, should he make waves? "I did have an appointment at six."

"I'm sorry to disrupt your plans." Mike stared at him intensely. "But you know this situation is an emergency. Your job requires—"

"I know. You're right." Judah swallowed his rebuttal. "I can help get the paperwork together." Hopefully, he could do the work quickly and not be too late for their meeting with the pastor. "What time is this special council session?"

"Seven o'clock," Mia answered.

"Not much time." Craig stood. "We'll jump right in and get it done for you, boss."

"That's what I want to hear." Mike jotted something down on a notepad, seemingly avoiding Judah's gaze.

Great. Why did there have to be more complications on the job when things were just starting to look up? He followed Craig out of the room, wishing he didn't feel obligated to stay. Why had the group called for another meeting? Did they discover evidence about the dike? Financial issues?

He paused and tapped a quick text to Paisley. *Working late. Sorry. Will try to make the session if I can.*

He stuffed the cell phone into his back pocket and strode into the work area where Craig and a couple of other guys were pulling up information on their computers. Mia scurried back and forth between them and the printers, laughing and chatting as if everything were normal.

Far from how Judah felt. He needed to be at that counseling session with his wife. If an emergency out on the ocean had happened, and he was rescuing people, that would be different. But, this, gathering files, most likely for Mayor Grant, instead of him meeting Paisley and Pastor Sagle? That tore him up inside.

He picked a computer to use in one of the spare cubicles and dropped into the chair to locate the necessary files. He went through the motions of doing the required research, even though something felt off about the whole thing. Why did the committee go back on their decision?

Judah knew exactly which blueprints to print out. Which ones required updates. Once they were spread out on the work-table and dry, he thoroughly checked over everything again. Some revisions were required. The group stayed busy doing their tasks until the accumulated project sheets and blueprints were ready.

Mia helped by clipping pages together. Then she rolled up the blueprints in a tubular bundle, putting a rubber band around them, and said she'd deliver them to the council meeting.

It was almost seven by the time they finished. Too late for Judah to meet up with Paisley for their counseling session. He checked his phone. Strange that she hadn't texted him back.

He strode past Mike's office en route to his own office so he could grab his coat.

"Judah, a word?" The manager called to him.

"Sure. How can I help?" He shuffled into the small room and sat down on the edge of the chair where he sat earlier.

Mike crossed his arms over his desk and leaned forward, squinting. "Didn't I tell you to be a peacemaker at last night's meeting?"

Judah cleared his throat, suddenly feeling uncomfortable. "Yes, you did." What was this about?

"I'm sorry, but I have to relieve you of your position," Mike said brusquely.

"What? Why?" Hadn't he done what Mike wanted? "What happened?"

"There's been an official complaint lodged against you."

"A complaint? You're kidding. About what?" He stood up. "Who lodged a complaint?" The mayor? Craig? Anger burned hot in his chest. If he did something wrong, he'd apologize. But he went beyond the call of duty to assist this company, to get the approval they needed. A firing, after all he did to get last night's vote, and his staying late tonight to help, was beyond unbelievable.

"It's not so much what you did. It's about your demeanor and pushing your agenda too far in last night's meeting. Overriding the mayor's wishes."

"The mayor's—" So Judah was right. "I don't believe it."

How long had Mike been planning this firing? Before he even asked Judah to work extra tonight? This was too much to stomach.

"What's this really about?" He leaned his hands against the desk and stared at the other man.

Mike shoved his chair back as if putting more space between them. "The complaint alleges you misrepresented C-MER's role in the community. That you were disrespectful to members of the council."

"Disrespectful? That is not true. I never—"

"It's only a formality, but when you leave, I'll have you escorted out."

Escorted? How humiliating. Was this what the mayor wanted? More manipulation. Putting Judah in his place. Why? Because he pushed for a vote to safeguard the public? "Mike, I didn't do anything wrong at that meeting. Ask Mia. Ask Sue Taylor. I got you the outcome you wanted. The one you demanded of me to keep my job."

"Now, that's not the way I remember it."

Judah could only stare at his boss. Why was he changing his story? And kowtowing to everything the mayor demanded? That Mike didn't even have Judah's back, that he shuffled players around like their lives and their careers didn't matter—and for what, money or prestige?—was despicable. He shouldn't have come back to work here. Or taken Craig's position. Hadn't he felt leery about that from the start?

Mike shook his head and muttered, "Bad break. Goes above my clearance. Craig will be reinstated to his position."

Judah ran his hand over his hair, down his face. The world felt misaligned. He'd thought his success in the council meeting guaranteed his position. Now, this? "I don't understand how this could even happen. I did what you—"

"I'm sorry. You're a good worker. You've been faithful to the company up to this point." Mike's face hued red like he was embarrassed. "I'll hire you back to your old position in ninety days if you're interested. And if the complaints are dropped."

"Is this so-called claim that I misrepresented the firm a ploy so Craig can resume his role? Because he lodged a complaint?" If so, that was an unfairness Judah couldn't tolerate. "Or is this the mayor's trump card?" No reason to keep quiet about his suspicions.

Mike clamped his lips shut and averted his gaze.

Judah would like to march out the door right now without an escort. His pride and wounded ego nearly strangled him.

"I'll put in a good word for you during the inquiry." Mike stood.

"There's to be an inquiry?" Oh, man. Could things get any worse?

"That's the word from headquarters."

He'd served the company for eleven years. Had risked his life on the ocean to make sure others were safe—even at the detriment of his marriage. Then they fired him, then rehired him, and now ripped the rug out from under him again? "You should call whoever's assigned to walk me to the door. I'm leaving now." He strode out the door.

"This may seem unfair." Mike followed him into the open space between the offices and work area.

"You bet it does." Judah gritted his teeth.

"I'm getting a lot of pressure from the higher-ups. I'm sorry."

Judah stared hard at him, too many emotions running through him. When Mike reached out to shake his hand, he'd never been so tempted to avoid shaking someone's hand before. But even in the face of injustice, even if his insides were seething with the unfairness dealt him, he gulped and reached out to shake the other man's hand.

He even drummed up something polite to say. "Thank you for the opportunity to try this supervisory position." Then he turned and strode into his office.

A few seconds later, Craig stood in the doorway. "Mike wants me to escort you out."

Silently, Judah gathered his cell, his coat, and the few books and supplies he brought to work this time around. Then he strode to the entrance of C-MER, keeping a few steps ahead of the person he didn't want trailing him.

He didn't glance back at the building where he proudly returned as a supervisor. He couldn't believe how upside-down his life had become in such a few hours. All because he shared the mayor's last name and dared to stand up to the town leader? He felt shell-shocked. Numb, except for the throbbing behind his eyeballs.

He'd head straight home. Sleep off the headache and the feeling of despair. He didn't even want to call Paisley and tell her about his rotten day. Wasn't he in a foul mood?

Fourteen

Judah woke up the next morning, Saturday, and the remembrance of yesterday's events hit him. He was out of work, again. He replayed all that happened over the last two days. Still couldn't believe it. If he did something wrong, he'd be scrambling to make amends. But he gave the best presentation he could to the council and thought he'd done well—until last night when Mike told him he was fired. How would he pick up the pieces and provide for Paisley and him now? He was embarrassed even to tell her about it.

He groaned and ran his hands through his hair.

What did Mike say? He could have his old job in ninety days. No, thanks. Time to look for other employment, if he could find another job thanks to being canned. Maybe he'd look beyond Basalt Bay. How far would he have to go to work where no one had heard of Edward Grant?

He shuffled into the kitchen barefooted and powered up the coffee maker. Coffee first. Then he'd sit outside on the veranda. Maybe look for a job through Craigslist.

He sighed and numbly went through the motions of pouring creamer into his coffee. Then shuffled outside. The wind blew strongly over the sand, sending particles into his eyes. He squinted and trudged to the edge of the pavers he and Paisley put in a few years back. He'd like to extend the space and make a patio large enough to have a picnic table. Then they could have barbecues back here. Maybe that's how he'd spend some of his jobless days ahead. That and getting the flooring finished inside.

Just two days until their vow renewal. *Focus on that, Grant.* He noticed he had a missed call from Pastor Sagle. The pastor probably didn't appreciate that Judah canceled two sessions. He never meant for that to happen. He'd have to stop by the church and apologize. Would Pastor Sagle still require them to do the three sessions? Was there even time before Monday? If they had one tonight, one tomorrow, and the last session Monday morning, it would work. He'd text Paisley and see if she was okay with that.

It was strange that she didn't text him back last night after he texted her that he was going home to sleep off a migraine. Was she angry with him? If so, he wouldn't blame her. He had some explaining to do.

Sipping his hot drink, he heard a car pull into his driveway. Paisley? It didn't sound like her dad's VW. He couldn't see a vehicle from the backside of the house, so he shuffled through the sand in his bare feet and rounded the corner. If it was her, they could talk things through, and he'd explain what happened at C-MER that put him in such a funk last night.

"Hey, Judah." Paige, not Paisley, strode toward him.

"Hello." They met near the front porch. "What's up?"

"Is Paisley here? I wanted to ask her about my maid of

honor dress." She put her hand over her eyes, shielding the sunlight. "She asked me to be an attendant, but we didn't discuss what I should wear. And she's not answering my texts."

"That's great that you'll be in our wedding party. But, no, she's not here. She's still staying at your dad's."

"That's the thing. I was just there." A frown crossed Paige's face. "Dad says she never came home last night. He thought she must be here."

"What?" Tension rippled across Judah's shoulders. "She didn't stay at your dad's?" Where else would she be? Surely, she didn't take off somewhere without mentioning it. Take off? *Oh, no* A wave of déjà vu hit him as solidly as if he'd been punched in the stomach. Did she leave again? Leave him? He hated that his mind leaped to that conclusion. "You're sure she's not at your dad's?"

"I'm sure, Judah."

What if his not showing up for two marriage counseling sessions made her think he was lacking in commitment? That he was putting work before her, before them, as he had several years ago. "Not again." He stared out toward the breakers crashing over the beach. "Surely she didn't—"

"What is it?"

"Don't you see?" He dumped out his remaining coffee on the sand, making a dark stain. "I don't know … I'm just … what if she ran again?" Dread and fear and rejection—and his disappointment over getting fired—smashed together into one awful feeling in his gut. He rubbed his palm over his forehead. He knew he was overreacting, but he couldn't seem to help himself. "I canceled two marriage counseling sessions we were supposed to have with Pastor Sagle. I didn't get a chance to explain why I had to work late, and she may have assumed—"

He dropped onto the porch step. He set the cup down next to him and covered his face with his hands. Groaned. "How could she do this without talking to me?"

Paige sat down beside him. "Calm down, Judah. We don't know that she left. There may be an honest explanation. Let's not assume the worst."

"You're right." He lowered his hands and exhaled a long breath. *Rational thoughts, Grant.* Why would Paisley leave, anyway? They were happy together. She was happy, right?

"You don't think—" Paige groaned.

"What?"

"I don't want to say it." She met his gaze with a troubled look. "What if she ran away … with Craig?"

"Why would you even say that?" He shot to his feet. "No way. *No way!* She would not go anywhere with Craig Masters. She would not do that to us." He tromped to his truck. "But I'm going to find out if he knows anything. If he touched her—"

"Wait, Judah!" She ran after him. "Stop. I shouldn't have even mentioned it."

"No, you shouldn't have. But if I find out that two-faced—" He groaned. "Please move your car. Even though I can't stand to think such a traitorous thought against my wife, I have to find out what's going on."

"Over a week ago, I sort of said some"—Paige swallowed like admitting this was difficult—"awful things to Paisley about … Craig."

"Maybe justified." Judah spit and felt like throwing up his coffee. "Everything was going great between us. Just two days until our vow renewal."

"I know. Don't lose hope." She tugged on his arm. "You should go back inside."

"No, I'm going to turn this town upside down, hunting, until I find her. Until I discover what happened. Where she is. Why she left without saying anything. Did your dad mention an argument?"

"No, he didn't say anything. Look—"

"Your car?" He opened the truck door. Good thing his keys were inside.

"Why don't you text Craig and ask him if he knows where she is?"

"No. I'm going to look him in the eye and see if he's lying."

"Maybe I should go with you, then, since I dated him." She seemed to be blushing. "I think I could tell if he's lying."

"Okay. Fine. Meet me at his house."

Paige still didn't head to her sedan. "First, go back inside. You can't face him looking like this."

"Like what?" No one was telling him what he could or couldn't do. Including his sister-in-law.

"Looks like you just got out of bed."

"So what?"

She pointed toward the sand. "What about those?"

He glanced down at his bare feet speckled with sand particles. "Oh." He still didn't have shoes on.

"You probably shouldn't be driving in your state of mind, either." She leaned around him and snatched his truck keys from the ignition.

"Hey!"

She dangled them in the air. "Take a shower and get dressed. I'll wait out here. Then I'll drive you to Craig's house or to C-MER in my car."

"You're awfully bossy this morning." He glared at her. She wasn't usually like this.

"Thanks, I think."

He didn't mean it as a compliment.

She kept squinting at him and holding the keys away from him. He could grab them from her, but she was probably right. He shouldn't be driving.

And he didn't want to have a showdown with Craig while he was dressed in his pajamas. "Fine. I'll be right back." He trudged through the sand, back the way he came, crossed the pavers, and entered the cottage. He didn't pause to wipe his feet.

He stepped into the shower and let the hottest water possible pelt over the top of his head. He thought about what had kept him from going to Pastor Sagle's office with Paisley last night. How she never answered his text. Didn't even question why he wasn't meeting her. Maybe she figured he was being a flake. Like he didn't want to talk about the difficult stuff with her in front of the minister. Then, when he came home, tired and frustrated after getting fired, he didn't contact her when he should have. He slapped the subway tiling several times.

If Paisley were upset with him, needing time to think things through, where would she go? She must have gone somewhere for the night. Not to Craig's. He gritted his teeth.

Did she just need some time by herself? Or did she, as he feared, as he dreaded, run away from him again?

Fifteen

After stopping by Craig's house, and no one answering Judah's knock, Paige drove him to C-MER. Even though it was Saturday, a dozen cars were in the parking lot. He leaped out the door before she turned off the engine, then barreled toward the business entry.

"Judah! Wait up."

Her shoes pounded the pavement behind him, but he didn't pause. He had one thing on his mind—finding Craig. Yelling at him. Maybe slugging him.

He plowed through the lobby without pausing to address Mia or ask for Craig's whereabouts.

"Judah?" The receptionist's eyes widened. She picked up her phone and punched the buttons. Probably calling security.

He'd better act fast. He tromped through the building that had been his second home for more than a decade, almost at a run.

"Security!" Mia shouted. "Judah Grant is in the building."

He got about two-thirds of the way across the open floor plan before Hank, the company's protection detail, and Jeff, his previous coworker, lunged at him and nearly tackled him. He fought against them, hoping to get close enough to Craig's office to call him out.

"I'm not here to do any harm."

"Sure you aren't," Jeff said gruffly.

The two guys dragged him back in the direction he came from with Hank muttering about disgruntled ex-employees not getting past him.

"Come on, you guys. I just need to talk to—Craig!" Judah yelled and yanked against their hold.

Mike Linfield strode from his office. "Why are you here, Judah? You know better than this." He stopped a few feet away as if Judah might be dangerous.

"I must speak to Craig."

"Judah?" Paige stood next to Mia with an intimidated look on her face. "Maybe we should leave, huh?"

He wasn't going anywhere without talking to Craig first.

Hank and Jeff reefed on his arms again, dragging him closer to the front door. It looked like he was failing at stopping them. "Let me go. I have to see Craig."

"Don't make any more of a scene than you already have," Hank grumbled.

"Masters! I need to talk with you."

"Vacate the building immediately." Mike pointed toward the door. "Or we're calling the police."

"I'm not leaving until I speak with Craig."

Mike nodded at the two guys, communicating for them to finish hauling him outside.

"Please, my wife is missing. I must ask him—"

"He's right." Paige stepped forward. Mia kept in step beside her like she planned to stop Paige if she tried something. "My sister is missing. We need to ask Craig if he knows anything about it. Is he here? Please, let me speak to him."

Judah's old office door opened. Craig shuffled out, yawning as if he'd been interrupted from a nap. He glanced at Paige, his eyes widening. "What's going on?"

"Were you with Paisley last night?" Judah spit out.

"What?" Craig glanced between Judah and Paige. "Of course not. Why would you ask such a stupid question?"

"Mia, call the police," Mike commanded.

"Of course." She scurried away.

"That's not necessary." Judah didn't take his gaze off Craig. Hopefully, his sister-in-law could decipher whether the man was telling the truth. "Did you spend time with Paisley last night?" He clenched his jaw. "Did you say or do something to offend her?"

"No, I didn't see her or talk to her." Craig dropped his fists onto his hips. "She made it clear she doesn't want anything to do with me. What's this about?"

"You didn't call her? Badger her? Force her—"

"No!"

"Paisley's missing," Paige said quietly.

"What?" Craig's shoulders slumped. He took a step toward Paige, but she moved closer to Judah. "Honestly, I don't know anything about that. If something happened, I didn't have anything to do with it." He held up both palms, but a tic twitched in his jaw. Hadn't Judah seen that happen recently? "You think it's the same as before?"

Judah groaned. Was everyone going to think that? Like he was to blame. That he couldn't keep a wife from running away from him. Yet, wasn't he even questioning that? Surely Paisley wouldn't do that to him again. She wouldn't leave. She loved him and wanted to marry him. But, if so, why wasn't she at her dad's, or at the cottage?

He'd done enough here. Made a big enough fool of himself.

"Go ahead. Take me away." He nodded toward Jeff. They escorted him the rest of the way from the building, and he walked beside them willingly.

He heard Mike telling Mia to call the deputy back and tell him not to come after all. Just a misunderstanding.

Once he was free to walk on his own, Judah plodded toward the car. He almost made it into the passenger seat before he got sick. He bent over the pavement and lost his coffee and whatever else he ate last night.

"You okay?" Paige asked from her side of the vehicle.

"No." He groaned. Wiping his mouth, he waited outside the car for a few minutes. He pressed his fist against his mouth and fought tears. He didn't want to fall apart in front of Paige. Why did one thing after another keep happening? Had Paisley left him? And, if so, why?

"What do you want to do now?"

"Where's Piper?"

"At a playdate with a neighbor." She stared at him over the hood of the car.

"Could you drive me back to my place?"

"Sure. You're not going to drive, are you?" There was that bossy tone in her voice again. "I can drive you somewhere else. Would you like to grab coffee? Soda? Something to settle your stomach? Piper is fine for a while." She got into the car.

"I'm okay." His stomach didn't roil as before, so he eased onto the seat. "Hopefully, that's the end of that."

"I'll say." She started the engine.

"Was Craig telling the truth?" He fastened his seatbelt.

"Yes"—she drove out of the parking lot—"and no."

"Which is it?" He shuffled on the seat to better see her.

"I'd say he answered truthfully about not seeing Paisley last night." She made a huffing sound. "But something was weird about him."

"You noticed that too?"

"I did." She stared forward as she drove. "Any chance you and Paisley argued?"

"No. Everything was great." He thought of their kisses from the day before yesterday. "But my bailing out of those counseling sessions might have sent her a bad signal."

Paige glanced sharply at him.

"It wasn't that." He lifted both hands. "Honestly, I didn't have a choice." But he couldn't get the thought out of his mind that he should have stopped by or called her last night. Did she forget his request for her to run to him instead of running away from him if she was troubled about something? He rubbed his palm over his stomach, still feeling queasy. "If I say, 'pull over,' do it quickly, okay?"

"Oh, sure." She shot him a worried look. "If my sister needed to get away to think, where do you suppose she'd go?"

"Out to the peninsula, but not overnight."

"That's what I thought too."

He yanked his cell phone out of his coat pocket. Then tapped in a text. Did Paisley even bring her phone along with her? Last time she didn't.

Call me, please. I'm worried. Miss you. We need to talk.

Paige brought the car to a stop in Judah's driveway. She laid her hand on his coat sleeve. "Why did those guys nearly tackle you back at C-MER?" She moved her hand from touching him. "I don't mean to pry, but it freaked me out."

"I got fired yesterday."

"Oh, no. That's terrible."

"Yeah, it is. An unfair thing that's happened to me, twice."

She shook her head and he saw sympathy in her gaze. "I'm sorry."

"Thanks." He nodded toward the cottage. "I should go. Thanks for the ride. Call if you hear anything, okay?"

"Yeah, you too."

He hopped out and marched down to the beach, needing a quiet place to think and pray about everything that had happened in the last twenty-four hours.

Sixteen

Paisley peered through the inky darkness, not seeing anything other than a sliver of light coming through a crack next to a door. She must be in a closet. Something pressed against her back—boxes or crates. Something solid was in front of her knees, too. The sensation of being imprisoned in the cramped, dark place brought back a flood of unwanted memories from her childhood. But even when she was locked up in the pantry, she'd never been tied up. Now, she could barely move. Trapped in a tiny space. Caged by tape and rope. How long would she have to stay here like this? Until she died? Ugh. Why did she have to think of that? Didn't Edward say he planned to get rid of her?

Panic crept up her throat. Her heart raced. Her temples pounded. She inhaled and exhaled frantically through her nose. *More air. I need more.* She closed her eyes and, using force of will, made herself breathe in and out, slower, calmer, and more evenly. *One. Two. Three.* Sometimes counting helped.

You're going to be okay. Just breathe. You'll get through this.

But, how?

When Edward brought her here—wherever here was—he'd kept her blindfolded. By the way the truck engine had revved, and he shifted gears, she imagined they were going uphill. He must have brought her to his mansion on the cliff. What did he plan to do with her next?

She shuffled on the carpet, moving half an inch, or so. The way her arms and legs were strapped with rope and tape kept her painfully immobile. She'd tried to break free for so long, at the coffee shop and when she first got here, that she exhausted herself. It seemed every part of her hurt from the strain, but she wouldn't give up. If she could break free, she'd run from this house—okay, maybe crawl—and hide in the forest that surrounded the Grant estate. Edward would never find her, then.

Hopefully, Judah would.

She drew in a long breath through her nose. She needed more oxygen. More movement for her limbs. The tape had better come off soon. She rocked back and forth, using her stomach and leg muscles, attempting to kick at the door or the boxes, anything her bare feet could reach. Where were her shoes? She lay still for a few minutes, too tired to move, listening. She couldn't hear anything other than her heart throbbing in her ears.

Why did her head hurt so badly? Oh, right. Edward hit her. Her legs hurt too. Didn't he kick her? *Scum of the earth.* No, she wouldn't think about him. She needed to move and keep blood flowing to her limbs, and not contemplate her captor. But how could she with the mummified way she was tied up? If Judah knew about this, about his father's abuse, he'd do something. He'd stand up for injustice, even if the person in the wrong was his dad.

She remembered the last time he rescued her. As if she were still caught in the whirlpool, the sea dragging her down into the depths of turbulent waters, she mentally relived the rescue. She would have died that day if not for Judah risking his life. Was he out there searching for her now?

How long had she been without food and water? She'd slept. Was it day or night? Had more than one day passed? What if she missed their vow renewal ceremony? No, that couldn't happen. But what if it did? She grimaced and the tape pinched her cheeks. *Ow.* What if, when she didn't show up at the marriage counseling session, Judah thought she skipped town? Ran away? Tears welled in her eyes. None of that. Otherwise, her nose would get stuffy and breathing would be impossible. Still, she fought the urge to weep.

Her stomach growled. She was thirsty and hungry. Hurt all over. She missed Judah. What if she never saw him again? Isn't that what Edward threatened? Judah had said their marriage would be stronger now because of God's love and grace. What if she never got the chance to fully reconcile with him? What if Edward got away with this?

No, he wouldn't.

Judah, don't give up on us. Please, find me. I want to be with you.

She closed her eyes and dozed off again. Then awoke with a start. She struggled to breathe. Her head hurt worse. Her arms ached. Her legs felt weird. Was she losing circulation to her extremities? She tried opening her jaws to pull her lips away from the duct tape, but her skin burned like it was on fire.

Her mouth was so dry. The acidic taste of tape on her lips and her tongue made her want to spit. But, of course, she couldn't.

Breathe. Just keep breathing. Don't panic.

If only she would listen to herself.

The darkness was so thick. Gulp. She had to think of something to pull herself out of her discouragement and anxiety. She couldn't see five things of beauty to focus on as she did sometimes when she was having a panic attack, but she could mentally picture them.

Judah's baby blues.

His tender smile.

The way he linked pinkies with her.

The peninsula she loved to sit on.

Her beautiful ocean.

If only she could sit by the sea right now. On her peninsula. With seawater pouring over her. With foaming spray arcing in the air like a waterfall. *Please, let me experience that again.*

Picturing her favorite place, a sense of calm eased through her. However, it didn't last long. Edward's cruel actions were never far from her thoughts. Left alone like this—tied up, without food or water, not enough oxygen in the room—how long would it take for her heart to stop beating? For the air in the stuffy room to be insufficient?

Edward said he wanted her gone. That she was unworthy of his son. Didn't he mention Mia taking her place in Judah's life? Something about her failing before. She knew one thing—Judah deserved better than Mia Till.

Once, she thought he deserved someone better than her. Not anymore. He should be with a woman who loved him with her whole heart, and she did. And he loved her. He'd keep looking for her. Didn't he do that before? He even hired a detective. He'd come after her this time, too, if he reached her in time. That was reason enough for her to keep breathing. Surviving.

Praying too. She needed to pray and trust God.

Lord, it's me again with my desperate, desperate prayers. Please, rescue me. Stop Edward from whatever harm he's planning to do to me. Don't let him get away with this evil. He's a terrible man. But I guess You love him anyway. Sorry, I can't seem to do that.

Thoughts of Edward's fiendish plans to get rid of her made her heart pound rapidly again. But she needed to stay relaxed. Calm. Thinking about God and His love. The mercy Judah kept talking about. The grace he gave her. Even when she didn't deserve it and messed up. Even when she doubted him. He kept extending grace and telling her God's love could change her, change them. *He* would help them create a beautiful marriage. And she wanted that chance with Judah. Oh, she wanted it. *Please, God.*

The Lord was here with her. He was! A strange, yet welcome, peace invaded her. As if suddenly she was breathing Him in. Breathing in His love like fresh air. And that was enough. Would always be enough. God was with her, comforting her. *Thank You, Lord.*

I'm sorry for … everything. For walking away from You and hardening my heart to You. Now, I want to be a true follower of Jesus for all the days, or hours, I have left. I want Your love in me. Judah's shown me such grace. I want to have that to give to others too.

God's presence seemed to surround her, wrapping her in a blanket of love. Peace, like she hadn't known in a long time, filled up the gaps inside her spirit with something warm, like oil. And while she didn't have any food or water, or even much air, she suddenly didn't fear what was still to come.

Seventeen

Judah walked along the seashore from the beach by his house down to Baker's Point where the gazebo used to be before the hurricanes, the same place where he first asked Paisley to marry him, and back again. As soon as he entered the cottage, he checked his phone. No voicemail. No text. Three years ago she didn't call, either. He pictured the note he flushed down the toilet a couple of days ago. She had left him a note the last time.

That's right. She wouldn't go away without leaving a note or message. He marched from the kitchen into the bedroom. Yanking both pillows off his bed, he hunted for a small piece of paper, maybe some stationery. When he found none, he was partly relieved, partly troubled.

Nausea, worry, and doubt plowed through him like waves crashing against his hope and resolve to believe for the best. What had happened to cause her to run again, if she did? And why wouldn't she have talked to him about whatever it was if she were so unhappy about something?

Where are you, Paisley?

He flopped down on the bed, flung his bent arm over his forehead, and stared at the ceiling. What now? He didn't have any leads. He could spend all day driving up and down the Oregon Coast, searching for her, and completely miss her. He couldn't imagine her walking away without talking to him, not when things were going so well between them. But why wouldn't she have been at her dad's last night? Where was she now?

He thought about how they recently talked over their past struggles, and she said she wished she never left him. He sat up. *She wished she never left me!* After saying that—what, six days ago—would she leave him without a word?

Not likely.

But still, he didn't know what to make of her disappearance. Or what he should do next.

Someone knocked on the door. Before he reached the living room, Mom entered the house.

"Oh, Judah. Is it true?" She rushed over to him and hugged him. "Did she leave again?"

"Who told you that?" His gut knotted up with more turmoil.

"Those gossips. Customers at Lewis's Super blab about everything." She clutched his arm. "Tell me. I want to hear it from you. What happened between you two?"

"Nothing. I don't know." He strummed his hands through his hair. "I can't imagine her leaving me again. But she didn't go home last night. Her dad and sister don't know where she is. Neither do I."

"The other day she was so happy and looking forward to your vow renewal ceremony." Hearing Mom say so was comforting. "How are you coping?"

"I'm worried and upset, as you can imagine." How much should he tell her? "On top of that, after a meeting at City Hall, I lost my job again."

"Oh, no. I'm so sorry, Judah."

"It's okay. Or will be." He paced across the living room. "All that matters is finding Paisley now. Us working out whatever happened to upset her, or whatever."

"What took place with your dad?" She gave him a look that said she knew this had to involve him somehow.

He stroked his forehead and sighed. "After my presentation, the group asked Dad and me to step out of the room so they could discuss the situation between the city and C-MER. He got mad. Probably called my boss."

"I can't imagine him getting you fired. He's proud of your work."

"I don't think he is." Judah didn't want to get into this with her. "Anyway, someone reported that I caused trouble at the meeting. Mike Linfield fired me. I'm at square one. No job and my wife is missing."

Missing. He stared at the floorboards. What if she didn't run? What if something bad happened to her? Like an accident. Acid crept up his throat. He swallowed hard, ridding his throat of the burning sensation. What if she went out on the peninsula, even though he warned her not to, and fell in the water again? "Oh, man."

"What is it? You're scaring me."

"I'm scaring myself. What if she didn't run away?" He faced her. "Ever since this morning, I thought she must have. But what if she didn't? What if she fell in the sea? What if the worst thing imaginable happened to her two days before our vow renewal?" The possibility of Paisley falling into the waves and getting sucked into a whirlpool again, alone, dug a trench of pain inside him. "Here I've been having these traitorous thoughts about her. When maybe all along—"

"Now, Son, don't think like that." Mom strode to him and wrapped her arms around him. "It will be okay. Let's believe in God's mercy and not expect the worst."

He knew she meant well. And he wanted to trust God. Man, he wanted to trust Him that good would come out of this. But sometimes bad things happened to people—they both knew that. Look at the glass window exploding, sending a shard into his leg. Look at how the hurricanes caused so much damage all along the coast. Even Mom had endured her own sea of pain. However, she was right too. God could still bring about good in this situation. Even a miracle, if they trusted Him.

Mom stepped back and smiled. "Aren't you the one who's always saying that God's grace can get us through anything?"

"That's what I usually say."

"How about some coffee to get your mind off things?" She scurried into the kitchen.

"I've had enough."

"I'm going to fix some anyway."

"Yeah, sure." He paced some more, listening to the sounds of her getting cups out of the cupboard and powering up the coffee maker.

Maybe he should drive to the peninsula and check for himself. Perhaps, after he texted Paisley that he couldn't make that appointment last night, she walked down to the beach. Did something happen there? Did anyone see her?

Mom brought him a steaming cup of black coffee. "Thanks." He'd be jittery if he drank any more today. He sipped it, appreciating the heat on his throat.

"Did anything troubling happen between you two?" Mom drank from her cup, but her gaze landed on him.

"Like a fight?"

"Mmm."

"No." He explained about missing the appointments. "Job stuff kept me away."

"Any chance she misinterpreted that?" Mom tipped her head, staring at him.

"That's what I thought earlier. Now, I'm not so sure."

"Have you asked the pastor if she called him?" She clutched her cup between both hands as if drawing the heat into herself. "Maybe find out what they talked about?"

"That's a good idea. I've been so baffled." He shrugged. "I mean, we're supposed to be renewing our vows the day after tomorrow."

"I know. Try not to panic. Paisley wants to wear that wedding dress more than anything. If only you saw how delighted she was to find a dress she loved." Mom patted his shoulder. "She wants to be with you, Judah. Married."

It was a relief to hear someone speak positively about his wife, about their relationship. "Thanks, Mom." He took a slurp of his coffee, then dropped the cup on the kitchen counter. He couldn't wait around here any longer. He had to do something. He ran for his room to grab his jacket. Shoving his arms into the sleeves, he rechecked his cell phone. Still, no word. "See you later, Mom." He dashed for the door. "Keep praying."

"I will. Keep in contact with me, okay? I want to know what's happened to our girl."

Our girl. He liked her claiming Paisley as her daughter. Their family.

Please, God, I need to find out what's happened to my wife.

Eighteen

Judah parked his truck in front of the Basalt Bay Peninsula and read the C-MER signs—*Stay off the peninsula! Danger! Keep off!* The notifications were strong visual warnings. Hopefully, people obeyed them. Paisley probably wouldn't pay a lick of attention to a sign telling her to stay away from the place she loved.

He turned off the engine and shot out of his rig. If she were sitting out on the point, like he'd found her other times, he'd see her from here. He didn't. Still, he tromped toward the rocks, his gaze searching the beach in both directions, and memories rushed through him. The time he held her here following the death of their baby. Then, a month ago, after returning to Basalt Bay, she collapsed here. Three weeks ago, she nearly drowned in the whirlpool and he rescued her.

What if he had to face losing her again? For the last few hours, he contemplated little else. If she ran away, it might be years before she came home again. But never seeing her? How could he survive that?

He trudged out on the rocks. He knew where to step safely. So did Paisley—he had to remember that. But what if, in her frustration or distraction, she didn't watch where she was going? Isn't that what happened last time?

Skirting around the rocks he traversed hundreds, maybe thousands, of times over the years, he approached the water's edge, but not too close. He didn't want to get soaking wet today. But he had to stand where he could see beyond the frothing seawater shooting white spray up into the air. Watching where the whirlpool had dragged Paisley down before, he observed it swirling and churning the water like an eggbeater attacking pudding.

"Judah!"

That sounded almost like—

He whirled around. Paige, not Paisley, stood where the land met the rocky peninsula. "Stay back!" No reason for her to come out here and possibly fall. "I'll be there in a minute."

"Okay." She waved at him before veering toward the parking lot.

The wind howled around him, shoving against him like it wanted to knock him into the drink. The water spray beat against the rocks, a perpetual roar as he stared into distant waters. What if the surf pulled her out there? Maybe he should borrow a boat and go searching. But the water was too cold for anyone to survive for long. Not that he wanted to think about that.

After watching the churning waves for long enough, he headed back. He jumped over one of the gaping holes where a large boulder fell into the sea after the hurricane, his shoes slipping on wet rocks. But he kept trudging forward.

"I was just at my dad's," Paige hollered as he approached her. "He said he doesn't know what may have spooked Paisley."

"No arguments between them?" He straightened his wind-blown hair, out of frustration more than any concern for how he looked.

"He said nothing was wrong. He's been watching out for her. She seemed happy. He doesn't think she'd wander out on the peninsula so soon after what happened before, either." Paige ran her hands over her arms as if to warm herself. "But she loved going out there. We all know that."

"Yeah. Not you, huh?"

"Mom warned me to stay away from the ocean. Same as Paisley and Peter, but they wouldn't listen." She let out a long sigh. "I never felt the affinity for the sea as they did. It was like it belonged to them and I wasn't invited."

"Sorry."

"Me too."

While she talked, he kept perusing the valleys and crests of the incoming waves.

"Even when I stepped on the rocks to speak with you, something foreboding came over me. I've never even been out to the point." Her voice went quiet. "Do you know how silly that makes me feel when I've spent my whole life in Basalt Bay?"

"It's okay. Too dangerous now, anyway."

"Judah, Paisley and I had an intense, awkward conversation two days ago." She groaned and her face turned rose colored. "You don't think that's why she left, do you?"

"What was it about, if you don't mind my asking?" Maybe this was a clue that would help him find her.

She gulped. "I'm sorry, but I do mind." She scuffed her shoes against the pavement. "It had to do with you." She glanced away, sweeping hair out of her face.

"Me? What did I do?"

"Nothing that you did. More about her leaving you." It seemed like she was struggling over whether to say anything else. "If our discussion caused her to run, I'd feel terrible. I'm so sorry, Judah. I just—" Her face crumpled into a sob, then she turned away and ran across the parking lot toward her car.

"Paige, wait!" But she didn't stop.

So, the two sisters had an 'intense' conversation? About him? Strange. But, even so, surely it wasn't a stressful enough conflict to make Paisley leave.

Sighing, he did a last visual check of the beach and the sea in front of the town, then trudged back to his pickup. Inside, he leaned his forehead against the steering wheel. The last time he did this was the night of the hurricane. The night he begged God to show him where Paisley was. And He had! Judah had considered it a miracle.

Lord, You know Paisley's missing. She could have hopped a bus to get supplies and was delayed. Or she could be upset about something. Or something far worse. She could be in danger or harm.

He stared out the windshield. "You are a God of second chances. You're a God who works miracles. I'm begging You to help me find her. Show me where she is. Please."

A few minutes later, he started the truck and drove to the church. He didn't know if the pastor had any information, but since Mom suggested it, he figured he ought to follow through and inquire. As soon as he turned off the engine, he jumped out of the vehicle.

Inside the foyer, he glanced in the chapel. The room looked welcoming, especially with the way the light flowed in through the windows near the altar. He'd like to sit down on the front pew and spend an hour praying for Paisley, for their marriage.

However, urgency propelled him down the hallway toward the pastor's office. Back to where he and Paisley talked with the minister four days ago. From the office doorway, Judah observed Pastor Sagle sitting in his chair with a book in his hands. "Got a minute, Pastor?"

"Oh, sure." The older man lowered the book. "Judah, I'm surprised to see you here."

"I wanted to apologize for missing our appointments. I had to work extra hours. I'm sorry for inconveniencing you."

"All right. Come in."

He strode to the pastor's desk and remained standing. "Have you seen Paisley since our meeting? Did she stop by or call?"

"Two days ago she came by." Pastor Sagle lifted a familiar-looking cream-colored envelope with Paisley's handwriting on it. "She gave me this and told me you wouldn't be able to make the appointment, so we rescheduled." He squinted at Judah. "You both missed our second session. I tried calling you."

"I know. I didn't mean to miss it, but a work situation came up. I thought she'd take care of it—"

"She didn't. No one called me."

That seemed strange.

"You both left me hanging."

"I'm really sorry."

Pastor Sagle shut his book and laid it on top of the calendar. "As far as I'm concerned, your ceremony is canceled."

"What?" The pastor's harsh words pierced Judah's heart. "Canceled" sounded like a nail being driven into the coffin of his hopes and dreams. "Don't end the ceremony. Not yet. Please."

"How are you going to make the three sessions I told you were essential with only two days left?" The pastor's eyebrows rose high on his forehead.

"I don't know. Paisley has gone missing. Don't—" He groaned. "Please don't cancel our ceremony."

"She's missing?" The white-haired pastor sat up straighter. "She left you again?"

Judah groaned. He could hardly get the next words out of his mouth. "She may have. And while it's possible we won't be able to go through with the vow renewal, that something may have happened, I don't want you to cancel yet."

"Judah, I had no idea."

"It might be"—he continued as if the pastor didn't speak—"that we'd have to do the counseling sessions after the ceremony. That could work, right? I'm begging you not to cancel before I know for sure what's going on."

He must sound pathetic, but finding his wife was what mattered, even if they couldn't go through with the ceremony. Maybe they needed more counseling than even Pastor Sagle could offer them.

"What happened? Tell me what's going on. Here. Sit down." The pastor pulsed his hand toward the chair.

Judah didn't want to take the time to sit down, but he dropped onto the chair and sighed.

"Start from the top. How did Paisley go missing, if she did?"

"I don't know. She's been so happy. We both have been. We were looking forward to our vow renewal. Being together, finally."

"I feared this would happen." Pastor Sagle shook his head and wiped his knuckles against his chin.

"Thought what would happen?" Judah tensed.

"People do this. Things get difficult … they run. You didn't like me asking her the question the other day, I could tell, but this was why."

Judah hated that the pastor assumed things about Paisley, about their marriage, that might not be so. And sitting here talking about his wife, as if there wasn't any question other than she left him, stung. He stood quickly.

"Don't leave offended, please." The minister gazed at him with a kinder expression. "Sometimes when people get in a rut of bad habits, that's what repeats itself. More bad habits."

"No disrespect, Pastor, but I don't want to believe that about my wife. That God can't bring about change and healing. I won't believe it."

"I'm sorry if it sounds abrupt and heartless, but it's possible this running thing is a pattern with Paisley, something you'll be dealing with for a long time."

Judah didn't want to hear such negativity coming from a spiritual mentor. He preferred to stay positive. Even for his own faith, speaking words of life and truth seemed vital. He'd already thought enough fearful thoughts today. "I'm determined to believe for the best. I confess my first reaction was that she ran too. But now I think something bad may have happened to her."

"What changed your mind?"

"A couple of days ago, she picked out a wedding dress. My mom went with her. She says Paisley was happy. Marrying me again is what she wanted, what she planned. She didn't intend to run away." Judah bit off a groan. "It just doesn't make sense why I can't find her." He tapped the toe of his shoe against the chair leg.

"What are you going to do?" Pastor Sagle stood on his side of the desk. "Do you think she could be injured? Didn't she fall into the sea recently?"

"Yes. That's what I'm most concerned about."

"Perhaps"—the pastor stroked his chin—"we should get an informal search party together. Rally some town folks to help."

"Really?" Hearing the pastor saying something useful was encouraging.

"We'll form lines and scour the shoreline." Pastor Sagle picked up his phone. "You know the drill. I'll make some calls."

"That would be great. Thank you." He headed toward the door.

"We'll meet by the peninsula."

"Sounds good." Judah rocked his thumb over his shoulder. "I'll talk to Paul. He'll want to be there too." He dashed out of the office.

But even if they turned the seashore upside down searching for Paisley, would they uncover any clues that would help him find her?

Nineteen

Judah stood on the beach in front of the town, amazed and humbled by how many people showed up to search for Paisley. News must have spread quickly. Even his father was there. Kathleen greeted Judah, as did his mom. James Weston and Paul stood beside Paige. He saw Pastor Sagle talking to a few shop owners.

"Did anyone see Paisley Grant since yesterday morning?" Deputy Brian called out, using a megaphone.

A few answered with negative responses. Others shook their heads.

Judah wanted to take charge and tell everyone to go ahead and start looking. But the deputy had his own way of doing things. A slow way, it seemed. But, then, Judah was impatient.

"Paul Cedars says Paisley was at his house early yesterday morning, but he hasn't seen her since." Deputy Brian cast a suspicious glance at Judah. "Up to that point, she'd been staying there. Judah Grant was the last person Paul saw with her."

The group's gaze turned toward him. Was the deputy implying he had something to do with her disappearance? Did the others think that about him? Heat infused his neck and face.

"Any reason to suspect foul play?" Leave it to the mayor to ask that.

"None as of yet." Deputy Brian perused the group. "Paul doesn't remember what his daughter was wearing, so we're uncertain if she was prepared to spend the night in cool weather. Probably not." Again he stared at Judah. "We'll split up into four groups. One will head north beyond Basalt Bay Peninsula. Walk in a line about an arm's length from each other, surveying every inch of coastline. If you find anything suspicious, don't pick it up unless the tide might damage it. Even then, take a picture with your phone before picking it up."

Judah inwardly groaned at what he might be implying.

Deputy Brian pointed toward the seashore in front of the town. "The second group will comb the beach from here out to the cannery. The third will start on the south side of the cannery and follow the coastline until you reach Baker's Point. Again, stand almost side by side and search thoroughly."

Judah contemplated his walk to the old gazebo earlier, a calming momentary distraction. He'd love to reconstruct the place where he asked Paisley to marry him the first time. Where other locals had celebrated proposals and baby announcements. Maybe he'd do that in his spare time since he didn't have a job.

People clustered into four groups.

The deputy waved his hands. "The last group will go through town, checking the streets and around the shops for anything unusual."

Which band of searchers should Judah join? What if someone found something and he wasn't there to see it for himself? He couldn't be in all the groups at once.

"Stay off the peninsula!" Still using the megaphone, Deputy Brian shouted. "I repeat, stay off the peninsula. It's dangerous. Observe the water from a safe distance."

"Judah!" Sal from Nautical Sal's Souvenirs trudged down the sand toward him, waving.

"Hey, Sal." He felt compassion for the man whose business had been ruined in the last hurricane. Maybe Judah could offer to help him in the days ahead. There, he'd already thought of a few things he could do in the absence of a job.

"Hold up, Judah."

"I will." He waited for the other man to catch up. "What's going on?"

Sal bent over huffing. "I just … got here. Sorry. Whew. Out of breath."

Judah glanced back and saw a line of people already walking perpendicular to the ocean, their heads bent as if perusing the sand. Farther away, another group of five or six made their way toward the far side of the peninsula.

"I wanted to tell you … I saw Paisley yesterday, early afternoon."

"You did? Where?"

"She was"—Sal held his hand over his heart like it was beating too fast—"walking past my shop. She always waves and gives me a kind look. I'm sorry to hear she's missing."

Judah stepped closer to him. "You're sure it was yesterday when you saw her?"

"No doubt about it. She was heading south. Maybe toward Miss Patty's or Bert's."

"Of course." Didn't they talk about her trying to get her old job back at Bert's Fish Shack? Bert wasn't among the searchers. Did he turn her down? Was she upset or disappointed by not getting a job? "Thank you, Sal. That information helps." He shook the man's hand. "When you get a chance, you should tell the deputy what you told me."

"Sure thing. I will." Sal rocked his thumb toward the lineup in front of the cove. "I'll join them, huh?"

"That would be great. I'm going to follow these guys." Judah pointed to the group heading toward the cannery.

He trudged along the beach to the pier. If Paisley went by Sal's shop yesterday, did she stop by Miss Patty's? Did the hardware store owner say something unkind?

Maybe Paisley's leaving didn't even have anything to do with him and her. But what could anyone say to make her take off like that, especially after their kisses two days ago? It didn't make sense. Which brought him back to the possibility of her having an accident along the slick rocks. If the tide came in while she was unconscious, anything could have happened.

His groan felt drudged up from beneath his ribs.

Farther down the beach, in front of the dunes, he approached the line of townspeople. Grit, propelled by wind gusts, flew into his eyes. Blinking rapidly, he fell into step to the left of Sue Taylor, the woman from the city council meeting. He had things he'd like to ask her if the task before him wasn't so ominous. No one spoke other than to mention a bit of old fabric someone found knotted around a stick. Looked to be a decade old.

While he didn't want his neighbors to waste their time, he hoped this was all a mistake. That maybe Paisley went to another town to get something for the ceremony and got detained. But wouldn't she have called or texted him? Could be he'd find her at the cottage, trying on her wedding dress. She'd want to do that, right?

But would they even have their vow renewal now? He groaned. He wasn't going to think that way. Not yet. He'd continue praying that Paisley, his love, his wife, was alive and safe. And soon they'd be together again.

Lord, help us find her before it's too late.

Twenty

Over the sound of the waves pounding the shore, Judah just barely heard someone calling his name. He swiveled around to see who it was.

"Judah!" Paige jogged down the beach toward him, waving something small in the air.

"What is it?" He strode toward her across the wet sand, meeting her halfway.

"Oh, Judah." She stopped and bent over breathing hard.

"What did you find?" He tensed, apprehensive of her news.

She handed him a tiny, stringy piece of cloth.

"What's this?"

She heaved a breath like she had to do that before she could speak. "There's a big … mess at my gallery … but I had to show you this."

"Big mess? What do you mean?"

"I'm on my way to tell the deputy about it." She tucked loose hairs beneath her hat. "Anything could have happened to cause such a disaster. Looters, maybe. But this seems suspicious to me."

"What are you saying? That Paisley might be involved?"

"It's possible."

He held up the piece of fabric to the sunlight. "Think it's hers?"

"I don't know. Do you?" She shrugged. "By the way stuff is thrown about in my coffee area, it looks like a struggle took place."

"A struggle?" Surely, Paisley wasn't involved in any skirmish at Paige's shop.

"I set a box on the counter a few days ago. Now its contents are spread across the floor. Coffee grounds everywhere." She clutched his arm. "What if Paisley went into the gallery and found someone looting the place? Not that there was much there. But sometimes that happens after a catastrophe. Looters, right?"

"Not usually this long after one. It's been a month."

"Still, she might have tried fighting someone off."

That sounded terrible. And far-fetched.

"The fabric might be a clue. Does she have a red shirt like this?"

He stared hard at it. "I don't know. We've been apart for three years. She has clothes and underthings I wouldn't recognize."

"Right." Paige tugged the material from his hand. "When I cleaned the gallery a couple of days ago, this wasn't on the floor."

"You're sure?"

"Absolutely. I would have noticed a red piece of fabric." She stared at it. "Looks like cloth torn from a tank top."

"Why would she be wearing a tank top?" He was still trying to work through what Paige was saying. "The weather's too cool."

"It adds warmth. Might have been tattered. Something she could tug loose. I'm not saying it's hers." She grimaced. "I found something else that I don't even want to mention."

"What is it?" He braced himself for more troubling news.

"Duct tape. A chunk of it." Her lips puckered like she was fighting a sob. "Oh, Judah, I'm afraid someone did something bad to her. She might have caught them in the act of stealing or doing damage. Maybe she tried to stop them. What if they bound her with duct tape?" Crying, she fell into his arms.

He patted her back in a brotherly way, his thoughts whirling with possibilities. Could this be what happened to his wife? Had she stepped into a burglary gone bad? His chest burned with fresh uncertainty and worry. If what Paige suspected had happened, what would the looters have done to Paisley? Just speculation, but still. A torn piece of cloth and duct tape? Might mean something. Or nothing at all.

"Do you normally have duct tape at your shop?" He set Paige away from him so he could see her face.

"Huh-uh. No reason to." She wiped her cheeks.

"You should find Deputy Brian and tell him about this."

"I will. Don't you want to come with me?" She pointed toward the other side of the beach where another group scoured the seashore.

"All right, but then I'll go by the gallery and hunt every inch of the place, just in case." At least this felt like a possible lead. Not a good one though.

"Okay. I could have overlooked something." She shivered. "Sorry. I didn't mean to fling myself into your arms. I'm just upset. Worked up over the idea that Paisley could have been mugged. Or—"

"I know. It's okay. We're both upset." Judah walked back toward town. "I have no idea which direction the deputy went."

Paige fell into step beside him. "I'm sorry this is happening right before your ceremony."

"Yeah, me too."

"I'd do anything to help, or get my sister back, or"—she whimpered—"take back what I—"

He glanced at her. "What did you two argue about? It might help us figure out where she is."

"Please, don't ask."

"What if it made her run?"

She shook her head. "I hope it didn't, but I don't want to talk about it. Besides, it got resolved. She asked me to be her maid of honor, didn't she?"

"True." Paisley had chosen a wedding dress *and* asked her sister to take part in their ceremony. That didn't sound like a runaway bride. Which brought him back to his thoughts about her having had an accident. Or did something happen at the gallery? A chill raced up his spine.

As they drew closer to the city beach, a couple of groups appeared to have already finished searching. People milled about as if listening for further instructions.

Mayor Grant stared back and forth between Judah and Paige with a strange glint in his eyes, as if he suspected them of something. What, romance? Good grief. This was Judah's sister-in-law. But he could picture where the man's evil mind may have wandered to, and it made his ears burn.

He strode to the far side of the group to avoid his father and to create some distance between him and Paige.

"Judah, find anything?" Kathleen walked up to him and smiled kindly.

"Not really." He wouldn't mention what Paige found at the gallery until he had more information.

"I'm still hoping for the best outcome." She patted his arm then continued moving toward the rest of the group.

"You should all go home," Mayor Grant spoke into the megaphone. "The tide's coming in, covering the sand and footprints. It's useless to keep searching." He returned the megaphone to Deputy Brian who thanked the group for their help.

Edward stomped across the sand toward Judah. "Someone in the group found shoeprints that looked like a woman's leading off into the brush beyond the dunes." His monotone voice sounded emotionless. "Unfortunately, the prints got lost in the blowing sand."

"Yeah, okay. Thanks." Judah glanced at his father and noticed a couple of cuts on his face. "Having trouble shaving these days?"

"Yeah, bad razor. Should sue the company." Edward trudged along beside him. "Where are you going now?"

Judah ignored his question. He couldn't forget that the mayor was probably the one who caused him to lose his job. And the one who'd hurt his mom. It wasn't like they were on friendly terms.

"I asked, where are you going?"

"I heard you." Why the sudden interest in his whereabouts? Edward kept staring at him as if demanding a response. Fine. "I thought I'd check out the gallery."

"Why? You think she'd go there?" The mayor's voice ratcheted up a couple of notches.

"Might, it's her sister's business."

"For now." Edward kicked his shoe against a clump of sand.

"Deputy"—Paige's voice reached Judah—"I may have found something of interest."

"What is it?" Deputy Brian asked.

"A piece of cloth was at the gallery that wasn't there before. And some duct tape."

Edward whirled around and huffed. "A little cloth and duct tape? So what? I'm sure it has nothing to do with the Cedars girl. She's a runner. We all know that. This is a waste of our time."

Annoyed that his father would speak so rudely about Paisley, especially with her being missing, Judah marched away from him and traipsed toward the rocks separating the beach from the town. Why did Edward even help in the search when he had such a grumpy attitude toward Paisley?

Out of habit, Judah grabbed his cell phone and checked for text messages. Nothing. What was that? Like the fiftieth time he checked since this morning?

Once he reached the gallery, he shoved his shoulder against the closed plywood door. It stuck then gave way suddenly. He strode into the dark room. Just enough light came in through the broken window facing the ocean and the setting sun for him to see into the coffee area. Like Paige said, boxes of coffees and creamers and to-go cups were scattered across the floor. Some bags of coffee grounds had burst open. Could the sea breeze blowing in through the open window have been strong enough to do this?

He shook his cell phone to activate the flashlight and shined it across the floor, around the coffee spills. He got down on his hands and knees, moving the light back and forth. Wait. What was that?

The hair stood up on the back of his neck. On the floor next to the small refrigerator, it looked like a word, although nearly illegible, was scratched into the dark coffee grounds. He leaned down closer. "Help"? Who wrote that? *Paisley?* A sickening feeling ran through his system. Had something bad happened that she needed help? *Oh, God, if Paisley's in trouble, help her. Show me what to do.* He snapped a couple of pictures of the word, his heart racing at the possibilities and the disconcerting thoughts colliding in his mind.

Was she here? What happened to her? He needed to talk to the deputy and get him to analyze the word. Get fingerprints. How long would that take?

First, he'd scour the building in case there were any other signs of a struggle. He shined his light around the walls and in every corner. He ran over to the small bathroom and thrust open the door. He flashed the light in a zigzag pattern across the tiny space. Nothing unusual.

If Paisley was here, possibly in trouble, did she tear off a piece of her shirt too? And what about the duct tape? Did someone tape her mouth or limbs? *Oh, Paisley.* He pressed his fist against his mouth at the conclusion his imagination was barreling toward, the one he couldn't bear to contemplate. Had she been kidnapped? Or harmed? Things like this didn't happen in Basalt Bay, a tiny town on the Pacific Coast. But if it was her, where was she now?

He charged over to the window and gazed down at the tide coming in. Had she fallen in? Been pushed? No, he couldn't go there. Crazy thoughts. Someone else may have written the word. Paisley might not have even been at the gallery.

He remembered what his father said about footprints being seen near the sand dunes. Should he hike out there and check?

Those indentations could have been from anyone's boots. Kids. Tourists. It might not have anything to do with Paisley, either. If she had stumbled into a bad scenario here at the gallery, where would someone take her? Would they demand a ransom? He checked his phone again. No texts. No messages.

He had to find the deputy—now. He ran out the door and sprinted toward the beach. When he reached the rocks leading down to the sand, the search party had already dispersed. Was that Paige out by the peninsula? A couple of people were clustered around the base of the rock pile. Hopefully, no one planned to go out on the boulders. He climbed down the rocks, then reaching the sand, took off running again.

"Judah!" Paige waved.

"You guys are staying off the peninsula, aren't you?" His past years of guarding people along the coastline were deeply ingrained in him.

"Yeah." Sal pointed at a C-MER sign. "We're avoiding the danger zone."

"Good."

"But what if she went out there?" Paige stared toward the rocky point. "What if she fell in?"

"We'd see her from here if she were on the rocks." Judah drew his sister-in-law away from the others. "Did you see a word written in the coffee grounds on the floor at the gallery?"

"No. What word?" Her wide eyes stared up at him.

"Help." He kept his voice low.

"What?"

"Your hunch might be right. I'm looking for Deputy Brian. Where is he?" He took several deep breaths, figuring he wasn't done running yet.

"He left with the mayor."

"Okay. I'll go find him. But first, look at this." He held out his phone with the picture of the word written in the coffee grounds toward Paige.

She cupped her hands around the screen and squinted at it. "Where'd you see that?"

"In the café at the gallery."

"Oh, my goodness. No, I didn't notice it. Do you think Paisley wrote this?"

"I have no idea. But—" He strummed his fingers over his windblown hair. "I've got to talk to the deputy."

"It's time for me to pick up Piper." Paige laid her hand on his arm. "If you find out anything, call me. You can come by and grab some food or rest for a while, too. Okay?"

"Yeah, sure." But he wouldn't. He'd be out searching all night, if need be.

"See you later." She jogged toward the parking lot.

The group dissipated, folks saying goodbye, offering sympathy, heading to their cars, or walking toward town.

Judah perused the coastline, checking one last time, then he strode back toward town and the deputy's office.

Twenty-one

A sound woke Paisley with a start, her moan muffled by the tape. Her tongue felt adhered to the duct tape. She could barely move her shoulders. Weak and stiff, even lifting her head an inch took an excessive amount of effort. Her arms were numb—at least they didn't hurt as badly as before. She needed to move them to keep her blood circulating. How long had she been twisted up on the floor like this? How much air did she have left in the stuffy room? Had she already been without water too long? People survived without liquids for three days, right?

Had Judah or Paige discovered the word she tried to write in the coffee grounds at the art gallery yet? She didn't know if it was even legible since she wrote it with her hands tied behind her back.

What was wrong with Edward to make him behave so irrationally? She remembered how soused he looked when she found him in the art gallery. Bloodshot eyes. Slurred speech. Tipsy. But when he turned on her, it seemed there was more to his monstrous actions than him drinking too much. Drugs, maybe. Meds and alcohol combined? Or pure, undisguised hatred. She shuddered.

The way he tied her up, hit her, kidnapped her, and possibly left her to die made her want to weep. That her father-in-law despised her so much was unfathomable. What had she ever done to him, other than pull a few pranks on him in her high school days?

Even though his animosity was palpable, she knew she couldn't hate him back, because that would be a sin. She didn't want to hold onto bitterness and resentment as she had before. At any moment, she might see Jesus, and she wanted a clean heart. If she survived and lived, and she hoped she did, she planned to act differently.

Still, how could the mayor do this to his own daughter-in-law? How could he cause such sadness to his son?

She still struggled with some of her negative feelings toward Edward—*Lord, forgive me*—but she was glad she prayed and made things right with the Lord earlier. She'd asked Him to forgive her for leaving Judah. For her anger toward God about Misty Gale's death. And she'd taken the first steps in forgiving her mother, too. If she had to leave this world, her heart felt more at peace. The heavy weight on her chest had lifted. *Thank You, God.*

Yet, one thing kept her from succumbing to the darkness, and possibly death—Judah. She didn't want him thinking she ran away from him or that she didn't love him, not after all he'd done to love her and welcome her back into his life.

And she didn't want him falling for Mia Till, either. Edward was dead wrong about Mia being a better fit for Judah than Paisley. He deserved a kind spouse. A faithful one. Paige cared for him—didn't she say so? If they got together after Paisley was gone, *long after she was gone,* Judah would be a good father to Piper. Paige would make a loving wife.

Ugh. Paisley didn't want to lay here imagining him marrying her sister, or them being happy together. She still wanted to be his wife. The mother of his children. Yes, she still wanted to experience being a mom.

What was that? She listened closely. Footsteps. A door opened and closed. Then silence. A toilet flushed. Muffled footsteps trudged up the stairs, coming closer. Edward?

She tried to swallow. Couldn't. Not enough saliva. She inhaled and exhaled, breathing in the smell and taste of duct tape. Fighting panic and fear at what her father-in-law might have planned for her, tears rushed into her eyes. At least there was still a little moisture in her tear ducts.

How could she defend herself against him? She had nothing to throw. No free hands to hit the cad. Too weak, anyway.

The door creaked open. A light blinded her, and she squinted at the pain. His shoe kicked her. Not hard, but it hurt.

"Still alive, I see." Was Edward disappointed to find her breathing?

She'd do what she had to do to stay alive. Including head butting. Tripping him. Kicking his kneecaps.

His fingers stroked her face. She jerked away. Didn't want him touching her. Thanks to the duct tape covering her mouth, she couldn't spit at him or yell at him. He pressed his hand on top of her head. She tried to pull back. *"Weave me awone."* Without warning, he ripped the duct tape from her mouth.

She screamed! Then wept. Her face burned. But she could breathe. Even though the strip of cloth kept her jaws open, she inhaled and exhaled, taking in gulps of air. More duct tape was stuck to the sides of her face and her hair, so she couldn't move much. She tried to tell him to undo the binding. "Pweethe un—"

"Be quiet."

She moved her tongue and tasted blood. The sides of her lips were cracked and swollen. Her throat ached.

"Here's water." He tipped a glass against her mouth, but she couldn't control her tongue or her swallowing reflex.

Gulp. Liquid sloshed over her lips, dripping down her neck and the front of her shirt. At least he brought her water—although it seemed he might be trying to drown her. She coughed and gagged.

"This is the way it's going to work." He shoved her onto her side and fumbled roughly with the duct tape and ropes at her wrists behind her back. Was he going to release her? "You'll be taken to Portland. From there, my associate will chaperone you on an international flight. Then I'll never have to see you again."

His associate? So, he didn't plan to end her life, just her life here in Basalt.

"Don't even think of doing anything suspicious. If you do, it will go much worse for you." He yanked at the duct tape, jerking her arms, her shoulders, her upper torso, and ripping off a layer of her skin and pulling some of her hair out of her scalp.

She screamed, again, then cried. He clamped his hand over her mouth, yelling at her to be quiet. She breathed noisily in and out through her nose as if the duct tape still covered her lips.

"If you want to live, be quiet!"

"Okay." She'd go along with what he said or appear to go along with it. Flying out of Portland? What a ridiculous idea. With the way she'd been tied up, could she walk? Would anyone even allow her on a flight?

He lowered his hand from her mouth and worked the fabric knot loose. When it finally fell away, she groaned in pain and relief. Her jaws hurt so badly she could hardly close them. "Why … are you … doing this?" Her throat felt parched. She struggled to swallow.

"So my son will have the life he should have had before you ruined it."

Did she ruin Judah's life? Sadness dripped through her like tears falling from her heart. She had left him. But she came back, apologized, and things were more beautiful between them than ever. She couldn't wait to start over with him. That didn't sound like she'd ruined his life.

"I have big plans for my son. And you aren't in them."

Big plans?

"He'll never become a leader if I don't push him into it." Edward yanked her upright to a sitting position.

She groaned but managed to remain seated and not topple over. Smoothing her right palm around her left wrist, she gently massaged where the tape had been. When her fingers encountered open wounds, she refused to make any whimpering sounds. She didn't want him to know how much pain he'd caused her.

"You were never good enough for my son."

"Yet, he loves me," she whispered.

"He'll get over it." He sneered. "You should have seen him and your sister, cuddling and holding hands, today."

Liar. Yet, she even thought they'd make a happy couple if she were out of the picture. Not that it pleased her to imagine it.

"Looks like they're finding comfort in each other's arms."

Why would Edward want Judah to be involved with Paige when he despised her family? She was a Cedars too.

"It's almost dark. Almost time for you to leave." He stood and shuffled through the doorway.

"But—"

"You'll do what I say, or something might happen to that little niece of yours."

"Leave her alone, you mons—"

"Uh, uh, uh. You will cooperate. Hear me?"

"I'm too weak … to travel. Even you"—in his crazy, delusional state—"must see that."

"Too bad." He started to shut the door, to obliterate the light from her.

At least her hands were free now. Could she stand up long enough to get the door open and escape?

"I need food. More water." She struggled to form the words.

He slammed the door. The locking mechanism clunked. So much for escaping.

If only she had her cell phone, she'd call for help.

In the darkness, she massaged her arms, glad to be free of the binding, and hoping to stimulate blood flow. Would he be so cruel as to hurt Piper if she didn't go along with his demands?

Twenty-two

Deputy Brian returned to his office, where Judah had been anxiously waiting for an hour, after inspecting the café in the gallery. He explained what he'd accomplished—took photos, labeled it a crime scene, and called in a team to take fingerprints and dustings. He told Judah how the findings from two examiners would have to match Paisley's fingerprint records for a conclusive ruling. "Now, all we can do is wait and see."

More waiting. Judah groaned. He already felt antsy and irritable from all the waiting.

Over the next hour, he alternated between pacing, sitting down and thumbing through an outdoors magazine, and trudging around the perimeter of the room some more. While he couldn't help but feel agitated, the deputy seemed almost unconcerned as he stared at his computer and drank several cups of coffee. Shouldn't he be out there investigating? *Doing* something?

For the umpteenth time, Judah strode past the door that led to the cell where he spent those hours locked up several weeks ago. He never wanted to experience a confined space, being caged like an animal, again. What about Paisley's situation? Was she safe? Did the word etched in the coffee grounds have anything to do with her? Maybe a kid was playing tricks on them. What if it was like the others thought, that she ran away again?

Man, he didn't want to go down that mental road again. Fresh air might clear his thoughts. "I'll be right back." Opening the door, he strode outside and walked quickly down the block toward Front Street.

On his way back, passing by City Hall, footsteps tapping the sidewalk alerted him that someone was following him. He glanced back. Mia approached him in her high heels. He groaned.

"Oh, Judah, I can't believe what's happened." She lunged at him, wrapping her arms around him like an octopus.

He shoved against her hold.

"When you came to C-MER and said Paisley was missing, I just thought, well, I thought she did the same thing as before." She hugged him again, rubbing her hands over his back. "With all the speculation, was a crime committed? Have you heard anything?"

"Not yet." He set her back from him, keeping her at arm's length. A hug of friendship was one thing, given the circumstances, but he wasn't falling for any of her tricks. "Thanks for your concern. Now, I have things to do."

"You're probably wracked with worry and loneliness. Poor boy." She smoothed her hand over his forearm. "I'm here for you if you need anything. Just ask."

Pulling away, he glared at her. "Stop, all right? I'm fine."

She linked her arm with his like they were pals, as if he didn't just tell her to stop. "If Paisley left a handsome man like you, I don't know what she was thinking. You're way too good for her."

"If you'll excuse me." Yanking his arm free, he strode back toward the police station. At least, inside the office, he didn't have to listen to Mia. He didn't need her callous comments, or her hints of flirtation, either.

"Judah, wait!" Her footfalls landed beside him again.

Her presence, and her clinginess, irritated him even more than usual. Without sounding like an ogre, what could he say to tell her to get lost?

"How about grabbing some food with me?" She smiled, her eyes twinkling like it was all a game to her. "I bet you're hungry. We could go to Hardy's—"

"No, thanks," he said abruptly. "Goodbye." He jogged back to Deputy Brian's office door.

The clackity clack of her heels followed him. "Judah, wait. Can I do anything to help you? I can see you're troubled, and I'm just hanging around waiting for your dad to show up."

"Where is he?" Not that he cared. Not now, when Paisley was missing.

"I don't know. He'll be back at his office any minute. Judah?" Her voice softened. "If Paisley left for good this time, do you think you can let her go?"

What a horrible thing to ask him. He squinted at her, barely holding in a stern rebuke. "Please, don't talk to me about that. It's too personal. And, quite frankly, none of your business."

"But if she needs to find herself"—Mia persisted—"or if she decides on living her life elsewhere, would you let her walk away?"

"What else could I do?" He gritted his teeth. He shouldn't

have said anything. Shouldn't have given her fodder for more comments or gossip.

"Exactly. And there are plenty of women—"

"I don't want to talk about that."

"If you need a friend, or more than a friend, I'm here for you."

Her implication that he might want to start up something with her riled him to no end. He'd never acted interested in her. Not once! One of these days he'd tell her outright, and yes, rudely, if necessary, to stay away from him.

Gruffly, he told her goodbye, again, and stepped into the jailhouse, relieved when she didn't follow him.

"Uh-huh. Right." The deputy spoke to someone on the phone. "So, no match?" Must be one of the examiners. "Thank you, sir." Deputy Brian ended the call.

Judah strolled to his desk. "So?"

"Sorry. Official business."

"Tell me. Please." Judah leaned his fists against the desk surface. "I'm in agony here. What did they say about the fingerprints? Are they Paisley's?"

The deputy stared at him. Then huffed. "Fine. Preliminary tests show that the fingerprints at the crime scene don't match hers with absolute clarity in either test. Therefore, the findings are deemed inconclusive."

Inconclusive. Not that it wasn't her. Not that it was.

"Either the prints had insufficient quality, or were overridden by other fingerprints, or she wasn't there." Deputy Brian shrugged.

"They're certain?" Judah sank down on his haunches and put his hands over his face. Another dead end. What now?

"Doesn't mean she isn't in trouble. But the prints on the fabric are inconclusive, too, since so many people touched it, including you." Brian glared at him like he still thought Judah was somehow to blame. "Anything you want to tell me? Anything you haven't reported?"

Judah stood back up. "No. Look, I'm sick with worry. I have no idea where my wife went or what happened to her. I want to find her. I have to."

"Okay. Just don't leave town." The deputy tapped a stack of papers on his desk. "I may want to question you if she doesn't show up soon."

"Let me know if you hear anything."

The deputy didn't answer.

Judah trudged outside and stopped on the sidewalk. What should he do now? For a second back there, he'd felt relief. Then the emotional tables shifted again. Did Deputy Brian think him capable of harming his wife? Or was blaming the husband routine protocol?

A car stopped beside him. Mom? She lowered her window.

"Judah, how are you?" She turned off the engine and got out of the vehicle. She hugged him tightly. "Have you found out anything about Paisley?"

"Not much. Other than a bit of torn fabric and someone fingered 'help' into some coffee grounds."

"Oh, my. You don't think—?"

"I don't know what to think, except apparently I'm a suspect."

"You're kidding." Mom glared at the deputy's office. "Tell me who thinks that, and I'll give him a piece of my mind."

"Thanks for the support. Right now, I can't think straight. Am I missing something? Where did she go?" He stared up into the darkening sky. Then he faced his mother. "Tell me honestly. Do you think she ran away from me again?"

"Absolutely not." She rubbed her palm over his coat sleeve. "Have you eaten anything?"

"No." Food didn't even sound good.

"Let's go get something, okay?"

Eating felt like another waste of time. He'd already spent too long waiting for Deputy Brian and the lab results. Inconclusive—what good was that?

"You haven't seen my new place yet. Why don't you come over to Kathleen's with me? I'll heat up some soup." She tugged on his arm.

"If I do, I can't stay long."

"That's fine." She waved him toward her car. "Ride with me."

"Okay." He probably shouldn't be driving in his frame of mind, anyway.

While Mom warmed up food in the kitchenette of the rental unit, Judah strolled around the tiny living room that wasn't much bigger than his old office at work.

The microwave timer chimed, then Mom brought him a bowl of steaming chicken noodle soup. "This should warm your insides."

"Thanks." He dropped down on an easy chair and spooned broth into his mouth, even though he wasn't hungry.

Mom returned to the kitchen, then joined him in the living room, working over a similar cup of soup. "What do you think of the place?"

"Small, but homey."

"Isn't it cute? Kathleen is such a sweetheart to let me stay with her." She pointed toward a table in the corner covered with a cloth. "She's working on a special mosaic piece. A present for you and Paisley for your vow renewal ceremony."

Thinking of the event he'd looked forward to with such anticipation, sorrow filled him. "That's nice." Tears flooded his eyes. He blinked fast to stop them from flowing and went through the motions of finishing his soup.

"We're looking to buy something bigger." Mom sighed. "Toying with the idea of a few ladies going in on a piece of real estate together."

Her voice made him focus.

"You are?"

"Yes." She set her cup on the coffee table. "I need to tell you something. This isn't the best time, I realize, but I've made a decision. I'd rather you hear it from me than one of the town gossips." She drew in a long breath then seemed to let it out all at once. "I'm going to move forward with divorcing your father."

"Oh, I see." He respected her need to put a safe distance between her and Edward, but it was tough to hear his parents' marriage was ending. "Whatever you need, I'm here for you, Mom."

"Thank you." Her voice sounded lighter. "It's great to hear you say that. Your thoughts must be whirling with terrible possibilities about what happened to Paisley. But I've barely stopped praying for her, and you, since I heard the news."

"Me, either." He set the bowl on the table and stood. "Now, I've got to keep searching."

Mom stood too. "You could sleep here on the couch. Get a fresh start at daybreak."

"Thanks, but, no. I'm going to check the beach again. Maybe drive along the coast."

Mom scooped up the dishes and hurried back into the kitchen. "Let me grab my coat and I'll join you."

"You don't have to do that."

"I know. But I'm going to, anyway."

He could use the company and was thankful for her offer, so he didn't argue. Except, he didn't want to talk. Didn't want to speculate what his life might be like without the woman he loved in it.

A few minutes later, Mom charged into the room, zipping up her coat, her eyes wide. "I just had the strangest phone call from your dad."

"What did he say?"

She waved her cell phone. "He said he was sorry for everything he's put me through, then hung up. What do you make of that? Him apologizing? I wonder what's going on." She stared at the screen. "His voice sounded odd too. Like he's drinking."

"It's nice he apologized, finally."

"It was. Not that it changes anything."

Twenty-three

"Where shall we start?" Mom unlocked her car door with a remote key.

"I was thinking we should talk to some people who weren't on the beach this afternoon." Judah stood on the passenger side, debating whether to get in or walk down the street. "Bert Jensen. Miss Patty. Callie Cedars. Maybe we should split up. Find out if anything happened with any of those that might have upset Paisley."

"Honey, I'd feel better staying with you. Let's not split up."

"All right." It was dark. Maybe staying together was a safer plan. "Looks like the hardware store is still open. We could start there." He walked in the direction of Miss Patty's business. In the past, she'd held a grudge against Paisley and was outspoken about it. Did she say something belittling to her like she did a few other times? Tension gnarled up Judah's spine.

He and Mom entered the brightly lit store and paused near the check-out counter.

"Hello, how can I—?" Miss Patty squinted at them. "What do you want?" Not a very nice greeting.

"Miss Patty." Judah forced a polite tone.

"We're looking for Paisley." Mom stepped forward, taking control of the conversation. "Have you seen her in the last couple of days?"

"I heard she left town. No surprise there."

Judah clenched his jaw. "Why do you say that?"

"Everyone knows she's a runner. With a mother like she—"

"Let's keep this conversation focused on what happened yesterday, or the day before, shall we?" Mom smiled, but the rest of her face tightened into her don't-mess-with-me look. "Did you see her? We're trying to piece together any information we can."

Miss Patty dusted a variety of tools on her counter before answering. "I haven't seen her since, let's see …" She glanced at the ceiling as if pondering her answer.

"What is it?" Judah leaned forward, his hands on the counter.

"I saw her outside her sister's shop."

"When?"

"Yesterday, early afternoon, she entered the building next door." Miss Patty continued dusting. "I saw her when I was helping a customer put a leaf blower in her car."

"You're sure?" Her time frame would collaborate with Sal's account.

"Yes, I saw her briefly." She threw him a glare. "An out-of-the-corner-of-my-eye sort of thing, but I saw her."

"Okay. Thanks." Judah expelled a breath. So Paisley must have been at the art gallery yesterday. What about the word written in the coffee grounds? Had she done that, despite the inconclusive results?

Mom patted his arm and nodded toward the door. "Let's keep going down our list."

He followed her, his emotions raw. What if something terrible happened to his wife? All day, doubts had plagued him. But what if she stumbled upon looters as Paige thought? A churning in his middle made him think his chicken noodle soup might not stay down.

When they got outside, he didn't go straight to Mom's car as she did. "I'm going back into the art gallery for another look. Give me a minute." Running to the next building, he flipped on his phone's flashlight and aimed it at the door. The deputy's crime-scene tape—that wouldn't stop him from entering—glowed yellow in the light. He shoved against the plywood door that felt jammed but not locked. Inside, he rushed over to the coffee area and shined the light across the floor. "Oh, no."

"What's wrong?" Mom had followed him.

"It's been cleaned up. Someone destroyed the evidence." He flashed the light over the whole area where the coffee supplies and grounds were previously scattered across the floor. No mess. No coffee grounds. "How could someone tamper with a crime scene like this?"

"Maybe Paige. It's her building, right?"

"Or Dad's." He opened his contact list and searched for Paige's name.

"Surely he wouldn't—" Mom gasped.

"What?"

"You said the building might be your dad's." Mom huffed. "Earlier, your father apologized. Now, the evidence is gone. A weird coincidence, or what?"

Just then a voice said, "Hello? Hello!"

Judah must have tapped Paige's name on the phone without realizing it. "Hey, Paige," he spoke into the cell phone. "Did you come by and clean the coffee shop in the gallery?"

"No. Why?"

"You didn't clean up the mess?" His concern increased.

"I haven't had time to go back." A silence. "What's going on?"

"It's been swept, and the stuff's gone." He looked around for a trash can. "There's not even any garbage."

"That's weird. Judah?" Her voice rose in a panicked tone. "Could you come over here to my house right now?"

"Why? I need to—"

"Someone's here. You must speak to him. I mean it. Get over here right away, please."

"Who is it?" He didn't have time for—

"It's Craig. Just hurry, will you?"

"Did something happen? Is this about Paisley?" He didn't trust Craig. Why should he drop what he was doing to run over and listen to whatever he had to say? "Paige—" But she'd already hung up.

Groan.

"What did she say?" Mom pursed her lips.

"Paige wants me to come over and talk to Craig, a guy I used to work with."

"Oh, I know who he is." What was with her sharp tone? Maybe she was tired and stressed, too.

"I should probably see what's going on over there." Judah took one last look around the dark area then strode toward the door. "May I have your key?" Mom passed it to him without comment. He wondered about her silence and seemingly moodiness, but he focused on driving to Paige's house in the subdivision. What did Craig have to say that Paige thought was so important?

"Should I wait here?" Mom quietly asked when he parked on the street.

"You can come in too. I won't be staying long." He exited the car and made his way through the carport where Paige's vehicle was parked. He heard the car door shut and footsteps. Mom must have decided to come along. He rapped on the back door.

Paige opened it quickly. "Judah. Come in."

"My mom's here too."

"Hello, Mrs. Grant. Welcome."

"Bess, please."

Judah entered the kitchen and Piper flew against his knees. "Hey, squirt." He lifted her. Despite the anxiety twisting through him, he smiled at the two-year-old.

"Unca Dzuda! Unca Dzuda!" She lunged up and down in his arms, laughing.

"I haven't seen you in a while."

"She misses you." Paige patted her daughter's back.

"What a sweetheart." Mom grinned. "You look good with a child in your arms, Judah."

He chuckled. Then felt a rush of sadness. He'd hoped that he and Paisley would have more kids.

Craig shuffled into the room from the hallway, then came to a halt and stared at Judah's mom.

She returned his stare. Something weird and awkward passed between them. How did they even know each other? Because of the mayor?

Judah set Piper on her feet and she dashed off down the hallway, dancing and singing. Paige left the room too, following her daughter.

"Can we talk alone?" Craig nodded toward the living room.

His eyes appeared clear, his movements normal, so he must be sober.

"Whatever you have to say, my mom can hear. She's helping me look for Paisley." Judah glanced at his phone to make sure he hadn't missed any calls or texts.

"Okay. It's about your father."

"Oh? What's he done now?"

"He's demanding that I do something … that sounds illegal." Craig cleared his throat. "I'm uncomfortable with what it might be."

"My father's doing something illegal?"

"I believe so. I won't be a part of any scheme to hurt anyone. Never again." Craig's voice went deeper. "Especially someone I care about."

Wait. Did he mean—? Head-to-heel tension rippled through Judah. "What exactly are you talking about here?"

"Paisley."

"What do you know?" It took every ounce of self-control he could muster not to grab Craig by the collar and shake the truth out of him. "Spit it out. What did my father want you to do? And what does this have to do with *my wife*?"

"I care for Paisley."

"I don't want to hear about that!"

Mom put her hand on his arm as if to restrain him.

"Judah." Paige entered the room, shaking her head at him. "Why don't you just listen to what Craig has to say?"

Was she involved in Paisley's disappearance too? Were they both? Ugh. Now he was thinking irrationally. But someone had cleaned up the evidence in the art gallery. "Tell me what you know!" He trembled with subdued rage.

Mom's hand slipped away from his arm.

Paige faced Craig, although she seemed to be keeping her distance from him. "Tell them what you told me, or I will. This is my sister. Her safety is at stake. We have to save her."

"Save her?" So Paige knew something. So did Craig. "One of you better tell me something now, or so help me—"

"Judah!" Mom and Paige both shouted at once.

"Okay. Just hurry up." If Craig or the mayor did anything to harm Paisley—

"The mayor wants me to drive a 'package' to Portland."

"A package?" Judah clenched his fists. *A package?*

"He's demanding secrecy. And loyalty. At ten o'clock tonight, I'm to arrive at his house in a rental car. He expects me to drive a parcel up to the Portland airport. Followed by an international flight to Europe." He grimaced and shook his head. "I can't say it's Paisley. I mean, I can't say with absolute certainty that he has her, or what condition she might be in if he does, but he has something he wants removed. Something that isn't an ordinary parcel."

Judah burst out the breath he'd been holding. Craig thought Edward was involved in a possible kidnapping? How ludicrous. It was, right? Yet, could there be a speck of truth to the accusation?

He met Mom's gaze, and a terrified look crossed her features, as if she were silently telling him she thought what Craig was saying might be the truth.

He faced the other man. "Tell me all you know about it."

"I've been summoned to assist Mayor Grant with a transfer of goods—or pay the consequences, which could be dire for more than just myself."

Hadn't Judah just seen his father this afternoon? He was

searching for Paisley. How could he be involved in her disappearance? The room spun. Judah staggered backward. Mom and Paige grabbed his arms and kept him upright.

"How could this be happening?"

"He may have snapped." Mom shuddered. "I've seen it before. His rage and hostility. Only this seems too bizarre even for him."

Snapped? Rage? Considering what he did to Mom in the past, and how mean he'd been in speaking to Paisley, had he been cruel to her too? Fear and turmoil mixed with disbelief inside of him. Then acceptance. And dread. "What time is the meet? I'll go in your place. I must go to her."

"No, Judah. Call Deputy Brian. He's the law in Basalt Bay." Mom pointed at him. "You cannot do this alone."

"Oh, I can." A fiery determination settled in the middle of his chest. He turned toward Craig, ignoring the plea in his mother's eyes. "Tell me the details. I'll go in disguise if I have to, but I'm going."

"He'll know it's you. In his condition—"

"Exactly. In his condition, whatever that is, he may have hurt my wife." Judah's limbs shook. His heart pounded so hard it felt like it could explode. "I'm the one who needs to face that, face him."

"Tell him the rest." Paige wrung her hands. "He has to know the rest. Tell him."

"What else is there?" Judah barked out.

Craig ran his hand across his forehead. "This could be something else. Might not even be Paisley. It's just—" He groaned and shook his head like he couldn't finish.

"He threatened P-Piper." Paige's voice broke.

"What?"

Craig patted her arm. "He threatened something *might* happen to her if I don't do exactly what he requires of me. That's why I didn't call you before. But I had to tell Paige." He stared at her, a soft look in his eyes. "I'm so sorry. I never thought he'd make me do something like this. I promised myself I'd never do anything underhanded or illegal for him again. Not even to save my hide."

Again? So, Craig had done things like this for the mayor before? That would have to be addressed later. But Edward being the mastermind behind Paisley's vanishing? Outrageous. Unthinkable. Judah knew him to be a cad, a control freak, and more recently, an abusive husband, but this—? Mom said he may have 'snapped.' Was that the case?

Mom hugged Paige. "Poor dear. I'm so sorry. Something isn't right in that man's head. I should have known after I left he might try something even more deplorable."

"No, Mom, this isn't your fault."

She covered her face, groaning.

Judah gave her a brief hug. "You did the right thing in leaving him. Even you couldn't have stopped this."

"Still, I wish I'd turned him in to the police before any of this could have happened."

Paige rubbed her hand over Mom's arm and whispered something to her.

Judah stepped beside Craig. "If Paisley is the package, then why? What's the deal? I know my father has treated her disrespectfully before, but why do something so vile?"

He shrugged.

"Tell me!"

"I don't know why." Craig kept his gaze aimed at Judah. "I know what is. Or what it seems to be. But not why."

Judah strode to the kitchen window, dealing with his frustration the only way he knew how. He gazed into the dark, collecting his thoughts and his turbulent emotions. He needed a minute to pray. Not just to react in fear and anger. *What should I do, Lord? Please, protect my wife. How could my father have done this to the woman I love? God, be with her.* Thinking of her possibly hurt or scared out of her mind sent chills racing through his body. He had to find her.

"We need to make a plan." Craig cleared his throat and rocked his thumb toward the living room. "Now."

"You're right. Let's make a plan." At C-MER, they'd created strategies to rescue people along the coastline. However, they'd never charted out how to rescue a woman from the clutches of an evil person. And that's exactly what he thought of his father right now. Evil. It seemed he'd been at odds with Edward for most of his life, but he'd never realized what kind of tyrant he could be. And for what purpose? What scheme was he perpetrating? This all had to be about some manipulation he had in mind. But, what?

In the living room, Judah dropped onto the couch. Mom and Paige stood beside each other near the doorway. Craig sat on the easy chair and pointed to a sketch on the coffee table. "This is what I've worked out so far."

Judah picked up a pencil-drawing of a map and noticed familiar markings. The long, narrow road descending from his parents' house. The two-lane road leading out of town. Highway 101 North.

"What happens after the pickup at Edward's?" Saying the man's name tasted bitter on his tongue.

"After the pickup, I'll stop here." Craig tapped the section of the drawing duplicating a stretch of highway where there wouldn't be any signs or buildings or lights that would reveal a switch—Judah knew the spot. "You can meet us there."

"What if he follows you?" Something clawed at Judah's throat at the thought of what Paisley might be going through. Panic attacks. Injury. Fear. *God, be with her.*

"Please, let's call the deputy." Mom's voice rose. "I understand you're worried about Paisley, and now the little girl, but I don't want either of you taking chances, either."

"We have to, Mom, don't you see?"

She whimpered and nodded, and Paige wrapped her arms around her. If anyone knew what Edward Grant could do, it was Mom. Imagining what his father might have done to Paisley thrashed his insides. But he had to think straight. Maybe this was all a mistake. How he hoped so.

"I'd rather go in your place." Judah stared at the map. Were there any routes better than the one Craig had in mind?

"I say we stick to the plan." Craig touched the map again. "Edward expects my cooperation."

"What if he trails you?"

"Then I'll figure out something else." Craig eyed him tersely as if he didn't like Judah questioning him.

"Hey, this is my wife we're talking about."

"I know."

Mom took a deep breath. "I'm sure he won't hurt either of you."

Judah glanced at her. "How can you be sure? Look what he did to you."

"I know. But you're … you're both—" She cut a glance at Craig.

What wasn't she saying? "What is it, Mom?"

"Even after all these years, I'm afraid of how he'll retaliate against me." She glanced between Judah and Craig, then stared at the floor, shaking her head.

"Mom?"

"Mrs. Grant," Paige spoke quietly, "were you going to say that Judah and Craig might be brothers?"

"What?" Judah glared at Paige. "That's not true."

Mom's eyes widened. "How did you know?"

"Know what?" Judah leaped to his feet. "You knew of this possibility? Of this absurdity?"

"I'm sorry, Judah." Mom pressed her fist to her mouth. "I wish I could have told you before now."

Craig stared at the floor. "You shouldn't have said anything, Paige."

"You're serious?" Judah glared from one person to the next. "You mean Craig might be my—" He couldn't even finish the statement or believe it.

"How did you find out?" Mom stared at Craig.

"Mia told me. But how reliable is anything she says?"

"Exactly." Yet, Judah's mother thought it was true? "Mom, you believe this notion?"

"Your father confessed to an affair years ago."

He pictured the way Edward flirted with Mia. His scoundrel-like nature. "Why didn't you say something before now?"

"He was the mayor. I was sworn to secrecy. He would have done far worse to me than he ever did if I told." She took off her hat and twisted it in her hands like she might do to a kitchen towel. "After his indiscretion, I forgave him. It wasn't until years later that I learned he had a child with … with Craig's mother." She glanced at Craig again. "It's not his fault who his father is, or yours."

Judah tromped across the room. Craig could be his brother?

Correction. Half-brother. Was this another manipulation on his father's part? Another lie?

"We should stick to the matter at hand. Do a DNA test at a later date." Craig tapped his fingers on the map. "Rescuing Paisley—if Edward has her—and keeping Piper safe. Those are the only things that matter tonight."

He was right, although Judah hated to admit that Craig was right about anything. He shut his eyes for a moment, gathering his thoughts, then he returned to the couch. Glaring at Craig, he forced himself to think beyond what he just heard. "Do you believe Paisley is the package?"

"I do. When Edward said 'package,' it sounded like something other than an object. And his tone was weird. Spiteful, or vengeful."

"Why would he do this to her?" Judah pictured how sweet Paisley had looked the last time he saw her. "Kidnapping in Oregon is a felony."

"Other than snapping?" Mom sat on the couch beside him. "He's had a grudge against Paul Cedars for most of his adult life. And he wants to control your future."

That last part wasn't news to him. "But, why? Why can't he accept the life I've chosen?"

"Who knows?" Mom's lips pressed together like she was stopping herself from saying anything else.

Emotion bunched up in Judah's throat. "Do you think he'll hurt her?"

"He's capable of doing anything to get his way." She trembled, perhaps recalling some of the things Edward had done to her.

If his father did anything to harm Paisley—

He gulped, unable to finish the thought. *Focus on the rescue,*

Grant. Like Craig said, nothing else mattered tonight. "If you pull over here"—he tapped a spot on the drawing—"and you find out you're being followed, what's Plan B?" In their C-MER planning sessions, they discussed alternative ideas for facing unexpected emergencies.

"On the south side of Newport, there's a gas station." Craig made an imaginary X on the map with his index finger, which would be about thirty miles north. "I'll stop to use the restroom and leave the car door unlocked. Meet us there."

"Too far. Pick me up here." Judah pointed at another location on the map between Basalt Bay and Yachats, five miles away.

"That's too close and too dangerous. It could get us both—"

"I don't care. She's my wife. I want you to pull over for a few seconds. I'll climb in the backseat with her."

"She might be in the trunk." Craig gnawed on his lower lip.

The pain in Judah's chest intensified. "Same plan, do, or die." Which was code for let's not talk about this anymore in front of the ladies.

"Same plan."

"Judah, please, don't do this." Mom gripped his wrist.

But he wouldn't reconsider. One way or another, he was finding his wife tonight. Then he'd deal with Edward Grant.

Twenty-four

Edward dragged Paisley down the stairs and shoved her onto a dining room chair. Stunned after being moved so roughly, and squinting at the bright lights in the room, she stared numbly at the bowl of cold rice he dropped in front of her on the table. Food, finally. But how was she supposed to bring her mouth close enough to eat it? Her arms and shoulders hurt too badly. She felt too exhausted to lift a spoon. Besides, she could barely close her jaws or swallow.

"Could I … have water?" Her voice came out croaky, her throat scratchy and sore.

Edward glared at her, then stomped into the kitchen and returned with a glass. He slammed it on the table too far from the edge.

"Move it closer, please?"

"Aren't you the pampered princess?" He shoved the glass so hard that water splashed onto her clothes.

She gasped at the sudden chill. Then, not wanting him to become angrier, she lifted the glass between her trembling fingers and raised the edge to her lips. She took sips. The water trickling down her throat burned. After she set down the glass, carefully, she picked up the spoon and scooped up a little food. With difficulty, she lifted the rice to her mouth. She stopped herself from weeping as she swallowed.

While she ate a few more bites, she took furtive glances out the windows. It was dark outside. If Edward got distracted, took a phone call or used the bathroom, she could possibly reach the door. Then she'd flee into the forested mountainside where he'd never find her. If only she could run. In her condition, could she even walk on her own?

He stomped past the table, staring at her like he suspected her of wanting to escape. "Isn't the food good enough for you?"

"It's fine." It would have been easier to eat if he heated up the rice. She was too tired and hurting to care about the bland taste.

It felt odd to be here in Edward's house without Judah or Bess being present. They'd never guess how abominably he could act. Except, Bess. She knew what kind of animal he was, even if he tricked others. She recalled the words from the pamphlet her aunt made her read. *A man of integrity.*

What a lie.

She picked up the spoon again and eased more food past her sore lips and into her mouth. She needed the sustenance.

"Hurry up and finish. It's almost time"

"Can I use the bathroom?"

He glared at her as if she'd asked for a thousand dollars.

"You kept me locked up for a long time." His scowl made her rethink her comment. "I mean, even prisoners get to use the bathroom." Her throat was so hoarse. Did he understand her?

He grew still as if listening for something. Was that a car? Suddenly, he grabbed hold of her shoulders—she flinched—and dragged her in the direction of the bathroom.

"Why are you—"

"Quiet!"

"Okay. Just don't—" *Don't touch me.* She didn't want to reveal how much his brutal grip on her arms hurt. "Why do you hate me so much?"

He shoved her into the mostly all-white bathroom before shutting the door without answering her question.

"Beast." Regaining her balance, she shuffled to the toilet. She used the facility, despite the effort of undoing her pants. Washing her hands in the sink under warm water felt both amazing and horrible. Her cuts stung where the duct tape had bitten into her wrists and chafed them raw. She stood there letting water pour over her wounds, thanking God for this small blessing.

She opened a few cupboard doors, searching for anything to hurl at Edward when he came back for her. TP. Towels. Soap. Nothing solid enough to do damage. But how could she throw anything when her arms weren't working properly, anyway?

Then she noticed her reflection in the mirror. Her pasty skin was pocked with raw sores around her mouth. Scratch lines crossed her cheeks where the duct tape had been. Would her face ever look normal again? Some chunks of hair were torn out of her head from when Edward yanked the duct tape off. Dark bags under her eyes made her look a hundred years old. Her eyes were bloodshot, probably from all the straining she did to try to free herself.

How much time had passed since she walked into the gallery to ask Paige to get her nails done with her? One day? Two?

She was shivering badly. Her teeth clanked together. She buffed her arms, needing warmth, but every movement hurt. A bath sounded divine. But not in this house, not with Edward nearby. She picked up one of the thick towels and tried … she groaned … to get it over her shoulders like a shawl. There. She sighed, feeling a little comfort.

The sound of male voices reached her. Edward's accomplice must have arrived.

She shuffled toward the exit to listen. Just then, Edward barged into the room and the door rammed into her. She stumbled backward, fell against the counter, her upper torso toppling over it. For a moment, she remained still, her arms crossed, her forehead leaning against her forearm. What would happen if she just sagged to the floor? Edward would probably drag her by her hair like a caveman. She didn't want him man-handling her again.

"Come on. Get out of here," he barked.

"I c-can't."

"Yes, you can. Move, now!"

Groaning, she pushed her hands against the cool surface, not quite succeeding. She tried again. Impatient as he was, Edward grabbed her sore arm, propelling her forward faster than her feet could catch up. She whimpered, but he didn't seem to care.

Her old hatred toward him bubbled up inside of her like a geyser ready to explode. While wrong, her angst might work for some good, might energize her. A burning desire for him to get the justice he deserved sprang up within her. He might ship her off to who knew where, but one day she'd find her way back to Basalt. *Get ready, Mayor Grant, your due is coming—just leave my niece alone.*

Edward picked her up, probably because of her slow gait, and hauled her back into the dining area. His jostling felt like torture. When he let go, her legs didn't hold her up and she collapsed to the floor. She moaned. Grabbing her tender arms, he jerked her to her feet.

At the front door, her escape route, a man stood in the shadows. Craig Masters was the mayor's accomplice? His stony glare reflected no compassion. No kindness. Why was he involved in this crime against her? Once, he told her he cared about her. *Liar. Fraud.* He and Edward were two peas in a pod.

Craig's jawline tightened like his teeth were clenched, but his gaze remained fixed on her. A blank stare. Wasn't he bothered by how Edward had mistreated her? Couldn't he see her wounds? How she could barely stand up? Would he help her if she begged him to?

Edward tore a piece of duct tape from the roll he carried, and the sound made her shudder.

"Please, don't put that on me again. I won't yell or make noise. I beg of you." She hated how pathetic she sounded. She appealed to Craig's decency, if he had any, with her gaze. "Please."

The brute just stood there watching. But then he seemed to stir out of his apathy. "Maybe you don't need to put that on her, Mayor. How about if you leave it off, this time?"

"Don't tell me what to do." Edward pressed the chunk of tape over her mouth, pressing his hand firmly against her cheeks as if to hurt her on purpose, making a show of who was in control. Although, he didn't wrap the tape around her head as he had before. Maybe she could work the single piece loose.

She shouldn't be surprised by Craig's involvement. Didn't he implicate the mayor in his attack on her that night at the bar? Partners in crime. Here he was doing Edward's dirty work again. Probably compensated for it too. Both were rats!

"You understand what you have to do?" Edward gripped the roll of duct tape again.

"I know what we discussed." Craig's gaze remained on her. "Take the backroads up to Portland. Catch our flight. Keep quiet."

"That's right." Edward jabbed his finger against Paisley's shoulder. She winced. "You listen to me, girl. Don't ever come back to this town again. If I hear that you tried contacting my son—I have ways of knowing whether you've followed my instructions, people who will do exactly what I say—you know what will happen. Don't think for a second that you could ever escape me."

More threats. Idle warnings? Or was he mad enough to follow through? Maybe he was, especially when he had henchmen like Craig to do his bidding. For her own safety, and Piper's, she nodded. She'd do anything to keep her niece out of harm's way. Edward was probably counting on that.

If only Paige could see the criminal activity her old boyfriend was up to. He and Edward belonged in prison. Would go there, too, if she had any say in the matter. But first, she had to survive. Maybe she could slip away from Craig in the airport. Or going through security, she could whisper to one of the TSA workers that she'd been abducted.

Edward tossed Craig a duffle bag. "Her passport and new identity are in there. Along with a change of clothes. Once she leaves the country, she'll be dead to all of us." He scowled in her direction. "And good riddance."

Never to be with Judah, or have a future with him? Never to see her dad? She swallowed hard.

"My contact will set her up with an apartment and a job, as long as she cooperates and remains silent." He tore some more duct tape and faced her. "This will be the end of our acquaintance, Paisley *Cedars*." Emphasizing her maiden name, he slapped the second layer of tape over her mouth. "From this day forward, you're dead to the Grants." He grabbed her left hand, startling her, and yanked off her engagement ring—and a layer of her skin.

"Noooo." She cried out in a muffled yell, not only from the pain, but because she didn't want to lose her ring. Judah's gift to her. Would Edward show it to him? Would he sneak the ring into their cottage and leave it where Judah might find it? Write a fake Dear John letter? She made garbled sounds of protest.

"Quiet!"

No, she would not remain quiet. But if she didn't obey him, what then? Would he rough her up as he already did? Would Craig stand there like a cold statue and watch the maniac do his worst? Edward was delusional if he thought any TSA worker would allow her on a jet looking as terrible as she did. The sores on her face resembled an infectious disease. And he was doubly delusional if he thought she wouldn't try to contact Judah.

"Make sure she wraps the scarf around her face. I put one in the bag," Edward told Craig. "That way no one will see her ugly face. Call me from each checkpoint."

"Yes, sir." Craig nodded, a tight look in his eyes.

"I'm heading down to Hardy's. Mia will be my perfect alibi, if you know what I mean." Edward guffawed.

Gag. As much as she disliked Mia, the woman didn't deserve a creep like the mayor for a boyfriend.

Edward grabbed hold of her again and propelled her forward. She clutched the towel that was still wrapped around her shoulders. Would he allow her to take it in the car? He yanked her arms behind her as if to tie them together again, causing the bath towel to slip to the floor. She tried to talk through the tape. "*Peesh, don-tie me yup.*"

"She can't cause trouble in her weak condition. She doesn't have to be tied up." Was Craig worried about her now, sticking up for her? He seemed to be avoiding her gaze. "Come on, Mayor. Let her rest in the backseat without restraints."

Edward squinted at Craig. "You're not falling for her, are you?"

"Never." A dark look crossed his face.

She'd call them both pigs if she could.

Edward yanked her arms together in front of her and wrapped tape around them, instead of tying them behind her back. A relief. However, the tape sticking to her wounds burned like crazy.

Craig's eyes appeared steely, yet it seemed there might be moisture pooling in them, too. Maybe he had a speck of human kindness in him. "You want me to do this?" He strode toward her, his arms extended as if offering to carry her.

"No. I'll take her out to the car myself." Edward shoved her forward, making her stumble.

She exaggerated a limp, hoping to make it difficult for Edward to haul her outside. As they passed the recliner in the living room, she toppled into it and curled up.

Swearing, Edward yanked up on her arms, pulling her to her feet. She cried out in muffled tones.

"Here, let me do it." Craig stepped forward and cupped his hands around her.

"I said I would." Edward gritted his teeth. But even she could see he was fatigued. Maybe this was her chance to fight him off and escape. Except Craig stood there looking strong and threatening like a security guard.

"Let me carry her," Craig persisted. He scooped her up quickly and strode to the door, ahead of Edward. He was strangely gentle with her. "Play along," he whispered in her ear.

She glanced up at him. What did he mean, "play along"?

He jostled her and squinted at her, acting like he was hurting her, but nothing about the movement was painful. "Stay still. Stop wiggling. You're coming with me."

She made garbled sounds of protest as if he were harming her when he wasn't. Was Craig feeling more compassionate toward her than he wanted Edward to know?

"Put her in the trunk." The mayor trudged toward the rear end of the vehicle.

What? No! Her noises of real disagreement were hindered by the tape. She wiggled, trying to get Craig to release her. If he did, she'd make a break for the trees. Under the cover of night, she might get away and hide where these two couldn't find her.

Craig jostled her again. "Be still."

She moaned, playacting, relieved that it wasn't Edward who held her.

"I can watch her better if she's in the backseat. We don't have to put her in the trunk." Craig's tone had a hard edge to it.

"Safer in the trunk."

"You can tie her up some more if you want."

What? Just when she thought Craig might be sympathetic to her plight, he had to say that. He dropped her roughly onto the seat. At least, he didn't dump her in the trunk.

Edward opened the other door. Both men worked at tying her with rope. She groaned.

"There." Edward huffed. "That should keep her still while you drive."

Craig met her gaze. *Traitor!* How could he treat her like this?

Both doors shut. The men spoke outside, arguing by the sound of it. Then the driver's door opened. Craig jumped in and started the engine.

Edward rapped his knuckles against the window. Craig rolled the glass down halfway. "Don't stop for the next hour."

"Why?"

"Do what I say and don't stop! Someone might be watching." He peered into the darkness, the whites of his eyes glowing. Was he paranoid? "Stick to the coastal highway. Stay away from the Interstate." He leaned down toward the window again, glaring at her. "Maybe I should do this myself. I've changed my mind. Get out of the car."

"What? No. I won't stop anywhere." Craig slapped the steering wheel. "I'm driving! Isn't Mia taking care of the rest? Isn't she expecting you?"

Mia. Paisley pictured the conniving flirt.

Edward mumbled something. Craig hopped out of the car and slammed the door. The two of them argued again, gesticulating, their facial expressions fierce.

If she could get to a police station, these two were going down. She tried stretching her mouth, pushing her tongue against the tape. It gave a little and she breathed easier.

Craig lunged back into the car, put it in gear, and zoomed off as if speeding away before Edward could change his mind. "Shoot."

He may have said another word, but Paisley wasn't sure.

"What's wrong?" The gap in the tape helped her words sound clearer. But the duct tape scraping the sores alongside her mouth made her not want to open her jaw again.

"He's following me."

Maybe Edward didn't trust Craig, either.

He increased the car's speed and the vehicle jostled on the curvy narrow road coming down from the mayor's house. Paisley locked her leg muscles, trying to stay on the bench and not slide into the gap between the seats.

They drove for a while in the dark. Lulled by the engine and time passing, she dozed, then woke up with a start, then slept again.

"Hey, Paisley!"

She jerked awake.

"Did he put anything on you? Like a listening device?"

What were they? In the CIA? "No. I don't know."

Silence again. More dozing. When she woke up the radio was going. Some '70s tune.

"I would have stopped before now and took the tape off. I'm sorry you had to stay like that for so long." Craig glanced back at her, and she saw the worry in his gaze. "The mayor told me to keep going, so I am. We're driving north on Highway 101."

Why was he telling her this?

"It wasn't supposed to turn out this way. He's been trailing me for an hour. I'm sorry for how he treated you."

If he were sorry, then why didn't he do something to stop it back at Edward's house? Couldn't he have slugged the guy and knocked him out? Why would he drive her away from Basalt, away from Judah?

"Honestly, I care about you and your sister."

Sure, he did.

He got quiet again, and she fell asleep to some almost-comforting lyrics about a country road taking them home.

Judah, where are you?

Twenty-five

Judah kept his gaze trained on the taillights ahead of him, staring into the night and the oncoming lights until his eyes burned and turned gritty, but he wouldn't let himself lose sight of Edward's vehicle and, ultimately, Craig's. Fortunately, this was a familiar two-lane highway heading up the coast. Earlier, when his father's truck pulled out and followed the rental vehicle, Judah knew their plan had changed and become more dangerous. He wouldn't give up believing he could be with Paisley tonight, but he had to be ready for anything. That his dad was involved in the kidnapping was beyond his comprehension. Maybe his mother was right. He should have called Deputy Brian and let him take care of this. Too late now.

He forced himself to stay far enough behind the other cars so the mayor wouldn't get suspicious. A nagging thought kept churning in him. Was there any chance this was all a mistake? Maybe Craig exaggerated the information about Edward for his own purposes. Didn't Judah mistrust the guy ever since Paisley told him about Craig's involvement in her leaving in the first place? It was hard to alter those opinions now. What if he was in as deep as Edward and trying to deceive Judah? He gripped the steering wheel tighter.

What if that business about them being half-brothers was a lie too? Something to get him feeling sympathetic toward Craig? But his mom knew about it, so there had to be some truth to the story, right? Unless Edward falsified the information to her in the first place. Judah wouldn't put it past him to do such a thing.

After trailing Craig's vehicle another half hour, Edward's truck suddenly veered off the road, heading toward a cluster of lights along the otherwise dark highway. Probably hitting a pub or a truck stop, or maybe he was low on gas.

"Finally." Judah narrowed the gap between his vehicle and the one in front of him, leaving space for a passing car to merge onto the highway. Ten miles later, he yelled, "Come on, Craig. Pull over." Why wasn't he stopping now that Edward's truck wasn't behind him? Did Craig fear he might still be back there? Or was he leading Judah on a wild goose chase?

A line of four cars and two trucks zipped past his pickup. Two merged into the lane ahead of him. Were any of the trucks Edward's? Too dark to tell.

A lone car turned off the road ahead. Craig's? How could Judah be certain considering the group of cars that just passed him? It looked like the same shape as the rental. Same shape as one of the vehicles in the lineup too. If he turned toward the gas station in the distance, then found out it wasn't Craig, he would have wasted precious minutes. He might not even be able to find him again in the dark.

At the last second, Judah turned sharply, exiting the

highway. He pulled up fast behind the other car. One person sat in the front seat. If that was Craig, where was Paisley?

The sedan crept into the gas station parking lot but didn't stop at a pump. Instead, the driver pulled around the far side of the building. What was he doing?

Judah followed slowly, waiting for Craig, if it was him, to step from the vehicle. He still wanted verification that he followed the right car. What if this was a decoy?

He veered into the parking space two lanes from the other car in case Edward swerved in too. Judah peered at the driver who had his sweatshirt hood pulled up. Why wasn't he turning this way? Waving, or something? If Judah had the wrong car, getting back to where the other vehicle was would take a high-speed chase.

He wanted to blast the horn to get the guy to face him. Was this Craig's rental? Was Paisley in there right now?

Finally, the driver turned toward Judah, although it was too dark to see his face. He pulsed his thumb toward the backseat. That had to be him.

Paisley!

Judah shut off the engine and leaped from the car. He charged over to the other vehicle's back door. Someone lay on the backseat, knees bent. Tied up? *Oh, no.* He grabbed the door handle. Locked. He banged on the front window. "Open up." *Paisley, I'm so sorry.* What did Edward do to her?

The locks clicked. Why wasn't Craig getting out of the car and helping?

Judah yanked open the car door. "Pais?"

She moved slightly, moaning, then glanced up at him with a dull vacant-looking gaze. Duct tape covered her lower face. Tape bound her hands. Rope held her legs together. Judah's heart broke into pieces. He wanted to weep, but there wasn't time. He squatted down beside her, leaning into the vehicle. "Paisley, are you okay? What have they done to you?"

His gaze flew to Craig's in accusation, but even he looked sick.

"This is the old man's doing. Not mine. This was the only way I could think of to help her."

"This was helping her?" Judah yelled.

Paisley's muffled cries came through the duct tape. "Oh, Judah. Help me. Hurry." He made out her indistinct words.

"I'm here now. Of course, I'll help you." He could only imagine what she must have gone through in the last thirty-some hours. "You're going to be okay now. I'm so sorry for what he did to you. This must hurt terribly." He tried to work the edge of the tape loose from her face, but his fingers shook. How could anyone do this to her? Let alone the culprit being his own father. He could no longer imagine that Edward might not have been involved in this crime. That realization gnawed at his core as he tried to tug the tape free without hurting his wife anymore.

"Hurry up," Craig ordered from the front.

"You could help me."

"I can't."

"Why not?"

"I'm keeping watch in case he comes back. If he does, be ready to shut the door. Because I'm taking off fast and trying to lose him. He won't let me get away with this. We both know that."

Judah groaned, working a little more tape loose, enough to hear Paisley crying and gasping. "I'm sorry, Pais. I don't want to hurt you. I'm so sorry." Tears blurred his vision. "I don't know how to get this tape off without causing you more agony." He still tugged on the edges, trying to be careful.

"You're going to have to pull it off at once." Craig huffed. "But her face is …"

"What?"

"Raw already."

"Turn on the light."

"No, man. Edward might be watching. He—"

"I don't care. Turn on the light!"

The dome light came on, splashing light over Paisley's raw, sore-looking, swollen face exposed around the silver tape. Tears flooded his eyes, making it nearly impossible to see. "Oh, Paisley." He felt sick.

"Just pull it off!" Craig shut the light back off.

"No." Judah wouldn't. He'd be as gentle as he could with her. She had external wounds. What kind of internal wounds and scars would she carry after this trauma? He wouldn't add to that by hurting her more.

His gut turned over at the broken look in her gaze as she peered up at him. Why hadn't he urged his mom to press charges against Edward after he injured her? If he had, this might not have happened.

"Just do it!" Craig said loudly. "I've got to get out of here. We all do." He peered out the window nervously, his hand gripping the steering wheel. "Think of Piper."

Judah swallowed. Craig was right. "I'm so sorry, Pais. This isn't working. I don't want to hurt you, but I don't know what else to do."

She scrunched her eyes closed and nodded. She grimaced like she was clenching her jaw. Then she made muffled commands telling him to do it. *Now*, apparently.

"I'm so sorry. So terribly sorry." He gripped the piece of loosened tape between his index finger and thumb, then he ripped off the rest in one yank. Paisley's scream tore him up inside. She toppled against him, sobbing, and he wrapped his arms around her, holding her to him, rocking her. Sniffing, with tears dripping down his face, he thanked God for rescuing her, for helping them be together again. Shuffling her on the seat so he could sit beside her, he dropped onto the cushion, enfolded her in his arms again, and shut the door. If Edward snuck up on them, Judah didn't want him to get the advantage on them before he had time to react.

"Thank you … for finding me." She lifted her hands toward him. "Please?" She nodded toward the bonds wrapped around her wrists.

"Of course. This might hurt too."

He worked with the tape at her wrists, checking her pupils, assessing whether she might be in too much pain, or possibly going into shock, while he tried to free her arms of the binding that had left sores on her skin. He kept tugging until the tape fell away. Then he fingered the rope knots that bound her legs, loosening them. He stared at her face, her beautiful face, that looked wet with the rawness of her injuries. "Oh, my sweet Paisley."

"You should go." Craig rocked his thumb toward the other vehicle. "Quickly. Go while you can."

He must think Edward was still in pursuit. "Where will you go?"

"Inland. Lay low until they find him." Craig shrugged. "He wasn't supposed to follow me. He had an alibi with Mia. But he must have suspected I might pull something like this. He'll be enraged, looking for retaliation. Finding it, unless I hide."

Judah knew his father was a difficult man, but doing all this underhanded, cruel stuff? It would take time to process.

"I'll text him as if I've made it to the next checkpoint. Buy us some time." Craig glanced back at Paisley. "You should take her to the hospital."

"I know." Judah cleared his throat. "Mia was waiting for him tonight."

Paisley glanced up at him, her dark eyes moist. "You were with … Mia?" Her voice sounded strained and cautious.

"Outside the deputy's office for a few minutes."

"That was planned." Craig tapped the steering wheel. "Mia Till is his alibi."

Paisley nodded.

He didn't know what Craig was talking about, but he didn't want to discuss Mia. "How are you, sweetheart?" Judah stroked Paisley's sweaty-looking hair back, being careful not to bump her wounds.

"So tired. Everything … hurts."

"I bet." He had to decide which hospital to take her to. They were about halfway between Portland and North Bend. Which one would be far enough away from Edward? "Craig, can you drive us to the hospital in North Bend?"

"Why don't you drive her yourself?" Craig squinted at him.

"I want to stay with her like this. Edward will expect you to head to Portland as planned. If you backtrack and go beyond Basalt Bay, he won't be suspecting that."

"I don't know, man."

"For Paisley's safety, please?" Judah shuffled her slightly on his lap so her legs could stretch out. Her muscles must need relief after being cinched together. "I'll leave my truck here."

"What if your father finds it?"

"Maybe he'll think it had a breakdown." He glanced out the window, checking for a black truck. "By now, the deputy should have a warrant out for his arrest. My mom will see to that."

"That's a start." Craig backed up the car.

"Wait. Do you have some water?"

Craig passed him a water bottle.

Judah opened it and tipped the bottle toward Paisley's mouth. "Here, try to drink some. You're probably dehydrated."

She sipped a little but seemed to have trouble keeping the water in her mouth. He put the top back on. He rested the back of his fingers against her forehead. A little warm. He pressed his fingers against her neck, avoiding the sores on her wrists, to take her pulse. Then he pulled her against him again, wrapping his arms gently around her, holding her close to his heart, right where he wanted her to be. Sighing, she closed her eyes.

"Do you think Edward will flee?" He had to find out what Craig knew. "If he goes into hiding, where do you think he'd go?"

"How should I know? For him to do this"—Craig jerked his head toward Paisley—"maybe he did snap, like your mom said. He seemed paranoid and delusional tonight."

Judah thought of how violent he'd become with Mom. "Something's probably been wrong with him for a while. Not that it excuses anything."

"Never know, Basalt might need a new mayor."

"I don't care about that. But I appreciate your help rescuing my wife. Sticking your neck out." He patted Craig's shoulder. "When I talk to the deputy, I'll put in a good word for you."

"I appreciate that."

"I can't help but wonder what Edward is holding over you to get you to go along with his foul schemes."

Craig met his gaze in the rearview mirror. "It's not an honorable tale."

"Still, I'd like to hear it."

"Another time, perhaps." Craig turned up the radio, ending the conversation.

For the rest of the drive to the hospital, Judah held Paisley and prayed for her. And, he kept glancing behind them, making sure a black truck wasn't following.

Twenty-six

In the North Bend Shoreline Hospital, Judah sat by Paisley's bed all night, holding her bandaged hand and praying. Dozing occasionally. A gray-haired nurse, who introduced herself as Joyce, and who surely meant well, suggested that he wait in the lobby so Paisley could rest better. But he refused to leave her side. When she woke up, he planned to be the first person she saw. Since they'd medicated her, she seemed to be resting fine, anyway.

For a while, he'd been staring at her face, observing, and angered by, the abrasions and bruises caused by the duct tape … and being hit, her doctor said. A crushing thought he couldn't stomach. But he had to face facts. Edward had been abusive to her. Hurt her. *Paisley, I'm so sorry.* No way was Judah leaving her alone. Hospital security would have to restrain him and drag him away to stop him from staying here in this chair, close to her. He failed to protect her before. Not happening again.

He'd been praying for her injuries, physical and emotional, and praying for them, for their marriage, that this horrible experience of the last two days wouldn't hinder them from spending the rest of their lives together. That he could be the strength she needed him to be in the days ahead. He begged God for mercy and grace for whatever they had to face as a couple, especially after this ordeal that his father had perpetrated.

Just thinking of Edward Grant laying a finger on his wife caused a surge of anger to rush through Judah. A couple of times, like now, he stood and paced to the window, unable to sit still any longer. He pulled back the curtain, just enough to see out, and stared at the ocean waves pounding the seashore on the other side of the street. The powerful force of the sea reminded him of the turbulent rage churning within himself. *"Dad, how could you have hurt Paisley?"* His heart thudded rampantly beneath his sternum. If his father were standing here, he'd be tempted to beat him up.

He'd have to spend some more time praying and asking God to help him forgive Edward. On his own, he didn't think he could muster the strength or will. *Help me to forgive.*

He strode back to his chair and sat down again. He laid his hand over Paisley's and asked God to touch her.

Besides her obvious wounds, the medical staff was treating her for dehydration, exhaustion, and possible infection. Doctor Clark said he'd like Paisley to remain in the hospital tonight and tomorrow, maybe longer, under observation. If all went well, they'd wean her off the drugs that were keeping her asleep and immobile later today.

Judah couldn't wait to talk with her. To find out how she really was and to assure himself that she'd be okay.

Last night, he'd texted Mom, letting her know Paisley was safe in the hospital. She texted back, expressing her relief that her "daughter-in-love" was found. He inquired about the warrant, and she said the deputy was taking care of it. Man, he hoped that were true. Hadn't he been suspicious of Deputy Brian's connections with the mayor in the past? Any chance he was under Edward's thumb like Craig said Mike Linfield and others in town were? Ugh. He didn't want to think about that.

In another text, Mom told him she'd filed for a temporary restraining order against Edward. She was worried he might come after her too. Considering his previous abuse, she planned to stay away from Lewis's Super until he was apprehended.

That seemed like a wise decision. Judah prayed his mom would be safe until his father was locked up. Imagining his dad going to prison was a harsh reality. But he couldn't see any other outcome, especially considering Paisley's injuries. His breath caught in his throat. "Lord, help me forgive."

Last night, Judah also texted Paige with the news of what happened and where they were. She said she and her father would make the drive south today, if she could find a safe place for Piper.

Another nurse, Karen, whom he met earlier this morning, came in and checked Paisley's vitals, cleaned her wounds, and reapplied gauze on her wrists. While she fiddled with the dials on the machines, she eyed Judah. "Wouldn't you like to go get some lunch in the cafeteria? We can text you when she wakes up."

"No, thanks." Judah nodded toward Paisley. "I want to stay here. Be the first one she sees when she wakes up."

"Ah, a romantic, huh? Good for you."

"We were supposed to get remarried tomorrow."

"Really?" The nurse took Paisley's temperature. "Like with a ceremony?"

"Yes. Small gathering. Not happening now." A pain burned up his chest.

"What a shame." Karen stared at Paisley then wrote something on her chart. "She'll need to stay here through tomorrow, at least."

"Yeah, I know." He'd already asked his mom to spread the word that the ceremony was postponed. He hated doing that. Paisley probably wouldn't like it, either.

The nurse exited the room quietly.

His phone buzzed. He glanced at the screen.

It's Paige. I'm here with my dad. Can we see Paisley?

Sure, he tapped. *Room 145. She's still asleep.*

Be up in a jiffy. So glad you found her.

He stroked Paisley's palm. "Your dad and Paige are here." How long would it be before the drugs wore off and she could talk to him? He watched the peaceful expression on her bruised and blistered face as she slept. He winced every time he thought of how Edward mistreated her. He whispered another prayer for her before her family arrived. *And, please, help me forgive the man I'm struggling to even accept as my father right now.*

Paige tapped on the door, then entered. Paul strode in behind her.

"Hey, Judah." Paige hurried to the opposite side of the bed. Gazing down at Paisley, her face crumpled, and she shook her head like she couldn't believe how battered her sister looked. "I'm so sorry this happened to you." She leaned over and kissed Paisley's forehead. "So sorry."

Standing at the foot of the metal-framed bed, Paul stared wide-eyed at Paisley. A myriad of emotions crisscrossed his features. Anger and sadness, maybe disbelief. "W-who would d-do such a thing?" His voice broke in a sob. "What kind of monster—?

Judah glanced at Paige. She hadn't told him? She shook her head discreetly.

"I'm sorry to have to admit this"—Judah swallowed—"but it was my father who kidnapped her."

Paul flinched then pushed his black-rimmed glasses up his nose. "Mayor Grant assaulted my daughter? He should be taken out and beaten!"

"Shhhh." Paige tugged on her dad's arm.

"I think you're right about that." Judah met his father-in-law's anguished gaze.

"My dear Paisley-bug. Is she going to be okay?"

"Yes, but it may take some time. If it wasn't for Craig, I don't know what might have happened." Judah shrugged. Had his father been deluded enough to think he could get away with such viciousness and continue being mayor?

"How long has she been sleeping?" Paige asked.

"Since after her exam last night. They're keeping her sedated for a while longer."

"Do you need a break? Maybe get some food? You look—" She stopped, didn't elaborate.

What? Terrible? He strummed his fingers through his hair. Yeah, he probably looked bad. He didn't sleep much sitting up. Too much on his mind.

"You say Craig is the one who knew where she was?" Paul stepped closer to Judah, obviously keeping his voice subdued.

"He played along so Edward would trust him." Judah released Paisley's hand. "He did a good thing for us, for Paisley."

"Where is he now?" Paige's focus was still on her sister.

"Hiding. Afraid of repercussions if the mayor gets to him before the law does."

"No wonder. Isn't he in trouble too?"

"Probably." Judah sighed. "He'll have to give a statement, might even be charged as an accessory, but I'll stand up for him."

"And the rest?" She met his gaze.

Did she mean about them possibly being half-brothers? "We'll figure out the rest later."

She nodded.

"Is Paisley safe here?" Paul patted the end of the bed. "In the movies, the villain always comes to the hospital to get the person."

"Dad—" Paige shot him a warning look.

"I doubt that will happen." Still, goosebumps skittered over Judah's skin. When he chose this smaller hospital, farther away from Portland, he hoped it would keep such a thing from happening. Paul's words of caution made him more determined to protect Paisley.

"What about the ceremony?" Paige asked softly.

"My mom's spreading the word that we have to postpone."

"Such a shame," Paul mumbled.

"If you want to take a break, grab a bite, or get cleaned up"—Paige fidgeted like she felt uncomfortable saying anything—"I'll text you if there's any change."

His first reaction was to decline, but he could use a bathroom break. Maybe grab a coffee. Paisley was safe with her sister and dad watching over her. "Okay. I'll be back in ten minutes." He leaned over and kissed Paisley's forehead, then left the room.

He found the nearest restroom and used the facilities. Then he dampened his hair and fingered it into place. What he wouldn't give for a toothbrush.

Down the hall, he located a few vending machines. The coffee wasn't bad. Or maybe, in his sleep-deprived condition, any coffee tasted fantastic. He used his coins to get a couple of pastries and made quick work of them before heading back.

In Paisley's room, everything was the same as before he left, only Paul sat in the chair Judah had vacated—a chair he wanted to reclaim. Paige sat in another chair she must have grabbed from the other side of the room.

"Feel any better?" She smiled. "You look more awake."

"Coffee helped." Despite the caffeine intake, he yawned.

"Is there anything we can do while we wait?" She nodded toward Paisley. "According to the nurse who checked on her—Karen?—it could still be a few hours until she wakes up."

Judah's phone buzzed before he could answer her. "Excuse me." He glanced at the screen and saw Mom's name.

Your Dad's truck has been found at the Portland airport.

Did that mean Edward left the country? Did he suspect Craig's deception, or that Judah was involved in last night's rescue?

"What's wrong?" Paige's worried expression reminded him of Paisley's facial features.

"My dad's truck is at the airport." He kept his voice low. "So he may have been on to Craig last night. Probably took an international flight. Just guessing. Who knows what he's up to?"

"Hearing that makes me feel better." Paige rested her hands over her heart. "I mean, that Piper is safe."

"Yeah, I hope so." At her startled look, he added, "I'm sure she is. It just won't be over until he's behind bars." Although, difficult to say, the man deserved prison time.

Thanks for telling me, he tapped into the phone.

I let everyone know the ceremony has been canceled. I'm so sorry.

Thanks. Couldn't be helped.

How is she this morning?

As good as can be expected. Still sleeping. He ended the texting session.

Maybe he'd sit down and close his eyes. Even with the caffeine boost, he felt exhausted. All his emotions and adrenaline were crashing. "The ceremony is officially canceled."

"I'm sorry." Paige's soft voice sounded sympathetic. "You both were looking forward to it."

"We were." It felt good to know Paisley had been eager to marry him again. That she wasn't running away. "Right now, her health is the most important thing. I'll wait however long she needs to recover from all of this."

"You're a good man." Paige patted his arm. "Thankfully, with Craig's help, you found her." She withdrew her hand. "It's good to know my sister has someone who loves her enough to look out for her. She's a lucky girl."

"I'm the lucky one."

Needing to find another chair for Paul, Judah strode back into the hall. He planned to reclaim the chair at the head of Paisley's bed. However long it took, he'd stay right beside her, waiting for her to wake up.

Twenty-seven

A couple of hours later, the door squeaked open and Judah jerked awake. How long had he been dozing? A figure dressed in dark clothes shuffled toward Paisley's bed. Judah leaped up. Out of the corner of his eye, he saw Paige stand too.

"Craig?" she whispered first.

"Craig?" he repeated.

The man pulled the hood off his head, revealing his face. "Hey."

"What are you doing here?" Judah stepped toward him, bypassing Paul dozing in his chair. Even though his previous coworker had helped get Paisley to safety, Judah felt suspicious of him and protective of his wife.

"I had to check and see for myself that Paisley was okay." Craig glanced toward the bed and grimaced. "She still looks bad."

"No, she looks wonderful." Judah wouldn't allow anyone to talk negatively about her. Even if her face was in a delicate condition, it would heal. Her trauma would heal. And she was beautiful, inside and out. "You shouldn't be here." He didn't mean to sound gruff, but Craig was probably in trouble for taking Paisley from the scene of the crime without notifying the authorities. Judah called Deputy Brian from the hospital last night and made his report. Craig probably didn't do the same thing.

"I had to see for myself what's going on." Craig nodded toward Paige. "Hello."

"Thank you for doing the noble thing and helping my sister." Paige raised her chin like she was forcing herself to speak up. "For helping Piper stay safe."

"You're welcome." Craig seemed to stand a little taller. "Any word on Edward's whereabouts?"

"His truck was located at the Portland airport." Judah shrugged. "Maybe skipping the country?"

"If so, this could hang over us for a long time." Craig shuffled back and forth as if antsy to get out of the room. "I should go." He rocked his thumb toward the hall. "Goodbye," he spoke softly toward Paige.

"Bye."

"Wait." Judah followed him, although he didn't want to be away from Paisley for more than a minute. He waited for a nurse to walk past them before speaking. "I want to say thanks again for all you did to help Paisley."

"What, you don't hate me now?" Craig's smirk was back, followed by a glance over his shoulder. Was he expecting security to grab him?

"We have some talking to do. Maybe a DNA swab test. But, no, I don't hate you."

"Paisley does. There are things—" Craig flexed his lips over his teeth. "At the least, I owe her an apology."

"That's the smartest thing I've heard you say in a long time."

Craig grinned crookedly. "I heard the two of you were getting remarried. That true?"

"It is." Judah still wished they were going through with it tomorrow. "Nothing will stop us once she's well enough." He remembered thinking almost the same words six days ago. *Nothing was going to stop them from being together.* Edward had done his worst to keep them apart, but he didn't succeed.

Thank You, Lord.

Craig nodded, his gaze trained down the hallway. "Sorry for all the trouble the mayor caused you both. And for my part in it, before."

Judah wouldn't comment on that, here. "I'll talk to Deputy Brian about what you did to help."

"Thanks. I was worried Edward might show up." Craig glanced in both directions as if keeping continual watch. "That he might try to take her again. But if his truck's been found, he probably left the state."

"Yeah, that's a relief. What are you going to do now?"

"Wait for news. Text me when you hear something, okay?"

"Will do."

"I hope she comes out of this okay." Craig strode to the elevator.

In all the time Judah worked with the guy—eleven years—he never saw any similar traits that would have made him think they were related. Did they have a comparable walk? The same chin shape? Both had dark hair, although not the same eye coloring.

Paige opened the door before he reached it. "Hurry, Judah. She's waking up."

Man, he'd missed being the first one she saw. He rushed back inside the room just as Karen scurried past him. The nurse spoke quietly to Paisley, asking her questions—What day was it? Who's the president? Did she know her middle name?—and took her pulse, then her temperature.

Paisley's dazed gaze met Judah's, and a tired-looking smile crossed her lips. He didn't stop walking until he stood right next to her bed. He bent over and kissed her forehead, wanting to avoid her sore cheeks. "Hey, sweetheart." He clasped her hand and knelt on one knee to be at eye level with her. "How are you doing?"

She shrugged slightly. Licked her lips. Then closed her eyes again.

"Guess she wasn't quite ready to stay awake." The nurse tweaked a couple of dials on the machinery. "She'll be in and out of consciousness for a while. Give her a sip of water if she asks for it." Then Karen scurried out of the room as quickly as she entered.

"Sorry." Paige groaned. "I thought this was it."

"That's okay. She'll wake up when she's ready." Settling back into his chair, Judah sighed. Was there any truth to the worries Craig, and even Paul, expressed about Edward possibly showing up here at the hospital? Not if he took a flight out of Portland, right?

Paul jerked awake, his glasses tumbling to his lap. "Did I miss anything?"

"Paisley woke up for a second"—Paige leaned forward, her voice quiet—"but she fell back asleep."

"I missed it?" He shoved his glasses back on.

"Don't worry. She'll wake up again pretty soon."

Judah's phone buzzed. He checked the screen. Mom again.

Deputy Brian wants to talk to you. Can you give him a call?

Later, I will. Being here with his wife when she woke up meant more to him than answering the deputy's questions.

It's important.

I'm sure it is. I'll call him later.

Okay. I'm praying for Paisley.

Thanks.

He checked for other texts. One from Mia? He was tempted to ignore it. He glanced at Paisley. Still asleep. Just in case it was an emergency message, he checked his screen.

Do you know what's going on with your dad?

Did that mean Mia wasn't aware of his plans? Or was her question another piece of Edward's alibi?

What's going on? he tapped in.

He didn't meet me last night. Do you think something might have happened to him?

Hard to say. He wouldn't lie. But if she was fishing for information, she wasn't getting anything from him.

I heard Paisley was found. Too bad about the canceled wedding.

That wasn't something he cared to discuss with her. He put the screen to sleep and slid the phone into his coat pocket. It vibrated a couple of times, but he ignored it.

After a while, Paige and her dad went to the cafeteria to get some food. They offered to bring something back for him. But he wasn't hungry. He'd spend the time praying. It might be a long night ahead, but he planned to stay alert in his chair. Nothing bad was going to happen to his wife on his watch.

Twenty-eight

Paisley opened her eyes slowly. A thin line of light streamed around the curtains. The dim room seemed blurry. Was something wrong with her eyes? She blinked a few times. Metal railings surrounded the bed. An IV tube was connected to a port in her arm. The white sheets smelled slightly of bleach. A machine near her head hummed. Why was she in a hospital room? Was she dreaming? Her mouth felt painfully dry. Her head throbbed. So the nightmare she'd been through must be real. She adjusted her shoulder. Everything ached, but why? Had she been in an accident?

Judah? Oh, there he was, leaning back in an uncomfortable-looking chair, eyes closed, mouth open, snoring. She smiled at how handsome he was even in sleep, but then her mouth cracked like a broken eggshell. Ugh. Maybe she shouldn't move any part of her body. Laying still, she watched him, loving him with her gaze, her heart. His hair was ruffled like he'd been strumming his fingers through it. Was he troubled? His chin looked shadowed like he hadn't shaved in a while. What day was this?

Water. She needed moisture in her mouth. Every movement caused an ache in her arms. If only she had the strength to reach for the glass on that portable table. "Ju …" She cleared her sore throat. Tasted something on her lips. "Jud—" She coughed, but that hurt too.

Judah sat up, closed his mouth, and met her gaze with a surprised look. "Pais, you're awake."

"H-help me."

He jumped up and leaned over her. "What is it? Are you hurting? What's wrong? Should I call for the nurse?"

She shook her head. "Wa … wat …" More stifled coughing.

"Right." He fumbled for the glass on the table, adjusting the straw to her mouth. "Here you go. It's great to see you awake. Just take sips."

She sucked, but the movement made her lips burn. Liquid spilled out both sides of her mouth. She didn't have much control over her tongue. "What's … wrong … with me?" She swallowed with effort.

"You've been injured. It may take some time for you to feel better. You were admitted to the hospital last night." He set the glass down. "Do you remember anything?" Leaning over her, he stroked her hair back from her forehead, gazing at her tenderly. Furrowed frown lines puckered his forehead. "What did"—he gulped—"what did my father do to you?"

The mayor? For a second, she had a mental image of him grabbing her, shoving her. But that couldn't be right. Her mind went blank. "I don't know." Another scene pulsed through her thoughts of Judah carrying her. Into the hospital, probably. "What do you think … he did?"

"He kidnapped you. I know that much." Judah took a long breath. "He hurt you."

"Oh?" Maybe her imaginings were right. They must have given her a strong medicine since she felt too woozy and light-headed to comprehend much. Did he say Edward kidnapped her? "Why would your dad do that?"

"Who knows?" Judah lowered the railing and sat on the edge of the bed, gazing down at her, his baby blues shining. "I'm so glad you're going to be okay. That you're here with me. That he didn't succeed at his evil plot. It never would have worked, anyway. I'd always find you. You know that, right?" He stroked her fingers and smiled.

She didn't know what he meant about Edward, but she could gaze into Judah's eyes all day. But then, her eyelids closed, too heavy to stay open.

When she woke up later, he sat in his chair again, sleeping. What had he said? The mayor kidnapped her? She pictured herself lying on the closet floor. Another image of her riding in the backseat of a car tied up in rope passed through her thoughts. Wasn't Craig driving?

"Craig."

Judah sat up. "You're awake." He yawned. "What about Craig?"

"He"—she thought hard—"helped me."

"You remembered something?"

"I think so." She stared at the bandages on her wrists and felt the soreness. Edward had put duct tape around her wrists. More memories came together like the pieces of a puzzle. "He threw my cell phone into the sea."

"I'm sorry. We'll replace it." Judah sighed. "Do you remember what happened to your ring?"

That recall rushed through her like a tornado. "He tore it off."

Judah tensed, then visibly relaxed as if controlling his response. "It's okay. You can tell me about it. I know Edward did some bad things to you. He's in a lot of trouble for it, too."

She nodded as thoughts returned. "He acted mean. Sort of crazy. Drinking. Maybe, drugs." She cleared her throat. "He tried to push me out the window."

Judah's eyes widened. "I'm so sorry, Pais."

"But then, he saved me, I think."

"What do you mean?"

Reality and fears jumbled together in her mind. "He took off his belt … I was afraid … then he wrapped it around me and pulled me back into the gallery." She coughed. "He wrapped my head with tape to make me stop shouting."

Judah bit his lip between his upper and lower teeth. "I don't know what to say, other than I'm appalled that my dad would treat you so violently."

She couldn't keep her eyes open for long, but she wanted to watch him. To hear him talking to her. His voice was calming and peaceful. "What day is it?"

"Our wedding day."

"Oh, Judah, really?" She closed her eyes, then jerked awake. "I'm glad I didn't miss our ceremony." She must have dozed again. She woke up, picturing herself strolling down the aisle in her wedding gown. "You didn't peek at my dress, did you?"

Judah chuckled. "No, I did not."

"Good. You said today is our vow renewal, right?"

"It would have been. I'm sorry but I postponed it."

"What? No. Why would you do that?" She coughed again, waiting for the dry ticklish feeling to go away. Didn't he want to renew their vows? "Why did you cancel?"

"Postponed. Because of what happened to you." He

touched her arm. "For now, you're where you need to be, healing, getting better. I'm staying right beside you."

"Please, can we still have our ceremony?"

"As soon as you're well enough, we will. I promise." His eyes sparkled with unshed tears. "You have to stay here. Doctor's orders."

"But—" She took a breath, then released it. "Can I have a mirror?"

A tense look crossed his face. "It's too soon. Maybe tomorrow, okay?"

"Please, can you get me a mirror?" She struggled to speak normally. "I want to see how I look today."

"You sure?" By his frown, he obviously didn't want her to see herself.

"Yes. I know I look bad."

"You look beautiful."

She appreciated his kindness, but she knew the truth. "Judah, please, get one for me?"

"I'll be right back." Sighing, he shuffled from the room.

Edward had called her ugly, and she remembered how ghastly she looked in the bathroom mirror last night. Was it only last night? She lifted her right hand, forcing herself to move it despite the pain, and stroked her cheek. Gooey stuff, medicinal cream, was on her face. No bandage. She tapped her lips. They felt swollen. Sores and scabs speckled her cheeks. She must look pathetic.

He reentered the room with a handheld mirror. "You sure about this?"

"I'm sure." She studied him, watching for any sign of his being repulsed by her looks. He met her gaze steadily without glancing away.

"I love you, Pais. Your scars will heal, so don't worry about how they look today, okay?" That was kind of him to say, but still.

"And if they don't?"

"No matter what, I love you and want you to be my wife, for better or for worse, forever."

"I'd prefer 'for better' rather than 'for worse.'" She pointed at the mirror. "Hold it up, will you?"

He sat down on the edge of the bed and held the circular mirror out toward her.

Ugh. She still looked terrible. Worse, if that were possible. Now, she had bruises. Red puckered sores lined her cheek. Would the raw patches of skin around the sides of her mouth leave scars? No wonder Judah didn't want her to see her face. She turned from the mirror, away from him. "Don't look at me, okay?"

"What do you mean, don't look at you?" He smoothed his hand over her shoulder. "Your being here with me like this is a miracle. Don't you know how out-of-my-mind worried I was when I couldn't find you? I begged God to lead me to you."

She heard him set the mirror on the table. Then the mattress moved up and down as he sprawled out on his side, laying beside her on the bed. The nurse might not approve of his street clothes touching the hospital bed. Even so, when he stroked Paisley's hair, running his fingers down her arm, she relaxed against him. "Pais?"

"Hmm?" With effort, she turned just enough to see him.

"I only want to be with you. I love you. You're in my heart forever."

His words poured over her like warm honey. His sweet smile made her want to smile back at him. How could she doubt for a second that he'd stick by her and love her, no matter how she looked? Edward was a liar. He didn't know what a great son he had.

"Thank you."

Judah gently stroked her back. "How are you feeling?"

"Just tired." She closed her eyes, glad that he was close to her. Thankful he wasn't repulsed by her. Then she remembered something. "When I was in the closet, I didn't know how many days had passed." She swallowed. "I was afraid you might think I ran away."

He slid some hair off her forehead, still gazing at her. "I confess the thought tore me up."

"You believed I ran?"

"I'm sorry, but at first I thought that." He closed his eyes. When he reopened them, moisture puddled in them. "I didn't know what to think when you disappeared. I thought the worst. I'm sorry for doubting you."

"It's okay." She'd doubted him too. About him and Mia. Even him and Paige. "You said Mia showed up, right?"

"Yeah. What about her?"

She blinked a few times, focusing on him. Trying to remember. She felt better, but the grogginess came over her in waves, stealing her thoughts. "Your dad mentioned lining up my replacement. Mia. That you wouldn't be sad for long because of her."

"Don't give that idea another thought." He leaned closer to her, their noses almost touching. "I choose you, Paisley Rose Grant. Doesn't matter what Mia does. Doesn't matter what Edward says. I choose you." His steamy gaze and wink sizzled warmth right through her, despite her injuries. "I hope you still choose me, too."

"I do. You're my …" She must have fallen asleep without finishing her thought.

When she woke up, Judah wasn't on the bed. A doctor was peering down into her eyes. He wiped something off her cheeks gently, then reapplied salve, or lotion.

"Any chance I can go home today?" Her voice still sounded croaky.

The doctor's eyes shone above the mask covering his mouth. "Hello, Paisley. I'm Doctor Clark. I'm the attending physician on this floor. And I'd like you to stay here tonight. Maybe tomorrow. At least, until you get your strength back."

"Isn't it better for me to recover at home? I have a great caregiver." She glanced at Judah, sitting in the chair, and attempted a smile, but her lips didn't cooperate. "We were supposed to renew our vows today."

"Is that right?" The doctor tipped his head and stared compassionately at her. "You mean you're missing your own celebration?"

"Mmhmm. Doesn't seem fair, does it?"

"Not really. I'm sorry." He patted her arm then strode toward the door. "I'll be back to check on you later." He left the room.

She groaned at not being able to influence him to let her leave.

The door remained slightly open and the smell of food, maybe hamburger meat, rushed in. Her stomach growled. "Are they going to let me eat anything?" She had to get her strength back quickly, somehow.

Judah pointed to the drip machine. "They're feeding you through your veins."

"Not helping. I'm hungry."

"You want me to go find you some oatmeal, or something?"

"Oatmeal? Come on. You can do better than that."

He chuckled. "It's nice to hear you sounding more like yourself. Really nice." He leaned over and kissed her forehead.

One of these times when he did that, she was going to tip her chin and meet his soft lips. *If* she could forget how terrible her face looked for three seconds. "Just get me some real food, will you? Then I'll get stronger. You'll see."

"I'll be right back." Grinning, he left the room.

Paisley forced her arms to move past the pain and reached for the mirror on the table. She wanted another look at herself without Judah watching her reaction. As soon as she saw her reflection, she grimaced at the bruises and cuts. No wonder he stared at her like she was an injured kid. She dropped the mirror back on the table. How long would it take for her to look like herself? Would she ever?

Judah returned a few minutes later with a bowl of food and proceeded to feed her like she was an invalid. Not romantic at all.

"Applesauce? That's what you got for me?"

"Nurse's decision." He put a half-filled spoon in her mouth. "How does it taste?"

"Blech." She'd rather have a burger from Bert's, or whatever was causing that yummy smell in the air, even if too much too soon might make her sick.

After she took a few more bites, Judah set the bowl on the table. "Your dad and Paige are here too."

"They are? Can I see them?"

"Uh-huh. I texted them. They'll be here soon. They're staying at a nearby motel."

"Where are we?" She tried to get more comfortable on the stiff mattress.

"North Bend Shoreline Hospital."

"The one built near the ocean?"

"Yes."

"That's so amazing." If only she could see the water from her bed and watch the waves pounding the seashore. That would make her feel better.

An idea came to mind. It might not work, considering she was stuck in a hospital bed, and her face looked like she'd been in a wreck, but it was worth giving it a shot. "Would it be possible for you to ask your mom if she'd come down here? Today, if possible."

"You want to see my mom today?"

"Mmhmm. You don't mind, do you?"

"No. I'm sure she'd drive down if I asked." His forehead creased with lines. "But, why?"

"Just ask her to bring some clothes for me, okay? I never want to wear the ones I had on again." Hopefully, he wouldn't read anything into her request. She didn't want to explain yet. "And tell her I'd love to wear my new shoes."

"I can do that." He got a puzzled look on his face. "Did you tear off a scrap of your shirt at the art gallery?"

"You found it?"

"Paige did."

"I'm surprised anyone saw it." She stared at the ceiling, thinking of how helpless she'd felt tied up on the floor. "My hands were behind my back, so I tugged on the shirt until the fabric gave way."

"That was brilliant. It was the first clue that you had been in the gallery."

She remembered her fear, her determination to get free, then the waiting in the dark, and all the yelling she'd done to no avail.

"And the word 'help'? Did you write that, too?"

"You saw that? I wrote it with my finger behind my back. I was sure I messed up the letters." She flexed her jaw, glad the medicine made it more relaxed and less painful.

"It was barely legible, but I knew what it said."

"That's cool." She decided to change the subject. "North Bend has some fabulous beaches. When I was tied up in the closet, picturing the sea comforted me."

"I'm glad." He sat down on the chair he'd been sleeping in before. He took her hands in his, and she knew he was trying to be extremely gentle with her.

"Also, I prayed."

"Good. Me too."

"No, I mean, I"—she thought for a minute—"I trusted Jesus. If I didn't make it back to you, and for a while, I thought I might not, I wanted to be ready to go to heaven." She met his gaze. "I needed to believe in Him again, not just because you want me to, but for me, for my own heart." A wave of emotion hit her, and she fought tears. "*He* was there with me in the closet. I'm so thankful."

"That's wonderful, Pais. An answer to my prayers."

"I'll never forget it." She linked her pinkie with his. "I prayed you'd find me. But if you couldn't, I still had to make things right with God."

"He answered both of our prayers. And He even used Craig." Judah blinked fast like he was absorbing tears.

Suddenly, her eyelids were too heavy to stay open. The last thought on her mind before she succumbed to sleep was hoping Judah didn't forget to ask his mom to bring her shoes.

Twenty-nine

Judah watched Paisley sleeping, her dark hair splayed out on the white, hospital pillow, and he thanked God for watching out for her through all that happened in the last few days.

His cell phone vibrated, and he checked the screen.

Don't forget to call the deputy.

He groaned at Mom's reminder.

I won't forget, he tapped in. *Paisley wants to know if you'll grab some clothes and bring them here.*

Which clothes? she texted back.

Grab anything. And her new shoes? Thanks.

Sure. I can do that. She added a happy face emoji.

Paige and Paul entered the room.

"Hey, Judah." Paige hurried over to Paisley's bed.

"She's still asleep?" Paul moaned and plopped down in the extra chair. "I had a terrible night's sleep at that motel. Worst bed I've ever attempted to rest in."

Paige seemed to be biting back a laugh. "Yet, he snored through most of the night."

Judah chuckled. The lighthearted moment was a relief after all the recent tension.

"How is she?" Paige stared at her sister as if willing her to wake up.

"She was alert for a while. Cognitive. Even hungry."

"That's wonderful news."

"Yeah, it is." Judah stood and moved toward the door. "Since you're here, I have a phone call to make, then I'll be right back."

"Sure. Take your time. Get some coffee, whatever."

"Get me some too!" Paul called after him.

"Now, Dad." Paige mentioned something about his blood sugar test being too high.

"I don't need you girls treating me like a child." Paul harrumphed.

Snickering over their familiar squabble, Judah made his way down the hall. He passed the nurse's station, nodding at Karen. He tapped the deputy's name that was still in his contact list from when he worked with C-MER and waited for the connection to go through.

"Hello. This is Deputy Corbin."

"Judah Grant, here."

"Didn't I tell you not to leave town?"

"I know." Judah sighed. "I had to find my wife."

A silence. "When can I interview Paisley?"

At least, the deputy didn't chastise Judah's decision.

"She's still in the hospital." He tried to keep his tone quiet. "Resting, per doctor's orders. She can't talk with you right now."

"I needed a statement from her yesterday."

"I apologize for the inconvenience." Time to change topics.

"Any updates about the mayor?" Judah would feel more peaceful when the man was taken into custody.

"Nothing conclusive. I've put out an all-state alert for him."

"Any bites, other than his truck being found?"

Joyce, the older nurse who'd been on duty last night, walked by and gave him a steely-eyed warning. "Please, keep your voice down. The lobby's that way." She pointed down the hall.

"Sorry." He lifted the phone, then replaced it to his ear. "I can't talk for long. Quiet zone."

"Where's Craig? Is he up to his eyeballs in this?"

"He rescued Paisley. Other than his intervening and successfully getting her away from Edward, I have no idea." Judah paused. "My father's the one who took Paisley against her will. Kept her tied up, and I'm not sure what else. Other than him plotting to send her to another country."

"Hearsay. I need an eyewitness account."

"Craig's an eyewitness." Judah's voice rose again. "Paisley's wounds are evidence too. Just ask her doctor."

"I will. Or someone will. Forest Harper is coming in to help gather evidence for the case."

"Forest?" Judah hadn't talked to the detective who helped him find Paisley in over two years. He'd be a great asset in this investigation. "I'm glad you're bringing in someone to get the situation resolved quickly." He was thankful to hear the deputy was taking Edward's crime seriously, too.

"So, why do you think the mayor did these things?" The deputy's voice deepened.

"I don't know. I wish I did." Judah glanced down the hallway. Someone in dark clothes, not a medical uniform, entered Paisley's room. "I have to go." He ended the call and ran down the hall. The guy who appeared to be a teenager was just exiting the room as Judah reached the door. "What are you doing in there?"

"I'm a volunteer with the hospital delivery service."

"Delivering what?" Judah was sorry about not giving the young man the benefit of the doubt, but right now he was suspicious of everyone.

"Flowers. What did you think?" The guy shook his head like he thought Judah might be crazy, then strode down the hall.

"Sorry. Just checking." He pushed open the door.

Paige met him and held up a card. "From *EG*." She glowered at a bouquet of red roses on a stand by the wall.

"EG. As in—?"

"I think so."

Paisley was awake now, watching him, but he took the card from Paige and strode to the stand before talking to his wife.

Too bad my plan failed. Better luck next time. EG

Judah groaned. "Does this mean Edward didn't leave the area? What about his car being found at the airport?"

"Part of his scheme to deceive everyone?" Paige shuddered.

"Maybe." Judah picked up the flowers and searched around the stems, just in case something weird had been attached, like electronic surveillance. He didn't find anything unusual.

"Why are you worried?" Paul stepped closer and pushed his glasses farther up his nose. "Do you think the mayor's here? Maybe we should spring her out of here." He nodded toward Paisley. "She's better off at home with me, anyway."

"Now, Dad. We're not medical professionals." Paige linked her arm with her father's. "This doesn't mean the mayor's anywhere near North Bend. You can order flowers online from anywhere."

"Better not be here." Paul scooted back near Paisley. "How are you doing, Paisley-bug?"

"Better, I think." Her voice sounded stronger. "Judah, what does the card say? Is it from … Edward?"

He met her gaze but didn't want to add to her worries or her previous trauma. However, to say "nothing" would be a lie.

"I wouldn't put it past him"—she coughed—"to try to steal me from my bed."

So, she realized the danger she was in? Judah couldn't hide his frown, nor the fearful expression that must have crossed his face.

"Is that what you think will h-happen?" Her voice cracked.

"No, of course not." Paul patted her hand. "We're only trying to second-guess what the mayor might do."

Judah knew how vital honesty was between them, so he read the card out loud to her.

"Next time?" she repeated in a hushed voice.

"Don't worry. That's not going to happen." He crossed the space between them and linked his left pinkie with her right one. She was supposed to be resting. Not getting stressed out. "Don't let it bother you. I'm here. We're all here for you."

"I appreciate that. But—"

"Any idea why he might be doing this?" Paige leaned toward Judah, a tense look on her face.

"That's what I'd like to know." Paul huffed. "I thought the mayor was supposed to be doing good for our community. What he's done here is unethical. Unworthy of any person serving as a mayor."

"I know." Judah met his wife's gaze and smiled, trying not to reveal the level of concern he had about Edward being aware of their location. While he hoped to extend comfort and confidence to Paisley, he felt like he failed epically. He was tired too. Spent from the extreme rise and fall of his emotions over the last couple of days. He could use a good night's sleep. But he wouldn't leave her side if he could help it. He let go of her finger and returned to his chair so he could sit close to her. He recalled his conversation with the deputy. "I talked to Deputy Brian. He's called in a detective to help him with the case."

"A detective?" Paige whispered.

"Forest Harper. You know him?"

"Isn't that the guy who found me?" Paisley spoke softly.

"Yes, he is."

"*He's* coming back to Basalt Bay?" Paige put her hand to her chest like she had heart palpitations.

"That's what the deputy said. You all right?"

"I can't believe he'd return. He said he'd never—" Her voice faded out. Dropping into her chair, she pressed her fingertips against her temples. "I don't believe this."

"What's wrong, Paige? You need me to get you something?" Paul strode to her and rubbed his hand over her shoulder.

"No, I'm okay, or will be."

Why did she have such a strong reaction to the news that Forest was coming back? Paige squinted at Judah, then nodded slightly toward her father, as if asking him not to say anything in front of Paul.

He wouldn't, but what was she so concerned about? A possible reason for her reaction crossed his mind. He might be way off, but was there any chance Forest Harper was the mystery man in her life? Piper's father? Probably not. But she obviously knew him. Of course, Basalt Bay was a small town. Everyone knew everyone.

Paige stood and ran her hands over her arms. "I'm going to get some fresh air. Want to walk with me, Dad?"

"Okay. Maybe get some of that coffee?"

"Sure, why not? I need some now, too."

The two of them left the room, leaving Judah with troubling thoughts as he watched his wife sleeping again.

Thirty

The mattress jiggled, or else someone touched her arm, waking Paisley up. Judah? She opened her eyes. He wasn't in his chair. The white-walled room appeared empty. A cart rumbled down the hallway with a squeaky wheel. Something smelled like meatloaf.

"You're finally awake." *Edward?* The man's voice made her skin crawl. "Stand up and come with me. We have to run some diagnostic tests."

She faced the screened-off area. He must be back there. She remembered the card with the flowers. *Next time.* This must be it.

Where was Judah?

"Sit up and put on the slippers that I left at the foot of the bed."

So, that's what awakened her. Had he been standing by her bed, watching her? Creepy. Where'd the call button go? She smoothed her hand over the blanket but couldn't find it.

"Get out of bed. You're coming with me." Edward stepped

around the screen, dressed in green hospital scrubs and a mask. Someone else might think he was a doctor. Not her.

"I'm not … going anywhere … with you." If he tried taking her out of the room, she'd kick him and scream. She clutched the sheets with both hands, but if he used force, her grip wasn't strong enough to resist him. Her heart picked up an erratic beat. Her temples throbbed. She swallowed several times, trying to control her reaction to seeing him.

"You're not the only one involved. You have your niece to consider." He leaned over her, his dark eyes gleaming like he knew the power he had over her. "Craig is outside her house prepared to do whatever I tell him to do. He won't go against me again. He knows better now."

What did he mean, "He knows better now"? Was Edward coercing Craig into doing another bad deed? While Paige was here with Dad, who was watching her daughter?

"All I have to do is send him a text, and he'll take the girl to a place where no one can find her." Edward tapped the cell phone screen.

"I don't believe you."

"No?" He squeezed her arm as if reminding of what he could do to her.

She winced and tremors of anxiety pulsated through her.

He held out the phone toward her and a video played of Piper dancing in Paige's backyard. Her cute voice sang "Mary Had a Little Lamb."

Tears flooded Paisley's eyes. Her throat tightened. Hard to swallow. Why wasn't Judah here? Didn't he say he'd protect her? She'd have to depend on her own wits and grit. And God's strength. She had that now.

"Put on those shoes." Edward pulled back her sheet. "Then

we'll slip into the stairwell around the corner. Don't cause any trouble. I'd hate to have to cover your mouth again." He smirked like he didn't mind at all, then pulled a roll of duct tape from his deep pocket.

Seeing the silver tape made bile roll up in her throat.

When she didn't move fast enough, he grabbed her arms and forced her upright. "Do what I say—now!"

The IV tube was already disconnected—he must have done that—but she still had the port in her arm. Barely able to use her fingers, she slid the slippers on one at a time. If she delayed long enough, Judah might come back. If only he'd walk through the door and knock his dad out cold.

"My son won't be your hero today. Or ever again."

"How do you know?"

"He's on a fool's errand. My deputy is talking to him right now."

His deputy. So, Brian Corbin *was* in the mayor's pocket like she suspected.

"Move!"

"Okay, okay." At least her thin gown covered her backside. She slid off the bed, nearly collapsing when her feet touched the floor. The blood in her head seemed to drop to her toes. She slumped over the mattress, gripping the thin blanket until the dizziness passed. "Why are you doing this?" She heaved a breath. "Your plan … failed before. It will fail again."

"No, it won't." Edward dragged her toward the door, even slumped over as she was. "Grants don't fail."

She tried to jerk her arms from his grasp. Even with the threat of Piper's well-being at stake, Paisley didn't believe Craig would harm the child.

Edward held out his video again. Hearing her niece's lilting voice tugged at her heart. Shouldn't she do everything in her power to keep the girl safe? At least make Edward think she was going along with him while seeking an escape? Then she'd go to the police.

"Shall I text Craig?"

"No."

"Then, come on."

Lord, please show Judah I'm in trouble. Keep Piper safe. I don't want my sister to go through the loss of a child.

She shuffled along in her slippers, deliberately going slow, with Edward forcing her down the hallway. She bent over and coughed, acting like she needed to catch her breath, hoping to make eye contact with someone. No nurses were at their station. No strong men were in the hall who could take Edward down. Suddenly, he clutched her around her middle and hauled her toward the stairway door.

"Heee*llllp*—"

He clapped his hand over her mouth. Her protests came out garbled.

Just before the stairwell door closed, a male patient walked by, gripping his IV stand and staring at her. Would he report what he saw?

Edward set her down roughly. "Don't try that again. Keep quiet." He clutched her sore wrist and dragged her behind him down the stairs. She struggled to keep up. Exhausted and breathless, she begged, "Please … let me … go."

"We're almost to the first floor. Keep your trap shut. We'll take the back exit. No guard there. I've been here before, so I know the secluded areas." He stood taller as if playing the role of a doctor. It seemed he thought he could get away with this masquerade. But didn't all criminals think they'd get away with their wrongdoing?

Edward led her into an empty hallway, and they passed several closed doors. "Hurry up." He kept her close to him, one arm gripping her elbow, the other one wrapped tightly around her shoulders, and pulled her through the exit that didn't have a guard, just like he said. But it had a security camera. She grimaced up at it and mouthed, "Help." Was a security person watching her?

Edward propelled her into the parking lot, going faster, now, and Paisley squinted into the bright sunlight. After being locked up in the closet, traveling by car at night, then staying in the dimly lit hospital room, the brightness outside was painful and made her eyes water. Even so, those first few moments in the seaside air invigorated her and lifted some of her mental fog.

Edward dodged around several cars, hauling her behind him.

"Wait. I can't … go that fast." She tried to catch her breath.

"Yes, you can."

If he kept dragging her along at this speed, she'd fall on her face. Her chance to get away from him was fading fast. The mayor's black truck gleamed in the sunshine not far ahead.

She had to think of a way to detain him. For her not to get into his truck. Maybe she'd ask him questions. Distract him. "Why are you doing this?"

"Isn't it obvious?"

"That you hate me? Yes." She shuffled her slippers along the pavement, forcing him to slow down. "Why is what I don't understand."

"Quit stalling. Keep walking." He gripped her wrist tighter and pulled more forcefully. "If you love Judah at all, you'll do as I say and get out of his life."

"What does any of this have to do with Judah?"

"Everything. He's destined for greater things." Edward huffed like he was tired too. "Because of you, he hasn't become the leader he should have been."

"I don't understand."

"If he never met you—" He groaned. "If only I never met Sue—" He clamped his teeth shut as if he didn't mean to say that part. "Things would be different, that's all."

Did he mean Sue Anne? Was this hate of his about what Aunt Callie talked to her about? And what kind of leader did he expect Judah to be?

"They're plotting to get rid of me." He prodded Paisley toward his truck. "But they won't succeed."

"Who's trying to get rid of you?"

"Don't act like you don't know." His breath came in huffs. "Stop asking stupid questions and walk faster."

"No. Leave me alone." She yanked against grip.

"Hold it right there!"

Edward froze, and Paisley stumbled into him.

Brian?

"Deputy Brian"—Edward's voice sounded snide—"turn around and pretend you didn't see anything just like you've done a hundred times before."

At least, Brian was here, standing up to Edward. Maybe he'd had a change of heart.

Whatever was about to happen, Paisley couldn't let Edward force her into his vehicle. She had to think of a way to fight back, maybe clobber him with her fist or elbow, even in her weakened condition.

Footsteps thumped the pavement. "Dad, let her go!"

Judah? *Oh, Judah.* He came for her. There he stood beside

Deputy Brian wearing a tormented look on his face. Seeing his concern for her, his love, she started crying. God sent him, told him where to look for her, didn't He?

"Stop that blubbering." Edward jerked her arm, shaking her. "It doesn't matter that he's here. Your fate is in my hands."

Her fate? Who did he think he was?

Edward yanked her up into his arms, clutching her around her middle. She tried to fight him, but it was useless. He was stronger than her. Still, she wouldn't give up.

"You'll never be good enough"—he growled in her ear—"for the future mayor of Basalt Bay."

What?

He shoved her against the side of his truck, his hand at her neck, while he opened the door with his other hand. She clawed at his arm, but it didn't seem to affect him.

"Dad, let her go! Now!"

At her husband's commanding tone, hope and pride infused her. Judah wouldn't let Edward get away with stealing her a second time. And she'd still watch for her chance to free herself.

"Edward, release that woman," Brian said gruffly.

"She's coming with me." Edward glanced back. "Put down that gun, Brian. You won't use it on me. I'm the mayor. *I* make the rules. It's your job to follow them."

"Not this time."

"Want to bet?"

"Judah?" Paisley called to him.

"Shut up!" Edward grabbed her hair with one hand and clapped his dirty hand over her mouth with the other one.

Judah lurched forward as if to attack Edward and rescue her, but Deputy Brian gripped his arm, detaining him.

Paisley sank her teeth into Edward's foul-tasting thumb. He cussed but removed his hand from her mouth. Then he pressed himself against her, forcing her toward the inside of his truck. She clung to the door handle with one hand and shoved against the steering wheel with the other. She didn't have much strength, but she was not entering his vehicle.

"Get in the truck!"

"No."

Edward thrust his right arm around her neck and clenched his arm muscles, squeezing her throat.

She gagged and wheezed. On the other side of the parking lot, the whirling blue lights on the squad car turned blurry.

"Dad, stop. You're hurting her. Let her go!"

Deputy Brian, with his gun pointing at them, and Judah, with his hands extended, narrowed the gap between them.

"Back up or I'll be forced to do something I don't want to do." Edward's arm cinched even tighter around her neck.

Her breathing became desperate. *Air. I need—*

"Please, Dad. I love her." Judah patted the air as if trying to calm his father. "She's my wife. I want to be with her."

"You were wrong to go against my wishes and marry her." Edward squeezed her throat like he meant to kill her. Did he realize what he was doing?

She sucked in a thread of air. Judah and Brian turned blurry too.

"You should want what's best for me." Judah had to see she was in distress, about to pass out. "Release her, now!"

Edward's arm loosened slightly. She inhaled a huge gulp of air and thanked God.

"I do want what's best for you. That's why I'm doing this. Soon, you'll understand."

"Understand what?"

If she elbowed Edward in the stomach, it might give Brian a chance to apprehend him. Did she have enough strength? Would the deputy take the shot?

Suddenly, Edward picked her up and shoved her toward the inside of his truck again. With her body halfway inside the cab, she knew it was now or never. She gritted her teeth and rammed her right elbow into his gut. Pain zinged through her arm.

"You wretched—"

Judah lunged against his father, wrestling him to the ground. Paisley's leg got caught in their tussle, and she fell too, but then she broke free. She crawled along the ground until she was clear of the men fighting. Before she could stand up, Judah picked her up and ran with her, putting several car lengths between them and where Deputy Brian and Edward were, now, scuffling. Finally, Deputy Brian subdued Edward on the ground.

"Pais, I'm so sorry. So sorry," Judah whispered near her ear.

Deputy Brian slapped handcuffs on Edward and read him his Miranda Rights. Then he led him toward the squad car. All the way across the parking lot, the mayor yelled, saying he'd tell all of Basalt about the deputy's darkest sins, offering him bribes, and continued to be combative.

Paisley exhaled a long sigh. It was over. It really was over.

"You'll never have to worry about him doing this again. You okay?" Judah gazed at her compassionately, but she saw he was tired too. Probably deeply saddened that his father would more than likely be charged as a criminal and do prison time.

For her, that was nothing but pure relief.

"I'm okay. Sleepy. Achy." She leaned her cheek against his shoulder. Then she remembered what Edward said. "Judah, have you ever wanted to be the mayor?"

"No way. That's the last thing in the world I'd want to do. Look at the trouble it's caused my family." He strode toward the hospital entrance, carrying her. "Let's get you back inside. Back to your bed."

"Okay." She sank against him. Edward was in custody. Piper was safe. The world felt like a better place.

A security guy, Doctor Clark, Karen, and another nurse, who was pushing a wheelchair, ran out of the building.

"Are you okay?" the doctor asked. "Randal, here, saw the video of you being abducted."

"We came as quickly as we could." Karen hurried over to Paisley and took her pulse.

Judah briefly explained what happened. Then, he gently set Paisley in the wheelchair.

Minutes later, thanks to the kind nurses, she was back in her bed with warm blankets snuggled about her and warm tea to drink. The doctor said her vitals were good, considering all she'd been through. He recommended more bedrest—and lunch.

A nap sounded heavenly, as did food, but, first, she had a question. "Any chance I could go home this evening?"

"I'm sorry, but, no." Doctor Clark patted her arm. "I think you should stay here so we can keep an eye on you. Especially after the stress you've endured today."

"Okay, fine. However, I have one tiny request."

"Oh? What's that?" Doctor Clark tapped the chart he held and eyed her.

"Could I be released for one hour?"

"Released?"

"Paisley?" Judah took her hand in his.

"Here's the thing. I have a ceremony I've been looking forward to, and I'd hate to miss it."

"Sweetheart, I canceled it, remember?"

"I know. But I didn't. Not in here." She rested her other palm over her heart. "Judah, will you still marry me today?"

"Of course, I would, but"—he glanced at the doctor—"you must stay here, doctor's orders."

"I know. But, please?" She stared at him, then aimed her gaze at Doctor Clark, then glanced at her husband again. "I don't want this day, the seventh day since I promised I'd renew my vows with you on this day, to pass without that happening."

Judah just stared at her, smiling.

"We do have a chapel here at the hospital." The doctor stared at the ceiling like he was thinking it over. "We even have a chaplain on staff. You could exchange vows there, if you'd like."

"What do you think?" Judah rocked his eyebrows. "Your dad, Paige, and my mom will be here."

"It sounds wonderful. But I have a better idea. A more memorable one."

"What is it?" Judah stroked her hand.

Doctor Clark squinted at her.

Could she convince these two, that after all she'd been through, she deserved to have one wish granted?

Thirty-one

Two hours later, Judah stood outside Paisley's hospital room door, dressed in his black suit that Mom had mysteriously brought from his closet. How did she even know to bring it? How had she deciphered Paisley's wishes and brought along her wedding dress and his suit after he texted her earlier in the day that Paisley wanted her clothes?

"Mother's intuition," she said. And something about "shoes making all the difference."

He tugged on the sleeve of his white shirt, wishing he had a proper tux for the occasion. But this would work fine for a beach wedding at dusk.

The doctor had given his blessing for Paisley's request for one hour away from her sickbed, if she was extremely careful. Of course, Judah was thrilled to accommodate her wishes. Far be it from him to deny her request to marry him again. He was eager too. After what his father did to keep them apart, and after all Paisley had suffered, he wouldn't deny her anything. The thought of his dad mistreating her still gnawed at him, but he couldn't dwell on it, or the weight in his chest would be too hard to bear. He and Paisley might both need counseling sessions from Pastor Sagle when they returned to Basalt Bay.

Ever since the doctor approved her mini-furlough for their ceremony at the sea, Judah had been working on what to say for his vows. He wanted to be spontaneous and sincere, but he also needed to have a few thoughts in his mind. *Paisley, you are the woman of my dreams. My heart …*

The hospital chaplain, Karl Lambert, agreed to perform the rites since, technically, they were still married. Nice of him to do that, especially after Judah explained the harrowing experiences Paisley had endured.

Mom slipped out of the hospital room, squeezing through a narrow opening in the doorway like he might try to see beyond her into the room where she and Paige were helping Paisley get ready. He might have too, so he could steal a peek at his wife. He'd never seen her in a wedding dress before, and he was eager to do so. He straightened his tie.

"Paisley wants you to go on ahead of her, then she'll meet you down at the beach. She'll ride with Paige."

"What? No way. I want her to ride with me."

"She's insisting."

"After all we've—"

"Exactly." Mom gave him one of her serious looks. "After all you two have been through, she wants you to be standing by the water's edge, watching her stroll down the aisle—the beach—toward you like the beautiful bridal moment she's dreamed of since she was a little girl." Mom smoothed her hand over his arm. "It seems she missed out on that the last time."

"Oh, right." He sighed, remembering. "I guess she did."

"Everything's going to work out perfectly. You'll see.

Now, I'll drive you." She linked her arm with his and drew him toward the elevator. He hated leaving Paisley. But his dad should be locked up in the Basalt Bay jail by now. All that was over. He could relax. They all could. So why did he still feel tense?

"Don't worry. She's eager to do this." Mom nodded. "Resolved, one might say."

Glad to hear that, Judah let out a sigh that felt like it had been lodged beneath his ribs for about fifty-six hours.

At the North Shoreline Beach, he and Mom strolled down the seashore to the prearranged meeting point. The sandy beach was peppered with some giant boulders. A couple of massive monoliths extended into the sea, making a gorgeous backdrop for their vow renewal ceremony. A typical, Pacific wind blustered hard against them. At this rate, he'd have to shout his vows for Paisley to hear him, but that was okay. They were finally going to do this—become husband and wife again. *Praise God.*

Thinking of remarrying the woman he loved, the woman he'd waited three years to reunite with, the one he'd prayed would survive the crisis they'd just gone through, made his heart pound out a wild dance in his chest. Of course, she still had to return to the hospital room in an hour. But he'd be right there with her too. All night, and tomorrow, however long it took.

Exchanging vows in the hospital chapel would have been fine with him. Probably safer. But he knew Paisley loved the sea. So did he. And this would make a fantastic setting for their vow renewal, a special memory they'd cherish forever. A beautiful ending to an otherwise horrific couple of days.

He sighed.

"Something troubling you, Son?" Mom wobbled in her dress shoes and clutched his arm.

Tightening his arm muscles, he kept her from tripping in

the sand. "I can't help remembering some of the bad things that have happened."

"Focus on the good things to come. You and Paisley." She leaned her head against his upper arm. "Your happily-ever-after. And children?" She glanced up at him.

"I hope so." He sighed, and it felt like more stress eased out of him. "Oh, no." A ring. He forgot about a ring!

"What is it?"

Judah groaned. "I didn't think about a wedding ring. I mean, it's back at the house, but Dad took off Paisley's engagement ring. What am I going to do?"

"Don't panic. She's not going to be worried about that."

"I know, but I need something to give her during the vows." He took a couple of steps away from Mom, searching the sand. There. He leaned over and picked up a long skinny piece of beach grass. "Help me with this, will you?" He stepped beside her and tore the strand into three semi-even pieces. He held up one end. "Can you make a braid out of this?"

"I'm sure I can." She quickly formed a tiny braided rope with the grass, which reminded him of the scripture about a threefold cord not being easily broken—him, Paisley, and God. "How's that?"

"Perfect." Judah guessed the size of her finger and tied off one side of the braid, making a slim circle. "That will work for now."

"Beautiful, too." Mom grinned. "I'm proud of you and Paisley." She leaned up and kissed his cheek.

"Thanks, Mom."

He glanced toward the parking lot. Chaplain Karl and Paige were heading toward them. Where was Paisley?

His sister-in-law waved.

"Where's my wife?" He couldn't help but be worried after the events of the last three days.

"She's hiding back that way." Paige pointed behind her. "She doesn't want you to see her yet. My dad is with her."

"Okay." Paul would be walking down the beach beside her. Everything was going to be okay.

Mom hugged him. "Just enjoy this moment. Today's Paisley's and your special day. A blessed day."

She was right. He was about to make brand new vows with the woman he planned to spend the rest of his life with. He focused on the parking lot, waiting for his first glimpse of her. It was a long way for her to walk considering today's ordeal. At least, she'd finally eaten something solid. And with the way she elbowed his father, she must have gotten some of her strength back.

Judah and Karl shook hands. Paige gave him a quick hug then stood to his right, leaving space for Paisley.

The wind gusted against them, blowing their hair and clothes. But Judah enjoyed the powerful sensation. He still had tension pounding within him. He needed to let it go so he could enjoy the next few minutes with Paisley. This would be a day they could tell their kids about someday. The day they promised each other forever.

God was so good to have healed them and brought them back together. To help Paisley fall in love with him again. And He had protected her. Edward hadn't gotten away with kid-napping her. And even Craig stepping in to bring about a rescue had to have been God working out good in their lives.

Oh, there she was! Paisley, dressed in a long, flowing gown, walked beside her dad. Judah's heart beat to a fast rhythm. He stood taller, tugged on the bottom of his coat.

At the edge of the parking lot, facing his direction, Paisley wrapped her arm around Paul's like she was hanging onto him for dear life. She waved at Judah, grinning. He waved back. Even from here, she looked gorgeous. So precious to him.

No music serenaded the bride's walk except the pounding of the surf, the in and out swishing of the sea as it kissed the sand over and over, and the ever-present caress of the wind. Paisley strolled slowly toward him—probably as fast as she could walk—but he'd wait all evening if it took that long. Although Doctor Clark agreed to only an hour. Judah would like to run to Paisley and scoop her up, so she didn't have to walk so far. Independent as she was, she probably wouldn't like that.

About ten feet from him, she stopped, and they just gazed at each other, smiling, almost laughing. She looked amazing. Her face was still red and sore-looking, but he wasn't focused on that. Soon she'd be healed, and her injuries would be a memory. But, for this moment, it was like he was seeing beyond her outer wounds, right into her soul, into who she truly was—a beautiful woman with a kind heart who loved him—and he loved every part of her. His face warmed at those thoughts.

"Who gives this woman to be reunited with her husband?" Karl spoke.

"I do," Paul answered solemnly. Then he kissed Paisley's forehead.

She walked toward Judah on her own. About halfway to him, she stopped again. Was something wrong? She tipped her head as if communicating with him. Did she need his help?

He rushed across the sand to her. "You look amazing, Pais. Thank you for marrying me again. Are you okay?"

"May I hold onto your arm?"

"Of course." He extended his arm, and she linked her hand around his elbow. "If you hold onto me for the rest of our days, I'd like that."

"Just what I was thinking." She winked at him.

The wind billowed her lacy wedding dress around her, the frills of her train wrapping around them as Judah drew her to stand by him in front of the minister.

Karl said some lovely verses about marriage. He commended them on renewing their vows and repledging their lives to each other. He said a prayer.

That's when Judah noticed Paisley was shivering. It was chilly standing near the sea with the wind cutting a swath around them. He slipped out of his coat and wrapped it around her shoulders.

"Thank you."

"My pleasure." It would be his pleasure to take care of her for the rest of their days. Oh, yes, God had answered his prayers.

"Now, the bride and groom will recite the vows they've prepared." Karl nodded toward Judah.

He cleared his throat, and facing Paisley, gazing into her eyes, he gently linked their pinkies. "You are the woman of my dreams. My heart … the other half of me. For the last few years, nothing felt right in my life until you came back to Basalt Bay." He paused, emotion almost getting the better of him. "We've talked about our failings and our hope for the future, but here and now, I pledge to you my faithfulness, my strengths, and my devotion. I pray for healing for us and for our families. That from today forward, our love will grow stronger with each passing day. You are the love of my life." He released their pinkies, then he slid the grass ring over her finger.

Gazing at the ring, she grinned.

"Sorry about that," he said quietly. "I didn't have the real one with me."

"This is perfect. Thank you."

"With this ring"—he continued the vows—"I pledge to you my love."

Chaplain Karl nodded at Paisley.

She enfolded Judah's left hand in both of hers, her thumb stroking his wedding band. "Thank you for your sweet words, your affection, your love for me that has wooed me and drawn me back to you." She sniffed a couple of times, and he felt his eyes water too. "Thank you for rescuing me, again. For always being there for me. I love you, Judah Grant, more than I ever realized I could love another person. I promise to stand by you, to stick close to you—to never run from you again—and to be the wife that you need me to be for the rest of our lives."

He swallowed down a gulp of emotion.

A mischievous expression crossed her face.

"What?" He smiled. Finally, he'd relaxed. He was so thankful for the loving way she gazed into his eyes, almost as if they were alone.

"Unfortunately, I have to go back to the hospital tonight."

"I know. But I'll be right there with you."

"Thank you for that." She took a breath as if speaking might still be difficult for her. "However, since this might not be quite the honeymoon night we wished for—"

"True, true." He chuckled, his cheeks heating up.

A few others snickered.

"Before the pastor tells you to kiss the bride—"

"Yes?" Could he kiss her? Were her lips well enough?

"Would you mind taking a walk with me?"

"You want us to take a beach walk?" He glanced at the others who were gathered with them, watching and waiting. "You sure?"

She slid his coat off her shoulders and handed it to Paige. "You and me and the sea?" She nodded toward the ocean and grinned. "Will you come with me, Judah?"

"I'll go anywhere with you. Oh, you want us to walk into the ocean?" He chuckled. The doctor might not approve of such a thing, but didn't Judah already think that he wouldn't deny her anything?

She giggled. "Yes. Let this be a seal to all we've promised each other. A sign of what we'll never forget." A pause. "What I'll never forget again as long as I live—that you were willing to walk into the sea with me during our vow renewal. And if you're willing to do that, it seems you must be willing to face all of this life with me too."

"I do, Pais, I do ... so help me God." He'd never forget this moment, either. Holding hands, they strolled side by side into the sea.

* * * *

With the waves splashing against them, the coolness spreading through her, and soaking the lower portion of her wedding gown, Paisley leaned in toward Judah and kissed his cheek. Paige had helped her put on a little mascara and gloss—maid of honor duties—but she couldn't do much about the redness on her face. She never wanted Judah or herself to forget not only the words said here, but what they meant, and what they did afterward.

She loved the way Judah gently held her hand, the ways he'd proven his love to her over and over. She prayed she could be the loving wife he deserved. When the seawater came up to their knees, they stopped and stared into each other's eyes, their backs toward their guests.

"For better or for worse," she said above the sound of the waves and the wind.

"For better or for worse. Do I get to kiss you now?"

"Yes." She was eager for his lips to press against hers in a married sort of kiss.

"Shall I kiss your forehead?" He grinned. "We have plenty of time to catch up on the other stuff later."

"You're sweet to suggest that. But, no way, mister. I want a real kiss from my groom."

"Okay, then." His chuckle, and the way he seemed a little nervous, made her smile.

"You may kiss the bride!" the group on the beach shouted.

Judah's moist gaze snagged with hers and she knew she loved him deeply. Judah and *her ocean*, what could be better? With the sweetest, most endearing look, he drew closer to her. When his lips almost touched hers, he paused a breath away, eyes glistening. "I love you, Pais."

"I love you too."

Then his lips fell softly over hers, moving ever so gently, sweetly and lovingly, and she melted into him, into his embrace. She never wanted the kiss to stop. She clung to him, strumming her fingers through his hair, pulling him closer, wishing for more.

He swayed slightly against her as the waves sloshed over their legs, making her feel as if they were slow dancing. When they leaned back from their embrace, their loved ones on the beach clapped and cheered. They both smiled and waved at them.

Hand in hand, they strolled through the water until they

reached the seashore. For a moment, Judah wrapped his arms around her and kissed the top of her head. He sighed, and she heard him saying something, praying, perhaps.

Then he whispered in her ear, for her hearing alone, "Whenever you're ready for us to celebrate, alone, I'll be waiting and ready." He kissed her lips again lightly. "No pressure. I just want you to know." He grinned at her like she was the most beautiful, precious person in the world to him.

Deep blue sea in the morning! She and Judah were married again! To have and to hold. For all their better days and worse days. Clinging only to him. She would be counting the minutes, the seconds, until she returned to the cottage with him as his wife.

Epilogue

Paige's journal entry:

Tonight was the sweetest vow renewal ceremony I've ever seen. Of course, I haven't seen many. It was wonderful and tender. I cried when Judah and Paisley walked into the sea together. I admit I was jealous of my sister. She has a handsome man who's crazy about her. A man who waited for three years for her to come home. Does Paisley realize how lucky she is? How women like me, and others in Basalt Bay, envy her?

I wish I had what she has. I wish I could find a man who'd love me as passionately as I love him. Does another man like that exist?

Today I heard some troubling news—chaotic heart-stopping news. Forest Harper is coming back. At the mention of his name, my lips craved to know what I once knew with him. To be held in his arms again. But that can never be. That's all in the past. Yet, my traitorous heart hasn't forgotten.

What will I do when I see him again? Scream at him for leaving me? Fall into his arms and profess that I still love him? Or will I tell him the truth?

Secrets have such a dreadful way of unraveling at the worst times.

If you enjoyed *Tide of Resolve*, or mostly enjoyed it, please take a minute and write a review wherever you purchased this book. They say reviews are the lifeblood for authors. Even one line telling what you liked or thought about the book is so helpful. Thank you!

~~~~

I took many creative liberties with Basalt Bay, my imaginary town on the Oregon Coast. To all those who live nearby, please forgive my embellishments. I enjoy the Pacific Ocean and the Oregon Coast so much that I wanted to create my own little world there.

~~~~

Look for this series to continue in 2021:

Waves of Reason

Port of Return

~~~~

If you would like to be one of the first to hear about Mary's new releases and upcoming projects, sign up for her newsletter—and receive the free pdf "Rekindle Your Romance! 50+ Date Night Ideas for Married Couples." Check it out here:

www.maryehanks.com
~~~~

A huge "Thank you!" to everyone who helped make this book a reality.

Paula McGrew – You have been a huge part of my writing journey. Thank you for your faithful assistance with grammar, story lines, and ideas. You have such an encouraging heart. Thank you for sharing your gift with me.

To my beta readers – Kathy Vancil, Kellie Griffin, Mary Acuff, Beth McDonald, Joanna Brown, and Jason Hanks – Thank you so much for the critique and encouragement. It always cheers my heart when I receive a positive response that you can help with another installment. Thank you for sharing your time, your thoughts, your words of praise, and the deeper notes of correction and guidance. You are all a blessing to me.

Susanne Williams – Thanks for always taking time to help me with cover design. I appreciate your eye for artistry and for seeing what works in the marketplace. Thank you for sharing your gifting with me, and my readers.

Jason Hanks – Thanks for the cheers and chats about my imaginary world. Thanks for being my sounding board and encouraging me to keep at it. I love you.

To my lovelies … Shem, Deborah, Philip, and Daniel … love you forever. I am so proud of you.

To Traci … my first daughter-in-love … you hold a special place in my heart.

(This story is a work of fiction. Any mistakes are my own. ~meh)

www.maryehanks.com

Books by Mary Hanks

Restored Series

Ocean of Regret

Sea of Rescue

Bay of Refuge

Tide of Resolve

Waves of Reason (2021)

Second Chance Series

Winter's Past

April's Storm

Summer's Dream

Autumn's Break

Season's Flame

Marriage Encouragement

Thoughts of You (A Marriage Journal)

Youth Theater Adventures

Stage Wars

About Mary E. Hanks

Mary loves stories about marriage restoration. She believes there's something inspiring about couples clinging to each other, working through their problems, and depending on God for a beautiful rest of their lives together—and those are the types of stories she likes to write. Mary and Jason have been married for forty-plus years, and they know firsthand what it means to get a second chance with each other, and with God. That has been her inspiration in writing the Second Chance series and the Restored series.

Besides writing, Mary likes to read, garden, do artsy stuff, go on adventures with Jason, and meet her four adult kids for coffee or breakfast.

Connect with Mary by signing up for her newsletter at

www.maryehanks.com

"Like" her Facebook Author page:

www.facebook.com/MaryEHanksAuthor

www.maryehanks.com

Made in the USA
Columbia, SC
16 May 2021

38048692R00167